Phineas Camp Headley

The patriot boy; or, The life and career of Major-General Ormsby M. Mitchel

Phineas Camp Headley

The patriot boy; or, The life and career of Major-General Ormsby M. Mitchel

ISBN/EAN: 9783337306465

Printed in Europe, USA, Canada, Australia, Japan

Cover: Foto ©Andreas Hilbeck / pixelio.de

More available books at **www.hansebooks.com**

LIVES OF

MODERN AMERICAN HEROES.

FOR BOYS AND YOUNG MEN.

BY THE POPULAR BIOGRAPHER

REV. P. C. HEADLEY.

I.

THE HERO BOY.

Being the Life and Deeds of General Ulysses S. Grant,

THE PATRIOT AND HERO.

Tracing his career from Boyhood to Manhood, from the Schoolhouse to the Battle-Field and Victory. 1 vol., 16mo, fancy cloth, 340 pages and nine Illustrations. Price, $1.50.

Extract from a letter received from Gen. Grant's Father.

Rev. P. C. HEADLEY:

DEAR SIR—I have read over carefully the Hero Boy, written by yourself. It is correct and well written, with direct reference to doing justice to all parties.

Yours, most truly,

J. R. GRANT.

Notices of the Press.

This volume is the first of a series for boys, entitled " The Young American's Library of Modern Heroes." It is full of entertaining incidents of Gen. Grant's early life, and contains sketches of his career in the Mexican war, on his farm, and in the whole course of our national struggle against rebellion. The book is illustrated with maps and plates, and will be, according to its design, a very useful and entertaining book for boys.—*N. Y. Observer.*

Of all children's books we doubt if any class exercise so direct an influence as the lives of eminent men; to emulate their example is often the first ambition of the young in the career which native genius indicates. Hence, it is of no small importance what exemplars are put into the hands of children. One of the most attractive and authentic of these contemporary biographies for the young is the " Hero Boy," or the " Life of General Grant," by Rev. P. C. Headley. It is a handsome duodecimo, written with spirit, well illustrated, and handsomely bour¬ It will prove a taking book for boys.—*N. Y. Evening Post.*

Gen. Grant is now the foremost figure in this war, and the whole nation is ea; to know his history. The narrative of his rise from a very obscure and hum position to his present high command, illustrates the character of our institutio and the certainty of the rewards assured to honest energy; and the eyes, not o; of the whole country, but of the world, are now directed toward him. The bi raphy before us gives a brief sketch of his early life, but is much more minute details of military operations since the war begun. The style is animated at graphic, and is well suited to its stirring them?.—*N. Y Independent.*

In the "Hero Boy," Mr. Headley has made his work a labor of love and honor —love for the boys and honor for the man. Gathering his materials with great care, and arranging them with the skill of a practised hand, he has really produced the very best outline of the General's career yet put in print; it is illustrated with maps, enriched with a glossary of military terms, and leads off admirably as the first of a series entitled "The Young American's Library of Modern Heroes."—*Chicago Journal.*

II.

THE PATRIOT BOY.

BEING THE

Life of Major-General O. M. Mitchel, the Astronomer and Hero.

1 vol., 16mo, cloth, 300 pages. Fully illustrated. Price, $1.50.

Extract from a letter received from Gen. Mitchel's Son.

Wm. H. Appleton, Esq.:

Dear Sir—I have read with great pleasure the life of my father, written by Rev. P. C. Headley, and just published by yourself. In every thing relating to the boyhood and early life of my father, the author has been most successful and correct.
Very respectfully yours,
E. W. MITCHEL.

Notices of the Press.

General Mitchel was a remarkable man. As an astronomer, he was one of the foremost of the age; as an orator, he had few peers; while as a general, he proved himself possessed of the highest qualities of leadership. His nature was strong and magnetic; there was no resisting the fascination of his presence. He was idolized by his troops; and had he lived, he would doubtless have disputed the honors with the most successful of our chieftains.

We are glad the life of this gifted man has been written with reference to the youth of our country. We know it will do good, and stimulate many an ardent youth to noble endeavor. The present volume should be placed in the hands of every boy in the country; for the subject of it is one that cannot be too prominently kept before the eye of the nascent generation. It is got up in beautiful style, and reflects credit on the publisher.—*Albany Evening Journal.*

We know of none who presents a nobler example to the youth of America than the illustrious Mitchel.—*N. Y. Evening Post.*

We had once the pleasure of seeing the subject of this biography in his observatory in Cincinnati, where he most affably explained some of his methods of exploring the visible heavens. He was not then a soldier, but the patriotic love of country was active within him, ready to be called into action at his country's summons. He became a soldier—and an eminent one—and in the service he surrendered his life. As an astronomer, and as a general, he maintained a Christian life, and his death was a transit beyond the stars. Mr. Headley, who has succeeded so well in other biographies, has raised a fitting monument to the great and good man, and he directs the eyes of our youth to contemplate it.—*The Presbyterian.*

The subject is a brilliant example to American youth. We are familiar with the career of Prof. Mitchel, and rejoice to see it graphically portrayed in this beautiful volume. We would put this book into the hands of a lad to show him what true greatness there is in a man who has knowledge, religion, and patriotism. —*New York Commercial.*

III.

THE MINER BOY and his MONITOR.

Being the Life of Capt. John Ericsson, the Inventor,

DESIGNER OF THE FAMOUS IRON-CLAD "MONITOR," ETC.

A DEEPLY INTERESTING AND INSTRUCTIVE BOOK FOR BOYS.

One volume, 16mo, fancy cloth, 300 pages. Fully illustrated. Price, $1.50.

Notices of the Press.

The idea of placing our prominent and most deserving men in a historic light before the actions which have made them illustrious are deprived of their freshness, is certainly a happy one; and the practised pen of Mr. Headley is just the one to produce biographies worthy of the subjects sketched. There is as much romance for the general reader, old or young, in the life of John Ericsson as in that of George Stephenson, and we undertake to say that the author has in the present instance been as faithful to the ingenious Swede as the talented biographer of the great railway man was to him. The text of this pretty volume is liberally illustrated, which never fails to heighten the interest of reading boys.—*Troy Daily Whig.*

We have no hesitation in saying that this is the most interesting and romantic of all the recent "boy books." It treats of a personage whose name is far more familiar to our people than his history—of a man who belongs to that class of great mechanics who are equally important and useful in war or in peace. Of course it will be said that the life of Ericsson is an example to boys, and it is as far as industry, honesty, and energy go; but it is of special interest to boys who have a genius for mechanics, and, in any event, is most entertaining and instructive reading.—*N. Y. Evening Post.*

A fascinating history of a man of remarkable inventive genius to whom the nation is under immeasurable obligation. None can tell what course the war might have taken, or what result might have been reached, had not the monster Merrimac been checked by the Monitor, and her early success turned into defeat in the ever-memorable battle at Hampton Roads. The great influence of Ericsson's genius in manifold inventions is also shown, and many interesting things are told concerning Sweden, his native land.—*Congregationalist.*

IV.

LIFE AND CAREER OF

LIEUT.-GENERAL W. T. SHERMAN,

"THE GREATEST OF LIVING CAPTAINS."

Being an Authentic History of his Early Life and Remarkable Career.

1 vol., 16mo, fancy cloth, 368 pages, fully illustrated. Price, $1.50.

This Life of General Sherman is among the most interesting in the series, full of life, incident, bustle, and movement. One of the greatest Commanders in History is shown as he is, and we are now more than ever astonished at the extent and variety of his achievements, when they are thus brought into the compact shape of a single volume. The book is not less attractive by its mechanical appearance, with its clear text, portrait, sketches, map, etc.—*New Yorker.*

The facts here, from the early life of Sherman, are obtained from the most authentic sources. It is full of the incidents of his younger days, illustrating his life and character. His career is one of the noblest in military annals. It is well to have such books, that fall into the hands of the young, written by men of excellent taste and judgment. Mr. Headley has done justice to his subject.—*Boston Post.*

4

V.

LIFE AND NAVAL CAREER OF

ADMIRAL D. G. FARRAGUT.

Mr. Headley is doing a good work in giving us biographies of our modern American heroes. The series already embraces Grant, Mitchel (the astronomer), Ericsson, Sherman, and Sheridan. He now adds Farragut. These biographies are not mere re-hashes from the daily papers, but veritable histories, derived from authentic sources, often from the families and personal friends of the parties described, nor are they dry compilations of dates and statistics, but are full of stir and animation, suited to fire the imagination and enlist the admiring interest of youth.—*Sunday School Times.*

We warmly commend the series of Biographies, of which Admiral Farragut is the fifth, and one of the most interesting volumes.—*Daily Evening Telegraph.*

VI.

LIFE AND MILITARY CAREER OF

MAJOR-GEN. PHILIP H. SHERIDAN.

A valuable contribution to the history of the war.—*Boston Congregationalist.*

There are few better biographies or better worth recording than that of General Sheridan.—*New Yorker.*

General Sheridan was one of the most dashing, energetic, persevering, and successful Cavalry Generals the world has ever known. The history of this gallant Union officer abounds in interesting and thrilling incidents and adventures, all of which are graphically described, forming a very entertaining work, combining all the interest of fiction with the more substantial elements of historical truth. Youthful readers, as well as " children of a larger growth," will read these volumes with absorbing interest —*Syracuse Daily Standard.*

The series, which is concluded by the life of our cavalry hero, forms one of the most interesting and impressive which has ever been given to Young America. It is by example that boys are roused to emulate the great, and the presentation to the public in a cheap form of the events of the career of those men with whose fame the world is ringing, cannot but have the effect of ennobling the efforts of our young generation. Mr. Headley is eminently qualified for the task of preparing for youthful readers the work before us. All superfluity and high-sounding phraseology is avoided and a straight, consistent narrative presented. We warmly commend the works as the best reading that can be given to our young people, and the whole series forms a most attractive gift to increase the enjoyment of the holiday season.—*Philadelphia Daily Evening Telegraph.*

The above Biographies were written expressly for Boys and Young Men. They are not mere compilations from Newspapers, etc., but *authentic histories,* Mr. Headley having been furnished by the heroes in question, their relatives and friends, all the material and facts necessary to make them complete and reliable, instructive and entertaining. —————

NOW READY,

NEW EDITIONS OF HEADLEY'S

Life of Empress Josephine,   *Mary Queen of Scots.*
Life of Emperor Napoleon,   *General Lafayette,*
Women of the Bible.

Price, $1.75 each.

WM. H. APPLETON, Publisher,

92 & 94 Grand Street, N. Y.

CROSSING THE COTTON PONTOON BRIDGE, p. 217.

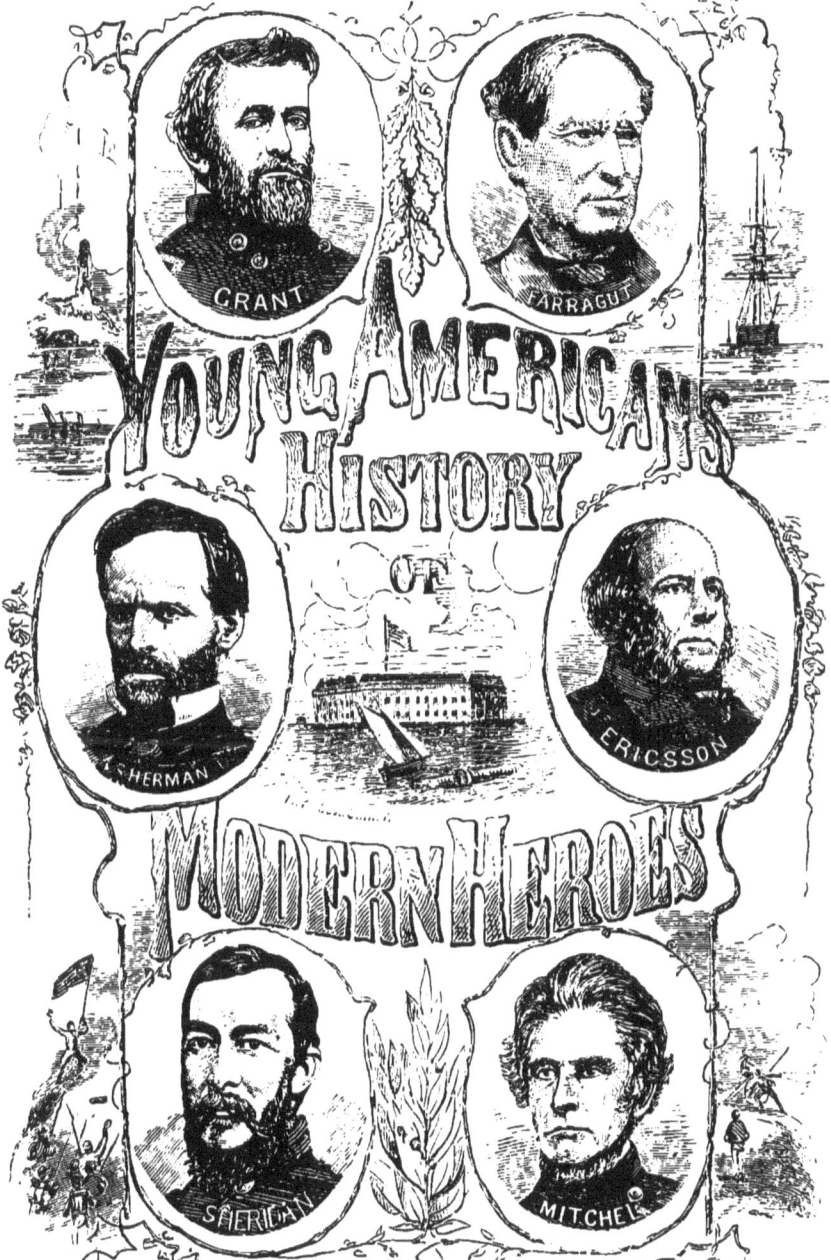

THE

PATRIOT BOY;

OR,

THE LIFE AND CAREER

OF

MAJOR-GENERAL ORMSBY M. MITCHEL.

BY

REV. P. C. HEADLEY,

AUTHOR OF "NAPOLEON," "EMPRESS JOSEPHINE," "HERO BOY," ETC.

NEW YORK:

WILLIAM H. APPLETON, 92 GRAND STREET.

1866.

J. B. S.*

THE WIDOW'S ONLY AND DUTIFUL SON,

AND ALL OTHER YOUNG AMERICANS,

WHO EMULATE THE EXAMPLE OF THOSE NOBLE MEN WHO

FOUNDED, PERPETUATED, AND HAVE DEFENDED

THE REPUBLIC,

THIS BRIEF RECORD OF A TRUE HERO

IS DEDICATED,

WITH A WARM INTEREST IN THEIR WELL-BEING,

BY THE

AUTHOR.

* See note on page 801.

PREFACE.

The "Young American's Library" would indeed be wanting in one of the most instructive and encouraging examples of the highest success in the midst of disheartening trials, of a resolute will and hopeful spirit, without the life of General Mitchel.

This volume is from authentic sources; and it is believed that in no important statement will the truthfulness of the narrative be questioned. Still the portraiture drawn must fall below the splendid original. For, while the records of his life are not full as we could wish, and as the "great departed" intended they should be for the sake of his family, it is no idle task to present, with fidelity, a life and character in successful activity and moral excellence so far above that of the majority of distinguished men.

Some latitude has been taken in the introduction of incidents and explanations, which, if not directly connected with General Mitchel's career, shed light upon the strong points in his nature, and on the conflict in which he sacrificed his noble life.

The author is indebted to Abbott's "History of the Rebellion," Pittinger's "Daring and Suffering," and to those who knew and loved General Mitchel, for many important facts.

Brief extracts illustrative of his brilliant oratory, and remarkable power to make astronomical science simple and attractive to the common mind, are taken from his "Sidereal and Planetary Worlds," "Popular Astronomy," and the "Bible and Astronomy," the only published works of the lamented author.

The most difficult part of the delightful task of writing the biography has been to give interest, and adapt to the juvenile mind, that portion of it which relates to his scientific career, without resorting to imaginary facts or conversations.

It is devoutly hoped that the narrative may stimulate to manly effort, and Christian fidelity, many youthful hearts in our land of "fiery trials," and of a glorious future.

NOTE.

The next volume in the "Young American's Library of Modern Heroes" will be the "Miner Boy and his Monitor," or the extraordinary life and achievements of Captain John Ericsson, the *American-Swede*, by the same author.

CONTENTS.

8 CONTENTS.

1*

CHAPTER I.

Y young readers who are very far in their "teens," heard of *Professor* Mitchel before the civil war made him a general. Nearly all of our officers were men but little known previous to the rebellion. Professor Mitchel, the astronomer and lecturer, was widely popular in the time of peace. He was justly admired for genius, and a character as bright, pure, and uniform, as the globes of light whose marches and motions he enthusiastically watched,

> " When marshalled on the nightly plain,
> The glittering host bestud the sky."

This fact will lend a charm to the record of his career, so worthy of your imitation.

The Mitchel family were originally Virginians. The father of our hero was an unassuming, intelligent, and enterprising man, of no ordinary mind. With a fine mathematical genius, he had a decided taste for astronomical studies; and, like many other youths who have not enjoyed the means of education, he might have gained a high position in the walks of science had he received the indispensable culture—perhaps have rivalled his honored son in splendid attainments. His wife was a remarkable woman. Over natural powers of a high order, and an attractive person, was shed the lustre and loveliness of unaffected piety. Mr. Mitchel was at one time in possession of a handsome property; but, besides raising a large family, by unavoidable reverses, he saw it pass hopelessly from his hands. Discouraged, and having sons who had never known the pressure of poverty, and were therefore unfitted to assist him in his efforts to retrieve his fortunes, he decided to leave Virginia, and go to the far West, to begin life anew. He disposed of his effects, and travelled slowly and wearily through what is now West Virginia, until he struck the Ohio River. The country was unsettled and wild. There were no railroads, and the only means of transportation was upon the flatboats of the Ohio. Upon one of these the family embarked, and went on their way to Kentucky. In this State Mr. Mitchel resolved to find a home. He bought land near Morganfield, Union County, erected a temporary house, and fairly commenced pioneer life.

In the new Kentucky dwelling, which the strangers

from the "Old Dominion" called their own, in the year 1809, was born Ormsby McKnight Mitchel. The father was a planter, and, consequently, had slaves to work the land; but often expressed his hatred to the system of labor that made it apparently necessary to own the negroes, and at his death gave them their freedom.

· This noble act, in advance of the public feeling even at the North, contributed largely to the embarrassment in business, which, with sickness attending a change of climate, had much to do with the life-struggles of the infant boy, all unconscious of the changes about him. There was nothing in Ormsby's experience different from that of other children until three years of age, excepting a premature interest, perhaps, in the moon and stars, calling forth exclamations of singular beauty. Then Mr. Mitchel was taken sick. The boy still played, unheeding the suffering and peril of the father.

Day after day disease did its work. Ormsby knew there was something strange and new in the dwelling. Mother's sad face, the physician's frequent calls, cast a shadow even upon the spirit of the child. And when he was told that father was dead, and touched the cold face, and then saw the coffin borne away, the boy wept with a grief which was caught from the faces about him—a passing shower of tears, succeeded by sunny smiles and laughter. It was years after, that he learned what he had lost—the meaning of the word *orphan.*

It is a sad thing, and a great misfortune in a human view, to be left early an orphan. But God often over-rules it for the highest benefit of the bereaved. This was evidently true in Ormsby's experience.

Having no nurse to aid the burdened mother, the youngest boy was taken care of much of the time by an older brother, who ever after cherished a strong affection for the object of his peculiar interest. Adversity had marked this household for peculiar trial. The chosen spot for a habitation proved to be sickly, and nothing of an earthly kind seemed to prosper.

Mrs. Mitchel and her family lived in Kentucky when it was a vast hunting ground. Some of the brothers became familiar with the romantic adventures of those early years. They often threaded the wilderness with the rifle. One of them served in the war of 1812 with the "Hunters of Kentucky."

The family, afflicted, and the means of support by the Providential discipline greatly reduced, broke up the sadly interesting associations in the Kentucky home, and started for that garden State of settlers from the East and South, Ohio.

Leaving on horseback, they travelled through the wilds of Kentucky to the banks of the Ohio. Little Ormsby rode in front of his eldest brother. At night they not unfrequently stopped in the forests where the Indian prowled around, fearing they should be murdered before morning.

COX & FAY. S.C. N.Y.

THE PLANTATION HOME, p. 15

They finally found themselves on the banks of the Ohio, and on the spot where Covington now stands, opposite Cincinnati, then only a few houses along the river side.

Under the very shadow of the hill upon which the Mitchel Observatory stands, the family attempted to cross in row boats. A fearful thunder storm burst upon them, and they all came near being lost. The first boat, containing the older brother, had gained the landing ; and he, the head of the family in fact, stood upon the bank watching the imperilled little bark. It finally reached the shore in the face of the tempest, wind, and current. After some hesitation, they concluded not to stop at Cincinnati, but pushed forward to Miami, a pleasant little town in Clermont County, in which, at Point Pleasant, you recollect, Lieutenant-General Grant was born.

Not long after, another move took the widow and her children to Lebanon, a thriving village in Turtle Creek township, and the capital of Warren County. It is between thirty and forty miles northwest of Miami. The country around Lebanon, which now contains three thousand inhabitants, is very beautiful and fertile.

A few miles east of the village, on the Miami River, is a great curiosity, which Ormsby often saw with wonder. It is an ancient fortification, nearly a mile in length, enclosed by a wall of earth. This enclosure is in some places ten feet high. It has more than fifty gates, or openings. By whom, when, or for what purpose the singular defences were built, is unknown. You know that all over the great western valley are scattered these relics of the past. Men of genius and culture have studied them, and volumes have been printed containing their speculations. Still we are in the dark. God limits our curiosity and knowledge on every hand. Wherever we turn, in our explorations, a voice comes at length to our inward ear, "Thus far and no farther."

Ormsby climbed over these memorials of past ages, as wise as the philosopher, in regard to their history, beyond plausible theories. Still his holidays were few, for he had neither time nor money to spend.

He had all the while a treasure more precious than a fortune; a gifted, devout, and loving mother. She threw over him an influence which was the true source of his success and greatness in after life. This he delighted to acknowledge through his whole history. Though left alone with her cherished offspring, and struggling to feed and clothe them, the heavenly atmosphere of her faith and love surrounded him continually.

We shall not know on earth the debt of gratitude which the Church and State owe such mothers—quietly, and caring not for human applause, doing their mighty work—then retiring into obscurity while their sons ascend to high positions.

Ormsby passed most of the years of early boyhood in Lebanon. Soon as the boy could earn money, he was ready to embrace every opportunity of adding a penny to the common treasury. Here his early school-days were passed. But the schools there were then poor. Ormsby, however, progressed rapidly. When eight years of age he was reading Virgil, and soon surpassed his country teachers. He often would say with regard to one of them, that after translating the most difficult passages he would ask him to read them; and upon his failure to do it, rendered them himself. At the age of twelve he entered a store as a clerk.

We come now to the most important crisis in his experience—the fountain of his highest eloquence—the seal of his true greatness and eternal destiny. He took his position in the world as a *Christian.* Thus early did he connect his studies, his ambition, his life, his everlasting state, with the cause of the Redeemer of mankind; and borrowed from Him strength " to will and to do."

His entire history from childhood till fourteen, is one of noble self-denying effort to lay a good foundation for success in life. His ambitious, aspiring heart, struggling with poverty, felt it no disgrace to stoop to what many would think a menial service. At one time you might have seen him running to the chamber or cellar of the store to get a broom, or gallon of molasses, for a customer. Then again you would have found him in his employer's house, doing the " chores" in and around it. The Kentucky orphan was the general waiter of the Ohio country merchant. A humble beginning for an astronomer and a major-general. But in this country, where we have no inherited nobility, our noblemen come oftener from the humblest and obscurest homes, than the mansions of the rich. I will let our hero tell his own story of this rough experience :

" I was working for *twenty-five cents a week*, with my hands full, but did my work faithfully. I used to cut wood, fetch water, make fires, scrub and scour in the morning for the old lady before the real work of the day was commenced. My clothes were bad, and I had no means of buying shoes, so was often barefooted.

" One morning I got through my work early, and the old lady, who thought I had not done it, or was especially ill-humored then, was displeased.

" She scolded me, and said : ' You are an idle boy. You haven't done the work.'

" I replied : ' I have done what I was told to do.'

" ' You are a liar,' was her angry reply.

" I felt my spirit rise indignantly against the charge ; and, standing erect, I answered : ' You will never have the chance of applying that word to me again.'

" I then walked out of the house to reënter it no more. I had not a cent in my pocket when I stepped into the world.

" What do you think I did then, boys?

" I met a countryman with a team. I boldly and

THE INSULT RESENTED, p. 20.

earnestly addressed him, saying : ' I will drive the leader if you will only take me on.'

" He looked at me in surprise, but in a moment said, ' I don't think you'll be of any use to me.'

" ' O yes I will,' I replied ; ' I can rub down and watch your horses, and do many things for you, if you will only let me try.'

" ' Well, well, my lad, get on the horse.'

" And so I climbed upon the leader's back, and commenced my teamster-life. The roads were deep mud, and the travelling very hard, and consequently slow. We got along at the rate of twelve miles per day. It was dull and tiresome you will believe ; but it was my *starting-point*. I had begun to push my way in the world, and went ahead after this. An independent spirit, and steady, honest conduct, with what capacity God has given me— as he has given you, boys—have carried me successfully through the world."

And now hear and always remember what he says to boys who have like himself, in early life, no friends to help with money, and must enter the busy world penniless. They are noble, inspiring words, spoken to a large assembly of lads in one of our cities :

" Don't be down-hearted at being poor, or having no friends. Try, and try again. You can cut your way through, if you live, so please God. I know it's a hard time for some of you. You are often hungry and wet with the rain or snow, and it seems dreary to have no one in the city to care for you. But trust in Christ, and He will be your friend. Keep up good heart, and be determined to make your own way honestly and truly through the world. As I said, I feel for you, because I have gone through it all : I know what it is. God bless you."

The fatherless boy had thus far been in a school of sad trial, yet blest with the kindly influences of home. In one view, he had no childhood; but took his place very early among men, to battle with poverty and pay his way.

The indignant and unceremonious desertion of his employer, you will notice, was not a rebellion against even tyrannical authority, nor a petulant refusal to do a servant's work in the honest endeavor to secure the needed compensation. It was the charge of falsehood, of unreliable character, which made him a homeless orphan. He felt even then that he could not, and would not, brook the insult to his sense of justice and his conscious integrity of purpose. The association with a nature so narrow and harsh was beyond endurance, and he went forth the *penniless* possessor of a fortune ; he had the wealth of a fine mind, lofty principle, and tireless energy of character. Brave young spirit ! God will bless always such a venture upon His providence.

And no part of Ormsby's life has a more important,

useful lesson for you, my young reader, than this very experience. It laid the foundation, so far as native character is concerned, of all his greatness. Those habits of patient industry, self-denial of present, transient pleasures, and a regard to the endless future which distinguished him, and gave him the noblest success, were formed in his boyhood. It reminds me of a youth in Yale College many years since, of similar spirit, who blacked the boots of the richer students to aid in the payment of his current expenses. One day they were around him at his work, talking over their future plans, when one of them said : " Well, K——, what are you going to be?" K—— brushed away, and quietly replied, " Governor of the State of New York." A laugh went round the little circle at his expense. The merry young men went forth from the college halls to be either a burden to society or comparatively unknown. The boy who was not ashamed to black boots to pay his debts, was heard in Congress, and was elected Lieutenant-Governor of the Empire State.

I must give you one more true and encouraging story. Thirty years ago, in the small academy at B——, was a boy faithfully devoted to the culture of his mind. But he was *poor*. Opening the drawer to his table you would have wondered and smiled, to see *a bowl of molasses well sprinkled with crumbs.* This was the student's whole provision for board. A loaf of bread, and the bowl with its contents, was the simple living. Now that lad is a popular author, whose beautiful cottage stands on the green banks of the glorious Hudson.

CHAPTER II.

OUNG Mitchel had improved his leisure moments. He early learned the value of these golden sands of time. Were you ever in the United States Mint? If so, you noticed a perforated floor, where the work in gold is done. Under this wooden net-work is the polished stone which catches the small particles. The woodwork can be removed, and the gold dust swept up and saved. The guide will tell you that nearly forty thousand dollars are thus saved every year in these *sweepings.* Young Mitchel caught the little fragments of time, and used them well.

When thirteen years old, Ormsby had acquired a considerable knowledge of Greek and Latin, in addition to English branches, including mathematics. He panted

2

—far from home, without money and without friends, which way he should turn if he were rejected.

While he was looking thoughtfully from his window, watching a sentinel pacing up and down, that stranger spoke kindly to him, asking him " if he was prepared for examination," and offering him all the assistance in his power. " Tell me what books I am to be examined in," said Ormsby, " and I will take care of the rest." Soon he was posted by his friend in regard to the text-books used in the severe trial before him. In a few days he had passed the ordeal with flying colors.

Being very young when he entered the Academy, his greatest ambition was to make each recitation as nearly perfect as possible. He had not been accustomed to the routine of study, like many of his classmates, who had reached even manhood. But his progress was steady and rapid. In his class was Robert E. Lee. Jefferson Davis was in the Academy at this time ; and being somewhat older than Mitchel, used to take him with him in his walks amid the magnificent scenery on every hand.*

From the cadet's barracks, where the young men had their rooms, he went to recitation, military drill, and mess hall or boarding-house, with promptness and regularity. His perfectly correct and abstemious habits kept him from the finely-constructed and managed *hospital* belonging to the Academy. He was no stranger in the engineering and model rooms, which contain the costly and

* See note on last page.

beautiful apparatus, and miniature forts, &c., for instruction in all kinds of civil and military engineering. In the riding hall, for exercises in horsemanship, he acquired equestrian gracefulness seldom excelled in the Academy. Nor did he neglect the elegant gallery of art, in which the marble and canvas seemed to breathe and speak. It was especially favorable to study at West Point when our cadet was there. The visitors were comparatively few. Railroad cars and steamboats did not then whistle at depot and wharf every hour. The tide of travel had not begun to flow toward that romantic spot; nor was it really thought of as a watering-place for the summer.

Every object, from the grand old mountains to Kosciusko's garden of beauty, interested him. He often sat near the iron enclosure of relics, itself the most suggestive of all—a part of the great chain which was drawn across the Hudson during the Revolutionary War. It was commenced January 20th, 1778, and finished April 11th of the same year. This gigantic chain weighed *one hundred and eighty-six tons*. The heaviest link weighed a hundred and thirty pounds.

Benedict Arnold, who commanded the position, had a link removed, pretending it was for repairing, to carry out his traitorous plan of giving, through André, the British possession of the stronghold—the key to the magnificent river.

Nothing will more forcibly show the depth of treason which .gave birth to the great Rebellion, than the *oath* taken by every cadet upon entering the Military Academy at West Point. It is a well-known fact that nearly all the leaders in the revolt were graduates of this institution. Jefferson Davis, as already stated in the biography, was a classmate of General Mitchel.

The cadets have been largely from the South. The result was, when the officers of the army and navy resigned their positions to join the ranks of treason, they furnished a larger number of commanders educated for the service at the expense of the United States, than were left to defend the Republic.

The following is the oath deliberately broken, and its national character denied and scorned by Davis, Beauregard, Lee, and other master spirits in the unexampled rebellion against constitutional law and order: .

" I do solemnly swear that I will support the Constitution of the United States, and bear true allegiance to the national Government; that I will maintain and defend the sovereignty of the United States paramount to any and all allegiance, sovereignty, or fealty I may owe to any State or Country whatsoever; and that I will at all times obey the legal orders of my superior officers, and the rules and articles governing the armies of the United States."

Young Mitchel wrote letters glowing with his earnest, affectionate nature, to his mother and brothers. Those to his mother revealed the characteristic tenderness and reverence to which allusion has been made. His large sympathies remind us of a great living divine, also widely known as a lecturer, who, when he was asked for the name of his gifted and devout mother, no longer among the living, wrote it in the following form :

" Elizabeth W—— H——, a name never spoken or written, without devout thanksgiving to God our Saviour, for her wonderful purity, piety, and charity ; that she was and *is my mother*."

How beautiful is such filial love ! The hue of a river's tide is often visible far out into the bay which receives it ; so in the manhood of these lofty minds clearly flows from the fountain at the cradle, the stream of affection for her who watched the dreamer there, and onward till the world was his sphere of action and influence—*her* gift to its struggling millions.

Cadet Mitchel graduated with honor. The highest mark of confidence in his attainments and character was, his appointment as assistant professor of mathematics in the Academy. This chair he filled for two years.

The next year after his graduation there was a revolutionary movement in France. Napoleon, you recollect, died on the rocky island of St. Helena in 1821. Charles X. succeeded him to the throne. He became unpopular on account of tyrannical measures, and the restless people, always changeful and unreliable, resolved to get rid of him.

When the outbreak of feeling came, and there was some prospect of a struggle for freedom, cadet Mitchel caught the fever of adventure. He wanted to have a hand in the strife. Day after day he thought of the arena of martial glory, and his dreams were haunted by its far-off enchantment. He wrote home, expressing his enthusiasm and his increasing desire to repair to France.

But the volatile Frenchmen soon dispelled his visions of valor and honor on their soil, so often red with the blood of revolution. In a few months Louis Philippe was seated on the throne of the empire, and the people were ready to shout, " Long live the King ! "

Leaving West Point, Mitchel joined the army in Florida, and was stationed at St. Augustine. His life became monotonous. The active mind of the youthful soldier could not endure the confinement, with no prospect of a larger field for the use of his culture, and the attainment of the reward of an honorable ambition to " make his mark in the world."

The occasional expedition—the many hours of idleness—the separation from social and religious scenes—all made him weary of a position which seemed to be of little worth to the country or to himself. He won a single victory which shed over his whole life a sacred halo of light. Miss Louisa Clark, of Cornwall, in which West

Point lies, had married Lieutenant Trask, who died. Her father was Judge Clark, at one time a member of the Legislature, and a gentleman of wide and deserved influence.

Mrs. Trask was a lady of fine intellect, rare culture, and of beautiful Christian character. This interesting young widow attracted the interest of the professor. His enthusiasm and noble character successfully won her hand, and they were married. The tenderly confiding nature of Mitchel found a congenial one in Mrs. Trask. Life from that hour became to him, who had the rough experience of orphanage, a new and blessed existence.

Resigning his place in the United States army, he went to the growing and charming city of Cincinnati, Ohio. The soldier became an honest attorney. For two years, old tomes and new, of legal lore, clients and courts, with the endearments and delights of home, which no one knew better how to value and enjoy than he, filled up the time.

Like poor Payne, who wrote the world-wide song,

" Home, sweet home,"

but was a wanderer all his days, Mitchel had a contrast to what he now enjoyed, to make that melody the very music of his soul. Wife, children, friends, around his table or hearthstone, were next to heaven in his affections.

This suggests the crowning excellence of his charac-

2*

ter; his consistent, unsullied Christian life. It brought no blush to his cheek, in any place or at any time, to "stand úp for Jesus;" everywhere giving the whole weight of his influence to the cause of true religion and human well-being.

Soon after he had taken up his residence in Cincinnati, he connected himself with the church of Dr. Lyman Beecher, and became a useful young layman under the eloquent teachings and practical activity of that distinguished divine. Here, also, ten years before he began his career as an astronomical lecturer; he made his first effort on the platform in the "Old College Building." The Rev. Thomas Brainerd, D.D., then pastor and editor there, relates, that his paper with others contained a notice that this stranger, a graduate of West Point, would lecture on astronomy. At the hour appointed the hall, lighted with candles by the friends of the speaker, contained an audience of *sixteen persons*. Though succeeding efforts were crowned with better success, he left the platform for the forum altogether, little dreaming of the splendid future before him as the orator of the stars.

CHAPTER III

Anecdote of our Hero—Is Elected Professor in Cincinnati College—His Enthusiasm in Astronomy—Is a Captain—He wants an Observatory—What is that?

ROFESSOR C——, who knew him well, related to me an anecdote illustrating Mr. Mitchel's enlightened views, and readiness to meet any objection to truth and duty. He was warmly interested in conference meetings, where the humblest voice could be heard in exhortation and prayer. The professor objected to them, because those would speak and pray who were either unsound in doctrine or otherwise unfit to lead a congregation. With the quickness of thought, and wonderful beauty of expression and manner peculiar to him, he answered his friend by narrating two incidents. One of them was to show the perversion of the freedom of such meetings, and the other, the vast amount of good which flows from them. Mr. Mitchel said: "A certain minister rose in a noon-day meeting, and with apparent sincerity told this story of his experience. Returning from a foreign coast, he prayed in faith that the Lord would give him ten souls the first meeting he should attend. He went to a religious meeting and made some remarks. The result was, ten persons became Christians. The man then snapping his finger, added, ' I might just as well have asked for *a hundred.*' " In contrast with such occasionally erratic and unhappy moments, Mr. Mitchel went on to say : " There was in the West a gentleman to whom another in a distant town was deeply indebted. This creditor wrote to a lawyer there, to collect the money due him. The attorney wrote back, that the young man who owed him was unable to pay, but struggling hard to get the means. The impatient creditor soon sent another demand for the collection of the debt. Again the considerate, compassionate counsellor at law, urged forbearance with the embarrassed, honest young pioneer. The indignant claimant replied, that the money was his rightful due, and he *must* have it. Time passed, and the debt was not paid. So off the angry creditor started for the lawyer's town and office. Entering the latter, he addressed his attorney excitedly, wishing to know why he had not collected the money. The kind appeal was once more urged; the exercise of mercy pressed upon the client. ' Right is right ;' was the unyielding response. ' I believe in justice, and all I ask is to have it done in this case. And now, I want to know whether you will get the money ? '

" ' I must if you insist—it is my business ;' the law-yer answered, ' and I will attend to it at once.'

" The gentleman left the office and strolled into the busy streets. Almost unconsciously he followed people going to the place of prayer. Soon after he was seated, a plain man arose, and repeated the passage, ' And what doth the Lord require of thee, but to do justly, love mercy, and walk humbly with thy God?' The speaker dwelt upon the grace of mercy, which was so often over-looked in the stern demands of justice. He impressively showed the deep meaning of the words of Christ, ' Blessed are the merciful for they shall obtain mercy.' The stranger was smitten with a sense of cruel *injustice*. The conviction of guilt became too strong for endurance. Rising, he astonished persons around him by his almost wild excitement. Pushing aside those in his way, he said, ' Here let me come—out of my way, I *must go !* ' Hasten-ing to the attorney's office, he inquired with anxious, earnestness, ' Have you collected the debt?'

" ' No,' was the answer ; ' but I was just going to see what could be done, and issue the warrant if necessary.'

" ' Don't you do it—don't you do it ! I have just found out that I haven't had the first idea of justice, or mercy either. I don't want the money, give it to the young man, for I'll have no more to do with it forever.' Thus the debtor returned to his home a better citizen, if not a Christian."

The lay-preaching had been the appeal more power
ful to the creditor than all the eloquence of the pulpit,
though indispensable in its high position.

In 1834, Mr. Mitchel was elected Professor of Mathematics, Philosophy, and Astronomy, in Cincinnati Col
lege, then just established.

From this time dates the beginning of his career as an
Astronomer. For ten years he filled with great honor
the chair which was the very one most congenial to his
taste. The students admired and loved him. His enthusiasm in the study of the starry heavens rose with the
growing familiarity of his mind with their glories. He
loved, upon a clear evening, to gather his class about
him, and with the poor helps they had—only inferior
instruments—to direct their attention to the wonders of
the firmament. With glowing words he would speak of the
"shepherdess of night, and her starry flock." He felt, and
tried to impress upon youthful minds, the language of the
still and radiant dome above their heads, sung by another :

> "Though voice nor sound inform the ear,
>   Well known the language of their song,
> When, one by one, the stars appear,
>   Led by the silent moon along,—
> Till round the earth from all the sky,
> THY beauty beams on every eye."

Not only in the college and the church was he active,
but interested in all the sources of public improvement.

. He was captain of a volunteer company ten years, drilling the men with the devotion to military order and discipline, of a colonel preparing his troops for the field of battle. It proved a valuable drill to him, keeping fresh and available his education at West Point. In other ways Providence was fitting him for his future and splendid, though brief military career.

In 1836 he filled the office of Chief Engineer of the Little Miami Railroad. Think of the Professor looking after the engines, tracks, and all the machinery for running the cars; learning lessons to be worth more than he dreams possible, nearly thirty years later on rebel soil, in his ever-active and valuable life.

The Professor's department of instruction of the college, and want of the helps needed, turned his attention to the *possibility* of having an observatory.

"And what is an observatory?" asks a young reader.

A general definition is, "a place appropriated for making observations upon natural objects." In astronomy, it is a building designed for making celestial observations. It has a dome for the optical instruments, which usually revolves; or a room in the upper story, with a movable roof, which can be removed when the heavens are viewed. The dome has openings with shutters. Its revolutions will sweep the horizon; and a single person can turn them just as he would the turret of a monitor.

The first thing essential is, to have the structure free

from *tremors*, or any motion.   To secure this, there are piers of solid masonry, built upon rock, or deeply imbedded, separated from every other part of the edifice, and rising high as the place for the instruments.   This, you will see, gives an immovable support for the heavy and nice telescopic apparatus.

The second consideration is, to avoid the effect of changes in the air.   So, places are selected secluded from the dust of travel and from fogs.

A third important consideration in putting up an observatory is, to have a free view of the horizon—a clear sweep of the circular base of the blue dome.

I hear another questioner inquire, "What is the *furniture* of such a house?"

An equatorial, or telescope, with which any part of the heavens may be seen by adjusting it, is the leading article in the costly furnishing.

There are two great classes, called *reflecting* and *refracting* telescopes.   In the former, the rays of light from a star, or any other object, pass down the large tube of the instrument, and fall on a metallic mirror, whose polished surface *reflects* them to a point called the *focus;* and there, forms a very luminous image of the object.   You then examine the image with a magnifying glass.   Of course, the greater the power of the lens, the larger will the object appear.

The refracting telescope has no mirror.   Instead of

this, the rays of light fall upon an *object-glass*, or power-ful lens, which brings them to a focus, and then you use the eye-glasses as in the other telescope.   Hear what he who has gazed many nights, while you were asleep, through the telescope, says about it :

" I will not here undertake to explain how it is that the telescope enables the eye to penetrate space.   That this power belongs to this magic instrument, no one can doubt who has ever seen a small, feeble star, converted by optical power into a magnificent orb, *forty times more ex tensive than the moon's surface*, as viewed by unaided vision.

" Who could have divined the nature of the revelations which would be made by an instrument giving to the eye a depth of penetration a *thousand fold greater* than it pos-sessed by nature ?

" If indeed the Creator is infinite, if His august pres-ence filleth immensity, then we had a right to anticipate that, no matter how deep the eye of man might pierce the domain of space, a point never could be reached wherein the evidences of God's presence would not appear.

" Such has been the result of the application of the tele-scope to sounding the mighty depths of the universe. Every.augmentation of power has served to reveal new wonders ; every increased depth to which the eye has penetrated, has evoked from the viewless depths of space, millions on millions of shining orbs, until the imagination is overwhelmed by the teeming numbers as by the mighty distances to which these island universes are removed.

" Conceive, if it be possible, of an object so remote that its light, flashing with a speed which no mind can comprehend, should still occupy a million of years in passing the mighty interval by which it is removed! and yet there is evidence that we now behold with the most powerful tubes, objects even ten, twenty, or thirty times more remote. We yield the point, and, in humble adoration, repeat the language of the sacred book, 'He inhabiteth eternity, His presence filleth immensity, and of His kingdom there is no end!'

" Such, indeed, is the effect produced by the telescopic explorations of the universe, that man has ceased to doubt the infinitude of God's empire, and now limits his ambition to a deeper penetration into its grandeur, without ever indulging the thought that he shall by any power pierce beyond its mighty limits. Lo! these are parts of His ways, but the thunder of His power who can understand?"

Besides this instrument, the next to it are the transit and clock for observing and keeping correct time, and the mural circle, which is used in measuring the distance of stars from the zenith, or point overhead—the central spot in the blue arch. There are also barometers, thermometers, &c.

And would you like to know when the first palace for a star-gazer was built?

It was commenced in 1667, and finished in 1671, at Paris, France, by Louis XIV. It was here that Picard, the superintendent, made calculations which furnished the great Newton with very valuable help in demonstrating the sublime law of gravitation, suggested by the falling apple. Leverrier is at the head of it now.

But where would you guess is the largest observatory?

Do you recollect who began the Crimean war, in which three empires were engaged?

Yes, the Emperor Nicholas.

In 1839, he had erected at Pultowa, ten miles from St. Petersburg, an Imperial Observatory. It cost half a million of dollars, and fifty thousand more are annually appropriated for its management. More than a hundred families are connected with its operations, and it is the best furnished and endowed in all Europe. The celebrated M. Struve superintends it. His name, as you will learn hereafter, is forever associated with that of the lamented Mitchel.

CHAPTER IV.

 FEW years since, we were entirely dependent on the Old World, especially upon England, for the discoveries in astronomy. The people of intelligence even, did not care for any thing so far above the business of a newly-settled hemisphere.

About the first thing that waked up scientific men in this country, was the transit of Venus, June 3d, 1769.

" What is *that?* " you inquire.

The word transit, you know, means a passing, as of goods over the country, from one point to another. When applied to Venus, the beautiful morning and evening star by turns, it indicates a wonderful event.

It has happened but *three* times, it is believed, since the creation of the world.

The path of the planet is across the sun's face ; that

is, it passes between us and the luminary of day, and looks like a little blot on its surface.

This phenomenon requires such a position of the earth and Venus in regard to the sun, that it can rarely occur.

The first time it was seen was in 1639, when a single person beheld the beautiful sight. Young Horrocks, living near Liverpool, England, suspected the thing would occur, and watched the result of his calculations. How intensely he waited for the grand spectacle; because never seen before, and attended with fresh light upon the science of astronomy. He could scarcely eat or sleep for days. But near the time for the expected wonder, the hour of divine worship arrived. Few, indeed, would have risked the loss by going to the House of God. Horrocks went—bowed to the "King of kings," and returning, looked through the tube of his instrument, and lo! the speck was in the "sun's eye!"

In 1761, the swift revolutions of the heavenly bodies brought again the transit. Astronomers from England, France, and Russia, were scattered round the globe, from Siberia to the South Sea, to be sure of clear, accurate, and varied observations.

Eight years later, the spectacle, it was predicted, would recur. In January, 1769, our scientific men began to get ready for the anticipated sight. They selected diferent points for watching the little black ball floating on the sea of fire. Temporary watch-towers were soon after erected, and aid to build better and permanent ones, was solicited from State Governments in vain. Money and politics, not stars, occupied the thoughts of legislators.

In 1825, John Quincy Adams, President of the United States, recommended in eloquent language, and urged with strong arguments, the appropriation of money by Congress, to build a national university and observatory.

And what did the people say? They treated the splendid project as the Romish priesthood did Galileo, because he said the earth turned on its axis, excepting the imprisonment of its advocates. They ridiculed the idle fancy—the proposed *waste* of Government funds.

The years vanished; for the world rolled on, and the sun and the stars swept along their high pathways.

Meanwhile Yale College, in 1830, placed a fine telescope in the steeple of a college building, which was almost a *prison* for it.

Williams' College, Western Reserve, and other institutions, followed in the erection of observatories, and putting in them good, but not the most powerful instruments. The Military Academy at West Point, ten years after Cadet Mitchel left its walls, built a noble edifice for the library, having three towers for the use of optical instruments. In 1842, Professor Mitchel determined to devote himself to the erection of an observatory that would compare with those in Europe—at least be entitled to the name. Congress, about the same time, began to act with reference to a national edifice for naval and astronomical purposes. He was *alone* in his enterprise. And now we come to a new exhibition of the energy and hopeful perseverance of the untiring Mitchel. You have another illustration of the great lesson of his useful life; the resolute will, seizing every opportunity for success in the noblest attainments, made sacred and sublime by his faith in God. No timid, vacillating, or selfish man would have conceived the enterprise of building an observatory which should have no superior in the country for years to come, and furnishing it with the best instruments the world could produce.

But how shall the professor, without fortune, begin the undertaking? The business communities care but little about the stars; the glitter of coin, or schemes that will make it, move the busy throng crowding the marketplace and thoroughfares of commercial activity.

The genius that knows no failure in a worthy cause, and had never repeated for himself the word " can't," thinks and dreams over the grand idea. He knows that it will seem to many like the extravagant scheme of an enthusiast. But he remembers that Columbus was regarded as a lunatic while he mused and wept over his mental discovery of a hemisphere, which none were ready to help him make a splendid reality. Kings and queens smiled at his harmless fancies, while he heard with his inward ear the shining surf breaking upon the shores of unknown lands, and saw the treasures of half the world lying at his feet. The navigator succeeded, because he thought not of final defeat. Professor Mitchel saw, in his imagination, the massive structure on some green summit, and himself behind the tube, whose glasses revealed resplendent and hitherto unseen wonders in the star-sown fields of ether. The edifice *must* be reared to science, the country, and God. He could devise no plan to get the ear and awaken the interest of the people, unless he could excite enthusiasm through the high themes which filled and delighted his soul.

One day it was announced by a " poster," in the hall of Cincinnati College, and a notice in the daily papers of the city, that Professor Mitchel would commence a series of lectures in the audience room of that institution. The astronomer finds it necessary to use his tact in this bait for the public. For however excellent the immediate instruction, his object is to catch his hearers in the golden meshes of his yet imaginary observatory. And just as you, young reader, have gone by yourself, tools in hand, to work out some ideal model of miniature mechanism, the professor goes to his study, to invent and construct a machine for exhibiting in brilliant light, and greatly magnified, the beautiful and wonderful telescopic views, on paper, taken in the silence of the night, when those whom they were to delight were asleep.

The evening for the first lecture came. Such had

been the efforts of friends of the man and the cause, that
before the hour had struck for the experiment, that had
disturbed the very repose of the lecturer, through the
open doors of the College Hall a large procession of intelligent citizens poured into the finely-illuminated room.

The extempore *Stereopticon* was a success, and is ready
for the exhibition. Manly, yet modest, is the bearing of
the " star-gazer " as he takes his position, surrounded by
members of the faculty and anxious friends—anxious, not
in regard to the quality of the lecture, but the effect of the
occasion on the scheme which suggested it.

And I am sure my intelligent reader will love to follow the astronomer through a few passages of this opening
and most eloquent lecture, and others which succeeded it.
How sublimely he walks among the ages past, and through
the starry depths !

" The starry heavens do not display their glittering
constellations in the glare of day, while the rush and turmoil of business incapacitate man for the enjoyment of
their solemn grandeur. It is in the stillness of the midnight hour, when all nature is hushed in repose, when
the hum of the world's ongoing is no longer heard, that
the planets roll and shine, and the bright stars, trooping
through the deep heavens, speak to the willing spirit that
would learn their mysterious being.

" Often have I swept backward in imagination six
thousand years, and stood beside our Great Ancestor, as

3

he gazed for the first time upon the going down of the sun. What strange sensations must have swept through his bewildered mind, as he watched the last departing ray of the sinking orb, unconscious whether he should even behold its return! Wrapt in a maze of thought, strange and startling, his eye long lingers about the point at which the sun had slowly faded from his view. A mysterious darkness, hitherto unexperienced, creeps over the face of nature. The beautiful scenes of earth, which through the swift hours of the first wonderful day of his existence, had so charmed his senses, are slowly fading one by one from his dimmed vision. A gloom deeper than that which covers earth, steals across the mind of earth's solitary inhabitant. He raises his inquiring gaze toward heaven, and lo! a silver crescent of light, clear and beautiful, hanging in the Western sky, meets his astonished eye. The young moon charms his untutored vision, and leads him upward to her bright attendants, which are now stealing, one by one, from out the deep blue sky. The solitary gazer bows, and wonders, and adores. The hours glide by—the silver moon is gone— the stars are rising, slowly ascending the heights of heaven—and solemnly sweeping downward in the stillness of the night. The first grand revolution to mortal vision is nearly completed. A faint streak of rosy light is seen in the East—it brightens—the stars fade—the planets are extinguished—the eye is fixed in mute astonishment on the growing splendor, till the first rays of the returning sun dart their radiance on the young earth and its solitary inhabitant. To him 'the evening and the morning were the first day.'

" The curiosity excited on this first solemn night—the consciousness that in the heavens God had declared his glory—the eager desire to comprehend the mysteries that dwell in these bright orbs, have clung to the descendants of him who first watched and wondered, through the long lapse of six thousand years. In this boundless field of investigation, human genius has won its most signal victories. Music is here—but it is the deep and solemn harmony of the spheres. Poetry is here—but it must be read in the characters of light, written on the sable garments of night. Architecture is here—but it is the colossal structure of sun and system, of cluster and universe. Eloquence is here—but ' there is neither speech nor language. Its voice is not heard,' yet its resistless sweep comes over us in the mighty periods of revolving worlds.

" Shall we not listen to this music, because it is deep and solemn? Shall we not read this poetry, because its letters are the stars of heaven? Shall we refuse to contemplate this architecture, because ' its architecture, its archways, seem ghostly from infinitude'? Shall we turn away from this surging eloquence, because its utterance is made through sweeping worlds? No; the mind is ever inquisitive, ever ready to attempt to scale the most rugged steps. Wake up its enthusiasm—fling the light of hope in its pathway, and no matter how rough, and steep, and rocky it may prove, *onward!* is the word which charms its willing powers."

How beautifully does the life of the orator illustrate these last words! He had been charmed to duty, and cheered in the trial of courage from his earliest boyhood, by the music of that single lesson of the stars, *onward!*

And the wonderful *orations*, we may call them, which week after week fell from his lips, carried the delighted hearers "onward" over the whole field of time. Like a dazzling comet, he went among the mighty systems of worlds, and led the mind along the track of discovery to the magnificent telescopic revelations of the present. With the first "star-gazers" he seemed to stand and watch the great over-arching sky, and decipher the fact that there was real and apparent motion there; that is, there were objects moving, and others which only seemed to be so, like the trees when the cars alone change their place: then he studied with them in the dim light of early ages, the revolutions of that nearest planet the moon, the grand march of the constellations, the flight of the terror-inspiring comets, and appearance of the dreaded eclipses, while the rays of science brightened along the track of discovery; till he looked among the glories which stream upon the vision of the latest "sentinels on the watch towers" of the starry heavens.

His strong and fiery imagination swept from the "hill-tops of Eden" to the heights of America, from which the inquiring eye has been lifted to the sky. How strange it is that we do not know, and shall never know on earth, when and where, and by whom the first intelligent observation of the heavens was made! Hear the sublime language of the professor:

" I would fain stand at the very source of discovery, and commence with that unknown godlike mind which first conceived the grand thought that even these mysterious stars might be read, and that the bright page which was nightly unfolded to the vision of man needed no interpreter of its solemn beauties but human genius. On some lofty peak he stood, in the stillness of the midnight hour, with the listening stars as witnesses of his vows, and there conscious of his high destiny, and that of his race, resolves to commence the work of ages. ' Here,' he exclaims, ' is my watch tower, and yonder bright orbs are henceforth my solitary companions. Night after night, year after year, will I watch and wait, ponder and reflect, until some ray shall pierce the deep gloom which now wraps the world.'

" Thus resolved the unknown founder of the science of the stars. His name and country are lost forever. What matters this since his works, his discoveries, have endured for thousands of years, and will endure as long

as the moon shall continue to fill her silver horn, and the
planets to roll and shine."

Here you have also a fine glimpse of our hero's character. Not anxious about the world's changing mood,
his great concern was to do his work well, and leave to
God and posterity his fame. Of the moon and the polar
star, he adds:

" Go with me, then, in imagination, and let us stand
beside this primitive observer, at the close of his career
of nearly a thousand years (for we must pass beyond the
epoch of the deluge, and seek our first discoveries among
those sages whom, for their virtues, God permitted to
count their age, not by years, but by centuries), and here
we shall learn the order in which the secrets of the starry
world slowly yielded themselves to long and persevering
scrutiny. And now let me unfold, in plain and simple
language, the train of thought, of reasoning, and research,
which marked this primitive era of astronomical science.
It is true that history yields no light, and tradition even
fails ; but such is the beautiful order in the golden chain
of discovery, that the bright links which are known, reveal with certainty those which are buried in the voiceless
past. If, then, it were possible to read the records of the
founder of astronomy, graven on some column of granite
dug from the earth, whither it had been borne by the fury
of the deluge, we know now what its hieroglyphics would
reveal, with a certainty scarcely less than that which

would be given by an actual discovery, such as we have imagined. We are certain that the first discovery ever recorded, as the result of human observation, was on the *moon.*

" The sun, the moon, the stars, had long continued to rise and climb the heavens, and slowly sink beneath the western horizon. The spectacle of day and night was then, as now, familiar to every eye ; but in gazing there was no observation, and in mute wonder there was no science. When the solitary observer took his post, it was to watch the moon. Her extraordinary phases had long fixed his attention. Whence came these changes? The sun was ever round and brilliant—the stars shone with undimmed splendor—while the moon was ever waxing and waning, sometimes a silver crescent hanging in the western sky, or full-orbed, walking in majesty among the stars, and eclipsing their radiance, with her overwhelming splendor. Scarcely had the second observation been made upon the moon, when the observer was struck with the wonderful fact, that she had left her place among the fixed stars, which, on the preceding night, he had accurately marked. Astonished, he again fixes her place by certain bright stars close to her position, and waits the coming of the following night. His suspicions are confirmed—the moon is moving ; and what to him is far more wonderful, her motion is precisely contrary to the general revolution of the heavens, from east

to west. With a curiosity deeply aroused, he watches
from night to night to learn whether she will return
upon her track ; but she marches steadily onward among
the stars, until she sweeps the entire circuit of the
heavens, and returns to the point first occupied, to re-
commence her ceaseless cycles.

"The long and accurate vigils of the moon, and the
necessity of recognizing her place, by the clusters or
groups of stars among which she was nightly found, had
already familiarized the eye with those along her track,
and even thus early the heavens began to be divided into
constellations. The eye was not long in detecting the
singular fact, that this stream of constellations, lying
along the moon's path, was constantly flowing to the
west, and one group after another apparently dropping
into the sun, or at least becoming invisible, in consequence of their proximity to this brilliant orb. A closer
examination revealed the fact, that the aspect of the
whole heavens was changing from month to month.
Constellations which had been conspicuous in the west,
and whose brighter stars were the first to appear as the
twilight faded, were found to sink lower and lower toward
the horizon, till they were no longer seen ; while new
groups were constantly appearing in the east.

"These wonderful changes, so strange and inex-
plicable, must have long perplexed the early student of
the heavens. Hitherto the stars, along the moon's route,

had engaged special attention ; but at length certain bright and conspicuous constellations, toward the north, arrested the eye : and these were watched to see whether they would disappear. Some were found to dip below the western horizon, soon to reappear in the east; while others, revolving with the general heavens, rose high above the horizon, swept steadily round, sunk far down, but never disappeared from the sight. This remarkable discovery soon led to another equally important. In watching the stars in the north through an entire night, they all seemed to describe circles ; having a common centre, these circles grew smaller and smaller as the stars approached nearer to the centre of revolution, until finally one bright star was found, whose position was ever fixed—alone unchanged while all else was slowly moving. The discovery of this remarkable star must have been hailed with uncommon delight by the primitive observer of the heavens. If his deep devotion to the study of the skies had created surprise among his rude countrymen, when he came to point them to this never-changing light hung up in the heavens, and explained its uses in guiding their wanderings on the earth, their surprise must have given place to admiration. Here was the first valuable gift of primitive astronomical science to man.

" But to the astronomer this discovery opened up a new field of investigation, and light began to dawn on some of the most mysterious questions which had long

3*

perplexed him.   He had watched the constellations near
the moon's track slowly disappear in the effulgence of the
sun ; and when they were next seen, it was in the east,
in the early dawn, apparently emerging from the solar
beams, having actually passed by the sun.   Watching
and reflecting, steadily pursuing the march of the northern constellations, which never entirely disappeared, and
noting the relative positions of these, and those falling
into the sun, it was at last discovered that the entire
starry heavens was slowly moving forward to meet and
pass by the sun, or else the sun itself was actually moving
backward among the stars.   This apparent motion had
already been detected in the moon, and now came the reward of long and diligent perseverance.   The grand discovery was made, that both the sun and moon were
moving among the fixed stars, not *apparently*, but *abso-
lutely*.   The previously received explanation of the moon's
motion could no longer be sustained ; for the starry heavens could not at the same time so move as to pass by the
moon in one month, and to pass by the sun in a period
twelve times as great.   A train of the most important
conclusions flowed at once from this great discovery.
The starry heavens passed beneath and around the
earth—the sun and moon were wandering in the same
direction, but with different velocities, among the stars—
the constellations actually filled the entire heavens above
the earth and beneath the earth—the stars were invisible

in the day time, not because they did not exist, but because their feeble light was lost in the superior brilliancy of the' sun. The heavens were spherical, and encompassed like a shell the entire earth, and hence it was conceived that the earth itself was also a globe, occupying the centre of the starry sphere.

" It is imposible for us, familiar as we are at this day with these important truths, to appreciate the rare merit of him who by the power of his genius first rose to their knowledge, and revealed them to an astonished world. We delight to honor the names of Kepler, of Galileo, of Newton ; but here are discoveries so far back in the dim past, that all trace of their origin is lost, which vie in interest and importance with the proudest achievements of any age.

" With a knowledge of the sphericity of the heavens, the revolution of the sun and moon, the constellations of the celestial sphere, the axis of its diurnal revolution, astronomy began to be a science, and its future progress was destined to be rapid and brilliant. A line drawn from the earth's centre to the north star formed the axis of the heavens, and day and night around this axis all the celestial host were noiselessly pursuing their never ending journies. Thus far, the only moving bodies known were the sun and moon. These large and brilliant bodies, by their magnitude and splendor, stood out conspicuously from among the multitude of stars, leaving these minute

but beautiful points of light, in one great class, unchange-
able among themselves, fixed in their groupings and configurations, furnishing admirable points of reference, in
watching and tracing out the wanderings of the sun and
moon.

" To follow the moon as she pursued her journey
among the stars was not difficult ; but to trace the sun in
his slower and more majestic motion, and to mark accurately his track, from star to star, as he heaved upward
to meet the coming constellations, was not so readily accomplished. Night after night, as he sunk below the
horizon, the attentive watcher marked the bright stars
near the point of setting which first appeared in the evening twilight. These gradually sunk toward the sun on
successive nights, and thus was he traced from constellation to constellation, until the entire circuit of the
heavens was performed, and he was once more attended
by the same bright stars, that had watched long before,
his sinking in the west. Here was revealed the measure
of the *Year*. The earth had been verdant with the beauties of spring—glowing with the maturity of summer—
rich in the fruits of autumn—and locked in the icy chains
of winter, while the sun had circled round the heavens.
His entrance into certain constellations marked the coming seasons, and man was beginning to couple his cycle
of pursuits on earth with the revolutions of the celestial
orbs.

" While intently engaged in watching the sun as it slowly heaved up to meet the constellations, some ardent devotee to this infant science at length marked in the early twilight a certain. brilliant star closely attendant upon the sun.   The relative position of these two objects was noted, for a few consecutive nights, when, with a degree of astonishment of which we can form no conception, he discovered that this brilliant star was rapidly approaching the sun, and actually changing its place among the neighboring stars : night after night he gazes on this unprecedented phenomenon, *a moving star !* and on each successive night he finds the wanderer coming nearer and nearer to the sun.   At last it disappears from sight, plunged in the beams of the upheaving sun.   What had become of this strange wanderer ? was it lost forever ? were questions which were easier asked than answered. But patient watching had revealed the fact, that when a group of stars, absorbed into the sun's rays, disappeared in the west, they were next seen in the eastern sky, slowly emerging from his morning beams.   Might it not be possible that this wandering star would pass by the sun and reappear in the east ?   With how much anxiety must this primitive discoverer have watched in the morning twilight ?   Day after day he sought his solitary post, and marked the rising stars, slowly lifting themselves above the eastern horizon.   The gray dawn came, and the sun shot forth a flood of light, the stars faded and disappeared, and the watcher gives over till the coming morning. But his hopes are crowned at last. Just before the sun breaks above the horizon, in the rosy east, refulgent with the coming day, he descries the pure white silver ray of his long lost wanderer. It has passed the sun—it rises in the east—the first *planet* is discovered! With how much anxiety and interest did the delighted discoverer trace the movements of his wandering star.

" Whatever light may be shed upon antiquity by deciphering the hieroglyphic memorials of the past, there is no hope of ever going far enough back, to reach even the nation to which we are indebted for the first rudiments of the science of the stars.

" Thus far in the prosecution of the study of the heavens, the eye and the intellect had accomplished the entire work. Rapidly as we have sketched the progress of early discovery, and short as may have been the period in which it was accomplished, no one can fail to perceive how vast is the difference between the light that thus early broke in upon the mind, heralding the coming of a brighter day, and the deep and universal darkness which had covered the world before the dawn of science. Encouraged by the success which had thus far rewarded patient toil, the mind of man pushes on its investigations deeper and deeper into the domain of the mysterious and unknown.

"In these primitive ages the heavenly bodies were regarded with feelings little less than thé reverence we now bestow on the Supreme Creator. The sun, especially, as the Lord of life and light, was regarded with feelings nearly approaching to adoration, even by the astronomers themselves. The idea early became fixed, that the chief of the celestial bodies must move with a uniform velocity in a circular orbit, never increasing or decreasing. Change being inconsistent with the supreme and dignified station which was assigned to him—what, then, must have been the astonishment of the primitive astronomers, who in counting the days from the summer to the winter solstice, and from the winter round to the summer solstice, these intervals were found to be unequal?"

CHAPTER V.

Y reader, have you seen an eclipse of the sun or moon? You know what it is? When the luminary of day is veiled, the moon has come between us and it, just where the *tracks cross;* that is, at the point in their orbits which brings them in a line with the earth. Of course we cannot see through the moon, and so the sun is obscured.

When the moon is eclipsed, the earth gets in a similar way between the sun and moon, and the light is cut off from the satellite of our world. You will be interested in the orator's description of the discovery of this simple fact that robbed the eclipse of the horrors which had terrified the people. A watcher of the heavenly bodies had become convinced that the dreaded darkness was caused by a natural law of revolution, and made calculations accordingly. Up to this time nobody knew or could guess what *blackened* the face of the sun and moon. It is not strange that the night coming at morning or midday, should alarm the inhabitants wherever it was seen.

I think we should be just as much alarmed were it not for the labors of that man ages since, and his successors in astronomical studies. Let us go back over long centuries. The prophet of such an event, explaining the dark marvel of the past since creation's dawn, has arisen. Every thing is ready for predicting the sun's hiding behind the moon. Says the eloquent Mitchel:

" He announces to the startled inhabitants of the world that the sun shall expire in dark eclipse. Bold prediction! mysterious prophet! with what scorn must the unthinking world have received this solemn declaration. How slowly do the moons roll away, and with what intense anxiety does the stern philosopher await the coming of that day which should crown him with victory, or dash him to the ground in ruin and disgrace! Time to him moves on leaden wings; day after day, and at last hour after hour, roll heavily away. The last night is gone— the moon has disappeared from his eagle gaze in her approach to the sun, and the dawn of the eventful day breaks in beauty on a slumbering world.

" This daring man, stern in his faith, climbs alone to his rocky home, and greets the sun as he rises and mounts the heavens, scattering brightness and glory in his path. Beneath him is spread out the populous city, already

teeming with life and activity. The busy morning hum
rises on the still air and reaches the watching place of the
solitary astronomer. The thousands below him, unconscious of his intense anxiety, buoyant with life, joyously
pursue their rounds of business and of amusement. The
sun slowly climbs the heavens, round, and bright, and
full-orbed. The lone tenant of the mountain-top almost
begins to waver in his faith, as the morning hours roll
away. But the time of his triumph, long delayed, at
length begins to dawn; a pale and sickly hue creeps over
the face of nature. The sun has reached his highest
point, but his splendor is dimmed, his light is feeble. At
last it comes! Blackness is eating away his round disc;
onward, with slow but steady pace, the dark veil moves,
blacker than a thousand nights—the gloom deepens—the
ghastly hue of death covers the universe—the last ray is
gone, and horror reigns. A wail of terror fills the murky
air; the clangor of brazen trumpets resounds; an agony
of despair dashes the stricken millions to the ground,
while that lone man, erect on his rocky summit, with
arms outstretched to heaven, pours forth the grateful
gushings of his heart to God, who had crowned his efforts
with triumphant victory. It is to me the proudest victory that genius ever won. It was the conquering of
nature, of ignorance, of superstition, of terror, all at a
single blow, and that blow struck by a single arm."

"Who," you ask, "was this wonderful man, whom

'his fellows must have regarded as little less than a god?'" His fame is "inscribed on the very heavens," but lost on earth. No one can tell his name or nation. Such is human glory! But great and good deeds *never die.*

"A thousand years roll by;" and in ancient and splendid Babylon the record of an eclipse is made, "which is safely wafted down the stream of time." A thousand years more have swept by, and among the fierce Arabs again the prediction is made, and the eclipse appears. And then after a thousand years are added to those already gone, the astronomer of Paris observes the same phenomenon.

Is it not amazing that the prophets of eclipses, whose records cover three thousand years, should exactly agree? That the Frenchman should study the record of the Babylonian who looked on the sun and moon so long before? You have learned how the great law of gravitation, the mysterious bond holding planets, suns, and systems together, was discovered by Isaac Newton. A falling apple led him to ask the natural question, "What brings it to the ground?" That apple was the key to wonders vast as God's universe.

Little thoughts and little things are not to be lightly esteemed; they have been the beginning of world-wide discoveries and eternal destinies.

We cannot follow the *celestial* orator through his unrivalled lectures. But since writing this a young lad said:

" Tell us about the comets, and the boys will be inter-
terested.   What did General Mitchel say about them?"
He had just read that a learned professor in Munich, a city
of which I shall have more to say hereafter, predicted
the burning of the world in 1865 by a comet.   Next
to the eclipse has this wanderer frightened the world.

The boy's questions were doubtless the same you
would ask, and I will give them with the answers.

" What are comets?"

" It is a very hard question to answer.   They suddenly blaze forth and sweep through the heavens with
amazing velocity.   Their aspect is often terrific.   Their
paths are irregular, and from all points of the compass
they rush toward and around the sun.   What they *are*
no man has yet been able to tell."

" I just recollect seeing one a few years ago ; but will
you describe their appearance?"

" The comet of 1858 was very beautiful.   It resembled a plume ; the trail of light flowing backward from
the splendid starlike brow.   Others. have been double ;
and the great comet of 1744 had six luminous trains,
which streamed above the horizon long after the globe of
splendor had sunk below it.   The Catholics, who were
afraid of the armies of the Sultan of Turkey at that time,
offered this prayer : ' The Lord save us from the Devil,
the Turk, and the Comet !' "

" Why were people afraid of comets?"

" Because they seemed to be wild and wandering messengers from distant regions, having no connection with our starry dome. They were regarded as omens of war, pestilence, and famine.".

· " How did astronomers find out they were not?"

" Observation proved that these fiery corsairs of the blue deep were, after all, governed by the same law of gravitation which binds all the worlds together. And though some of them plunge away for several hundred years into space, and then return, they had their appointed periods, like the earth and moon."   .

" Is there really any danger that a comet will destroy the world?"

" Newton, Mitchel, and others think not; at least that the collision is not likely to occur. If it did they believe the curious body is too light, or cloudlike, to jostle our planet out of its orbit, or set it on fire. Yet none can deny that God could make it a torch to kindle ' nature's funeral pile.' "

The lad looked thoughtful. The possibility of the world's meeting with a comet troubled him. I could only cheer him with the assurance that a sincere trust in Him who created the comet, would give us

" A heart for any fate."

He then inquired about the milky way, made of resplendent suns, so far away you cannot separate them with the eye.   And many of the nebulæ. or luminous clouds floating in the blue depths "blaze with countless stars" when a powerful telescope is directed to them.

Professor Mitchel seemed to forget that he was on earth, in dwelling on the boundless grandeur of the universe, which he had viewed during the "night watches," and talked as if he were among the resplendent worlds and discoursing *from* the skies.   He was like the imaginary traveller of the German poet, quoted by him to express his overwhelming visions of Jehovah's power, wisdom, and omniscience in the celestial vault.   Here is the singular and beautiful fancy :

"God called up from dreams a man into the vestibule of heaven, saying, 'Come thou hither and see the glory of my house.'

" And to the servants that stood around the throne, he said : 'Take him, and undress him from his robes of flesh : cleanse his vision, and put a new breath in his nostrils : only touch not with any change his human heart—the heart that weeps and trembles.'

" It was done ; and with a mighty angel for his guide, the man stood ready for his infinite voyage.   From the terraces of heaven, without sound or farewell, at once they wheeled away into endless space.   *   *   *   In a moment the rushing of planets was upon them ; in a mo-'ment the blazing of suns was around them.   On the right hand and on the left towered mighty constellations, forming triumphal gates and archways that seemed ghostly from infinitude. Suddenly, as they swept past systems and worlds, a cry arose that other heights and other depths were nearing, were at hand.

" The man sighed, and stopped, and shuddered, and wept. His overladened heart uttered itself in tears, and he said : ' Angel, I will go no farther. Insufferable is the glory of God. Let me lie down in the grave, and hide me from the infinite ; for end I see there is none.'

" And from all the listening stars that shone around issued a choral voice—' the man speaks truly ; end there is none that ever yet we heard of.'

" ' End is there none ?' the angel solemnly demanded. ' Is there indeed no end? and is this the sorrow that kills you?'

" But no voice answered that he might answer himself. Then the angel threw up his glorious hands to the heaven of heaven, saying :

" ' End there is none in the universe of God. Lo ! also there is no beginning.' "

I will only add the closing passages of these unequalled lectures :

" Look out to-night on the brilliant constellations which crowd the heavens. Mark the configurations of these stars. Five thousand years ago the Chaldean shepherd gazed on the same bright groups. Two thousand years have rolled away since the Greek philosopher pronounced the eternity of the heavens, and pointed to the ever-during configuration of the stars as proof positive of his assertion. But a time will come when not a constellation now blazing in the bright concave above us shall remain. Slowly, indeed, do these fingers on the dial of heaven mark the progress of time. A thousand years may roll away with scarce a perceptible change ; even a million of years may pass without effacing all traces of the groupings which now exist ; but that eye which shall behold the universe of the fixed stars when ten millions of years shall have silently rolled away, will search in vain for the constellations which now beautify and adorn our nocturnal heavens. Should God permit, the stars may be there, but no trace of their former relative positions will be found !

" Here I must close. The intellectual power of man, as exhibited in his wonderful achievements among the planetary and stellar worlds, has thus far been our single object. I have neither turned to the right hand nor to the left. Commencing with the first mute gaze bestowed upon the heavens, and with the curiosity awakened in that hour of admiration and wonder, we have attempted to follow rapidly the career of the human mind, through the long lapse of six thousand years. What a change has this period wrought. Go backward in imagination to the plains of Shinar, and stand beside the shepherd astronomer as he vainly attempts to grasp the mysteries of

the waxing and waning moon, and then. enter the sacred
precincts of yonder temple devoted to the science of the
stars. Look over its magnificent machinery; examine
its space-annihilating instruments, and ask the sentinel
who now keeps his unbroken vigil the nature of his investigations.

. " Moon, and planet, and sun, and system, are left
behind. His researches are now within a sphere to
whose confines the eagle glance of the Chaldean, never
reached. Periods, and distances, and masses, and motions, are all familiar to him; and could the man who
gazed and pondered six thousand years ago stand beside
the man who now fills his place, and listen to his teachings, he would listen with awe, inspired by the revelations
of an angel of God. But where does the human mind
now stand? Great as are its achievements, profoundly
as it has penetrated the mysteries of creation, what has
been done is but an infinitesimal portion of what remains
to be done.

" But the examinations of the past inspire the highest
hopes for the future. The movement is one constantly
accelerating and expanding. Look at what has been
done during the last three hundred years, and answer me
to what point will human genius ascend before the same
period shall again roll away? But in our admiration for
that genius which has been able to reveal the mysteries
of the universe, let us not forget the homage due to Him

4

who created, and by the might of his power sustains all
things.   At some future time, I hope to be permitted to
direct your attention to this branch of the subject.   If
there be any thing which can lead the mind upward to
the Omnipotent Ruler of the universe, and give to it an
approximate knowledge of His incomprehensible attri-
butes, it is to be found in the grandeur and beauty of
His works.

  " If you would know His *glory*, examine the inter-
minable range of suns and systems which crowd the
Milky Way.   Multiply the hundred million of stars
which belong to our own ' island universe' by the thousands of these astral systems that exist in space, within
the range of human vision, and then you may form some
idea of the infinitude of His kingdom ; for lo ! these are
but a part of His ways.   Examine the scale on which the
universe is built.   Comprehend, if you can, the vast dimensions of our sun.   Stretch outward through his system, from planet to planet, and circumscribe the whole
within the immense circumference of Neptune's orbit.
This is but a single unit out of the myriads of similar
systems.   Take the wings of light, and flash with impetuous speed, day and night, and month and year, till
youth shall wear away, and middle age is gone, and the
extremest limit of human life has been attained ; count
every pulse, and at each speed on your way a hundred
thousand miles ; and when a hundred years have rolled

by, look out, and behold ! the thronging millions of blazing suns are still around you, each separated from the other by such a distance that in this journey of a century you have only left half a score behind you.

" Would you gather some idea of the *eternity* past of God's existence, go to the astronomer, and bid him lead you with him in one of his walks through space ; and as he sweeps outward from object to object, from universe to universe, remember that the light from those filmy stains on the deep pure blue of heaven, now falling on your eye, has been traversing space for a million of years. Would you gather some knowledge of the *omnipotence* of God, weigh the earth on which we dwell, then count the millions of its inhabitants that have come and gone for the last six thousand years. Unite their strength into one arm, and test its power in an effort to move this earth. It could not stir it a single foot in a thousand years ; and yet under the omnipotent hand of God, not a minute passes that it does not fly for more than a thousand miles. But this is a mere atom ; the most insignificant point among His innumerable worlds. At His bidding, every planet, and satellite, and comet, and the sun himself, fly onward in their appointed courses. His single arm guides the millions of sweeping suns, and around His throne circles the great constellation of unnumbered universes.

" Would you comprehend the idea of the *omniscience*

of God, remember that the highest pinnacle of knowledge reached by the whole human race, by the combined efforts of its brightest intellects, has enabled the astronomer to compute approximately the perturbations of the planetary worlds. He has predicted roughly the return of half a score of comets. But God has computed the mutual perturbations of millions of suns, and planets, and comets, and worlds, without number, through the ages that are passed, and throughout the ages which are yet to come, not approximately, but with perfect and absolute precision. The universe is in motion—system rising above system, cluster above cluster, nebula above nebula—all majestically sweeping around under the providence of God, who alone knows the end from the beginning, and before whose glory and power all intelligent beings, whether in heaven or on earth, should bow with humility and awe.

" Would you gain some idea of the *wisdom* of God, look to the admirable adjustments of the magnificent retinue of planets and satellites which sweep around the sun. Every globe has been weighed and poised, every orbit has been measured and bent to its beautiful form. All is changing, but the laws fixed by the wisdom of God, though they permit the rocking to and fro of the system, never introduce disorder, or lead to destruction. All is perfect and harmonious, and the music of the spheres that burn and roll around our sun, is echoed by that of ten millions of moving worlds, that sing and shine around the bright suns that reign above.

If, overwhelmed with the grandeur and majesty of the universe of God, we are led to exclaim with the Hebrew poet king—' When I consider thy heavens, the work of thy fingers, the moon and the stars which thou hast ordained, what is man, that thou art mindful of him? and the son of man, that thou visitest him?' If fearful that the eye of God may overlook us in the immensity of His kingdom, we have only to call to mind that other passage, ' Yet thou hast made him but a little lower than the angels, and hast crowned him with glory and honor. Thou madest him to have dominion over all the works of thy hand ; thou hast put all things under his feet.' Such are the teachings of the word, and such are the lessons of the works of God."

CHAPTER VI.

HE pictorial illustrations of the lecture were very beautiful. The splendor of thought and diction were the more surprising, because unaided by manuscript in the delivery. The audience were fascinated. Week after week the throng gathered around the gifted astronomer, who meanwhile, in private conversation and in his solitary moments, was maturing a plan to secure the object which led him to the platform of oratory unrivalled in that, or any other college.

When the last lecture was announced, he was requested to repeat it in one of the largest churches of the city. This was the opportunity toward which all his efforts had been tending. Two thousand people assembled. The simple yet lofty eloquence enchained the mass which packed the spacious temple to the last echo of the orator's voice. When the strain of thrilling address ceased, the professor came down from the glory and music of the spheres to practical business, and requested the audience " to give him a few minutes of time, for the explanation of a matter which it was hoped would not be received without some feelings of interest and approbation." He was now among the " money changers." Business-like, he goes right to their sober, practical judgments with the *terrestrial* part of his work. It is amusing to think of such a transition—from the star-lit dome above them, to the counting-room and *safe*. After a simple, honest statement, he went on with his appeal in these words: " You look at Europe, and find rapid advancement in astronomy, and all over the world costly observatories are erected. In Russia, Germany, France, and England, there are instruments in great variety and magnificence, while there is an utter deficiency in our own country in every thing pertaining to the science of the stars." The fact that monarchs lavished treasures on the temples of science, that the people must build them here, was urged; the assertion that the reliance on these would be a vain one, suggested; and finally, the assurance given that the question would now be tested and settled. For he had determined to devote *five years* of faithful effort to secure the projected observatory.

This was always a quality of General Mitchel's character. He never said *go* simply, in a good enterprise, but "come with me." It was his rule to lead, as well as point the way.

A murmer of applause went through the vast assemblage. The plan was submitted. The amount needed was to be divided into shares of twenty-five dollars each; nothing was to be done till three hundred names were obtained, and each subscriber was to have the privileges of the observatory. This was accomplished, and the heroic spirit of the founder of the star-tower, was assured of triumph. Hear the pure and inspiring words of his lips :

" Two resolutions were taken at the outset, to which I am indebted for any success which may have attended my own personal efforts. *First*. To work faithfully for *five years*, during all the leisure which could be spared from my regular duties. *Second. Never to become angry* under any provocation while in the prosecution of this enterprise."

Let every youth catch the spirit of perseverance and patience breathed in these resolves, which were faithfully kept by him. He believed and tried the truth of the heavenly counsel, " He that is slow to anger is better than the mighty ; and he that ruleth his own spirit than he that taketh a city."

Soon as the three hundred shareholders were obtained by quiet effort succeeding the lectures, the association thus formed gave him permission to visit Europe, to see what the old world had accomplished in astronomy, and what it might have for him. It was a happy day for the professor when he turned his face toward Europe. No purer earthly delight could make a great heart beat with quickened pulsations. How wide the contrast between the barefooted errand work of Miami and Lebanon, and the scientific mission to the capitals and royal observatories of the mightiest kingdoms of the earth! He could sympathize with Columbus when his vessel's prow was pointed toward the untravelled seas where continents lay.

He hastened to New York, the port of departure, and June 16th, 1842, sailed down the bay. With loving eyes he watched the receding spires of the great Metropolis, and the shores on either hand, till Neversink faded from the view. His vision dimmed with the dew of feeling, for his idolized family and native land were disappearing, perhaps forever, from his sight. But his Christian faith hung a bow of promise over the darkness of distance behind, and "flung the light of hope" on his pathway over the sea. The flashing waters at night were the beautiful foundation of his floating observatory, from which he gazed with affection which they seemed to reciprocate, upon the bright friends of his nightly vigils, for whose sake he was self-exiled for a time to a strange land.

No moments are wasted on the voyage. The traveller has made activity the highest pleasure. Between the world of stars above, the wonders of the deep, the books,

4*

and a few intelligent friends, and the intense thinking over his plans for getting *into the heavens* and seeing for himself what was there he had not beheld, the days flew past.

Sights and sounds of land again began to appear. Soon after, the shores of England greeted his vision, and a glow of new enthusiasm spread over his fine face. He was near "Fatherland" and the object of his many anxious thoughts, a *window* to the starry depths.

He went to London and the Royal Observatory of Greenwich, to find the treasure that lured him across the Atlantic, an object-glass of the largest size. In the description of the telescope, you recollect this expensive part forms the distant object, bringing it before the eye-glass, through which the observer gazes upon the remote orb, as if it were comparatively near.

The gay capital of France, to which he longed to go when Charles the Tenth was dethroned, and draw the revolutionary sword, next attracted his steps. How different his errand! Not the soldier's glory, nor the pleasures of art, nor yet of sensual indulgence, stirred his ambition. He wanted a piece of *rounded glass;* and Paris, with all its dissipation, had gifted devotees of science, and splendid instruments for its service. But here, also, he was disappointed. He looked in vain for the creation of skill which should open to him when in the tube prepared for it, the marvels and glories of the canopy-studded with globes of light.

That scientific centre of the German States, Munich, was the next goal of his hopes. The name, I think, must remind you of a very fine poem, well nigh spoiled by its repetition, so often poorly, on the stage by school-boys: Campbell's "Battle of Hohenlinden." In that the shout is raised,

> "Wave, Munich, all thy banners wave,
> And charge with all thy chivalry."

This ancient city, the capital of Bavaria, is beautifully situated on the Isar River. This stream flows through an extensive plain, whose rich landscape environs the city.

The Park, *Max-Josephs-Platz*, is one of the very finest in Europe. But there were objects of greater interest to Professor Mitchel in the ancient city.

The museums of art are wonderful. For days you can see magnificent paintings, even if you look but a few moments at each. There are nearly half a million of *engravings*.

The university, about the time Professor Mitchel was there, contained 1,471 students, taught by *seventy-six professors*. In our country half that number of students would be a very large attendance upon college instruction by less than a dozen professors.

The Royal Library has six hundred thousand volumes. Another library has two hundred thousand books.

with four hundred manuscript works, *i. e.*, every word written with a pen.

The cathedral is a wonder. It was built nearly five hundred years ago ; and has two towers three hundred and thirty-three feet high—taller than any spire you ever saw, I think.

The view from these lofty towers is grand and beautiful. And there is in one of the squares an obelisk, or kind of pyramid, one hundred feet in height, made of *cannon* taken by the Bavarians in their wars.

This city is the residence of ambassadors from all parts of Europe. They live in splendid style, and make the old city seem like the home of a score of kings.

But turn aside from all these attractive scenes to that plain pile, and enter its doors, and you will see the centre of the professor's thoughts ; it is the manufactory of optical instruments.

Munich has long been famous for its fine lenses, and every thing pertaining to telescopes, and all similar aids for scientific men.

No manufacturer of these instruments was more famous than Frauenhofer. To walk through his cabinet, or any similar one, would interest the youngest of my readers. Such a variety of beautiful mechanism for making observations of earth and sky ! M. Mertz had succeeded the renowned worker in these instruments to annihilate space, and measure the visible universe. Yet

it was all the same to Mitchel.   No sooner had he entered
the cabinet, than his eye rested on the polished crystal
he sought.   There it lay, a foot in diameter, or three feet
in circumference, the prize of his pilgrimage.   But to
mount it, that is, to finish the instrument, would require
ten thousand dollars and two years of time.

The money could and *must* be secured.   Mr. Mitchel
made a bargain, but with conditions that would protect
M. Mertz against loss if he failed to raise the ten thousand dollars.

He then hastened again to Greenwich, England, to
become a pupil there.

It may be interesting to the reader to know more
about this home for a while, of Professor Mitchel.

Greenwich is in Kent County, three and three-fourth
miles southeast of London Bridge, and contains one hundred and six thousand inhabitants.   It is an old city,
with narrow, irregular streets, some of which are lower
than the River Thames.

If you are *not* an astronomer, the first object which
would attract your curiosity, would be the Naval Hospital.   It is designed for veteran, disabled, and unfortunate seamen.   The pleasure-loving, dissipated Charles
II., built it for a palace, on the site of the Greenwich
House, which was erected in the year 1300.   In it the
queen-daughters of Henry VIII., Mary and Elizabeth,
were born.   Here Edward VI. died.

The pile was converted to its present benevolent use in the reign of William and Mary, and opened for inmates in 1705.

The situation is beautiful, on a terrace above the river. The four squares which form the whole, bear the names of the sovereigns who completed them—Charles, Anne, William, and Mary; and with all the buildings, cover forty acres. The magnificent establishment is the largest of the kind in Europe, and I suppose in the world.

But Professor Mitchel gave only a small portion of time to this splendid monument of charity. Not very far from it stands the Royal Observatory, formerly Greenwich Castle, also founded by the gay king, Charles II., in 1674.

Here Flamsteed studied the heavens, and gave Sir Isaac Newton discoveries, which aided him greatly in unfolding his theory of matter; thus one noble intellect wakes up another to still higher efforts.

Professor Airy, Astronomer Royal, that is to say, appointed by the king or queen, welcomed his gifted friend and pupil, whom he had invited to come and reap any benefit he might be able to secure there. Professor Airy saw at once a rare intellect and a rare gentleman, in the American rival to the honor of new discoveries in the vast fields of ether.

The stranger had gladly accepted the compliment which he richly merited. The days and weeks went too swiftly by, while the books, instruments, and nightly star-gazing occupied his thoughts.   He was not ashamed to take his place once more as a learner at the feet of another, whose riper culture and experience might add a single new truth or idea to his own brilliant attainments.

CHAPTER VII.

THE mellow light of October, 1842, lay upon the rich landscapes of Old England, always wanting in the brilliant coloring of our autumnal verdure, when Professor Mitchel embarked for his home on the banks of the Ohio. His objects of travel were obtained.

With a grateful and buoyant spirit he bade adieu to the British Island, and sailed for New York.

Look where he might on ocean or sky, he saw often, and even in "visions of the night," the solid, transparent circle, lying in the cabinet of M. Mertz. He saw in fancy more; the temple it would yet adorn, rising on some fair summit near the Queen City of the West.

Arriving at New York, he hurried on to Cincinnati. A meeting of the society which sent him abroad, and of other interested citizens, large and enthusiastic, as-

sembled to hear his report. All were interested deeply
in the professor's story, and the hopeful beginning of the
work to which his ardent soul was devoted. But a commercial crisis had come upon the country during his
absence of four months.

" What is a commercial crisis?" a reader inquires.

A general depression in business, arising from failures
among men controlling largely the money market. The
causes are various. Sometimes it is the result of speculation and extravagance. The awful waste and expenditure of the war are pressing heavily on thousands in
our country, which, with the mania for speculation,
threaten much financial distress before peace is restored.

In this paralysis of business, the most enthusiastic
friends of the astronomer felt troubled, and some of them
too poor to do all that they had intended and promised.
Such an enterprise—purely scientific, and expensive—
offering no opportunity for speculation, needed the most
prosperous times.

And what shall the undaunted worker do? If he
could get to West Point without funds, he can get to his
observatory, at length.

Day after day he called on wealthy citizens, urging
the claims of the observatory. See him now, with elastic step and brightened brow, preparing his remittance of
a payment to M. Mertz in Old Munich.

Three thousand dollars! So much is sure, and soon

on the way to Europe. This amount was demanded to
secure the object-glass and the completion of the telescope, when the remainder of the price was to be paid.
"The die was cast." The order had gone with the
money to finish the magnificent instrument, which *must
have a house* in which to keep and use it.

And now the unresting brain and heart and hands
are directed to this edifice. As yet not even a site, a. foot
of land for its foundations, was procured. The professor
turned for help to a very wealthy and enterprising gentleman, who owned some of the verdant highlands near
the city.

He stated to him in honest, earnest words, the wants
and embarrassments of the Astronomical Society. The
listener was Nicholas Longworth, Esq., whose vineyards
covered many acres.

"Well, Professor Mitchell, the enterprise must not
fail for want of ground. Select *four acres* on the hill in
my twenty-five acre lot, and enclose it. It will give me
great pleasure to present it to the association."

"I can present you, sir, in the name of the society,
their warmest thanks. Of all eligible points for an observatory it is the most desirable."

With a lighter footfall, and more sunny brow than at
any moment since the struggle began for his watch-tower,
he left the presence of the munificent donor.

With a loving eye he looked away to the lofty hill,

lifting its ample swell four hundred feet above the streets of the city. From its top, the vision could sweep the entire horizon without an intervening object. Below lay the beautiful metropolis of the West, with its elegant buildings and hum of business; and around it, in every direction from the broad and glorious Ohio, were spread the plains and slopes, dark with vineyards and verdure, and dotted with tasteful dwellings. It was as rare a spot for the building, as was the splendid glass for the instrument that structure was to protect.

Two grand steps *onward* toward the goal of the astronomer's hopes are taken. The next is to build. No time is lost by him. He soon has the carpenters at work on the fence, and a road cut to the summit, making access by teams with material, quite easy.

The spring and summer of 1843 had rapidly passed to him, under the pressure of this great work, and college duties. An auspicious and exciting day has come. The ninth day of November was set apart for laying the corner-stone. That stone is to be a part of the pier, or masonry, supporting the telescope with its harness for service.

The anticipated morning dawns. The throng at an early hour begin to gather on the height. And now the moment for the ceremonies arrives; and who is that calm, venerable, majestic man, more than fourscore years of age, attended with so much reverence to the platform?

He is the orator of the day. Many hundred miles has
the noble pilgrim travelled, to lift his voice once more in
an oration to his countrymen. How softly the light of a
late western autumn, falls on the bald head fringed with
silver hair! All eyes glance fondly, admiringly toward
the central figure. Even the noble, yet modest astronomer, to whom it is an inauguration day of the greatest
enterprise of his laborious life, is forgotten. The opening services are finished, and JOHN QUINCY ADAMS
rises amid the hum and cheers of the concourse. With
tremulous lips, and clear accent, he pays his tribute to
the founders of the Observatory, to science, and then to the
country he loved—the home of a free, enterprising, and ·
intelligent people. The only cloud that hung darkly to
his discerning eye, on our horizon, was that whose lightning has fallen upon us, and whose thunder of retribution
is rolling day and night through the heavens.

For the last time did the veteran statesman, scholar,
champion of freedom, and Christian, open the treasures of
his gifted mind and large heart to the multitude. Memorable occasion! Do you think the bright boys who
saw that scene, and heard the words spoken, will ever
forget it? The influence of it will bless the land, till
its hills are swept with universal desolation, or " melt
with fervent heat."

The multitude dispersed. There lay the single piece
of granite. Around it were broken ground, and materials

for building. Winter is nigh, and this hindrance, with the want of funds, compels the suspension of labor for the season.

Do you not believe, my reader, that very few men would have held on, resolved to succeed, with such weariness of effort and discouragement? The secret of such unsurpassed energy and perseverance, is found in the struggles, good habits, and high aims of the boy in early life.

No one but Professor Mitchel himself knew the expenditure of labor it cost to save the imperilled object of many years effort. The winter of 1843 and 1844 was the trial-period of the whole undertaking. He thought, and prayed, and worked. The bloom and fragrance of May were never more grateful to him, who saw his intense and painful toil crowned with success for the time. The thousands of dollars more due to the makers of the telescope, were collected and sent to Munich.

What now shall be done? The treasury is empty, and eight thousand dollars more are wanted to finish the building. Fertile in resources, he resolves to appeal to intelligent mechanics, and go to work. Without money, and with *three* workmen, the summer sun sees the structure slowly rising. The second week finds the expenses of the previous one paid, and six hands on the torn hill-top. They toil on till Saturday night. "How stands the account?" asks the Professor. The treasurer replies, "Enough to pay up, and double the number of men."

Thus six weeks passed away. And during their long days, you might have seen the professor—*where?* Walking over the broken ground or sitting upon some stick of hewn timber, to see the work progress? No! he was not afraid of any kind of honorable labor, nor to show the callous palm. See him now driving the team which drags the "stone-boat," or handling, like a born *ditcher*, the pickaxe and shovel. A stranger would have found it difficult at a sufficient distance to conceal his noble forehead and face, to distinguish him from a son of the Emerald Isle. In this, too, he resembled strikingly General Grant, who in or out of the army scorns all tinsel, and appears like the commonest soldier or citizen.

The mechanics of Cincinnati acted magnanimously, indeed. Many of them subscribed stock, in other words, became members of the Astronomical Society, taking shares in the amount invested by it, and paid it in work.

In a quarry owned by the society, the stones were blasted and hewn for the growing edifice. Oh! with what keen delight did the brave, unselfish Mitchel, hear the rude sound of hammer, iron bar, pulley, and voices of command to the silent, faithful brute workers. More pleasant than the odor of summer flowers, was the smoke of the lime-kiln on the hill, in which the lime to cement the masonry was burned.

Nothing was refused in subscriptions to the object,

whether a day's work or a due bill, which could be bartered for something else that would pay.

The months wore away, and again autumn returned. The observatory walls were built, and a roof covered them, with no debt on them. And now a new difficulty arose. Mr. Longworth required the Society to finish the structure in two years, or forfeit the land. The time would expire in June, 1845. Either the period must be lengthened—a favor it would not be pleasant to ask—or the association run in debt. Professor Mitchel's private means were expended, for he *always* set the example in whatever he desired others to do. But the building went forward to completion. He hoped that in a brief time after a monument of scientific love and labor stood in the beauty of finished proportions, the money with which to meet all engagements could be obtained.

February, 1845, was another proud day. The professor is not on the hill. Along the streets he is passing, while mysterious burdens are carted from the general storehouse of commerce. What new turn has his activity taken? From Munich to Cincinnati that splendid object-glass, tubed and ready to be lifted to its place, has travelled. The mails had taken bits of paper ; a ship brought with its ponderous fixtures the crystal windows to the far depths of ether.

The telescope is actually in the city ! No victor ever exulted with a higher and purer triumph of genius and high endeavor, than did the astronomer from his unfinished temple, which was to enshrine the telescopic eye to pierce the heavens.

Boisterous March came, and his rough winds seemed to sing with joy around the finished structure, consecrated to victories over time and space.   All things were ready for the high priest of the sanctuary of science devoted to God and humanity.

THE MITCHEL OBSERVATORY.

THE DOME UNCOVERED, WITH HALLY'S COMET BEFORE THE TELESCOPE,
p. 96.

CHAPTER VIII.

HE building is eighty feet long and thirty feet broad. The front is two stories, while in the centre of the structure there is a third story for the telescope and other instruments. The roof can be taken off during the time of observing the heavens. It is a beautiful building, crowning well the summit on which it stands.

Dr. Bache, the superintendent of the U. S. Coast Survey, *i. e.*, a department for tracing coast boundaries, distances, &c., gave to the Observatory a large transit instrument and a sidereal clock. Professor Mitchel has used them well in dividing and numbering stars.

But he was to learn another and sadder lesson of trust than any hitherto known. He must feel the truth, that,

" When calmest on life's wave we ride,
    Oft rolls behind a gloomy tide."

5

A darkly mysterious providence was at hand. His last dollar was gone. And hark! on the still air rises the cry of "*fire! fire!*" "Where? What is it?" are the responses from the startled people. "The College! the College!" in another moment, is on every lip. The flames curl in the chill wind around the walls, until, in spite of streams from the engines of faithful firemen, they stand charred and desolate. With the College went the professor's salary. He was nearly as penniless as when he started for the Military Academy. He had engaged to superintend the Observatory for *ten years* without salary, depending on that from the College.

The cherished Observatory must not at last be abandoned. What shall he do? His wonderful faith, hope, and energy, will surely conquer in the trial of them all. Years would be necessary to rebuild the pile which had been the food of the flames. Again he thought and prayed—then *acted*. The enthusiastic reception of his lectures in Cincinnati encouraged him to try them abroad. His familiar and repeated conversations with his classes on astronomy, and with citizens about the Observatory, its design and uses, had taught him to speak with force and simplicity on the marvels of the sky. This strengthened his confidence and purpose more than any other consideration. To speak plainly and well at any time is a great attainment; but to do so when the motions and glories of the uncounted stars are the theme, and the

"common people" the hearers, is a rare attainment.
Because of this power the multitudes two thousand years
before heard the Creator of the world "gladly." The
astronomer turned his back on the temple, surmounting·
the lordly hill of all the region, and, with his baggage,
startèd for the great cities of the Union. It is no private
speculation—no mercenary aim that tears him from home
and his telescope.

Reaching Boston, the notice of his first lecture on the
starry heavens since his course in the College, and one in
the city church, was given. Indeed, he regarded the occasion as his entrance upon public life as a lecturer. The
hour came—the hall was not full. But he had charmed
the few; and without the least unbecoming pride, he said
to a friend afterward, "he felt sure every listener would
bring another the next evening." He was not disappointed. The question of success was answered: "The
Athens of America" had decided the claims of this apostle of science devoted to religion, to his high position.

In New York the Music Hall is thronged night after
night to hear his impassioned eloquence, poured in an unbroken flow of "thoughts that breathe and words that
burn," on the excited thousands. A sublimer spectacle
in lecturing was never seen. The object, the theme, the
orator, the intellectual audiences, the wrapt attention, the
almost painful intensity of feeling, all crown him the
prince of lecturers. Not a line of manuscript lies before

him. Yet he never hesitates, never repeats, never chafes the liveliest sensibility of any hearer.

Listen to even the boys as they walk homeward, and you will hear them saying :

" Father, wasn't it splendid? " Another exclaims : " If I could ever talk like that, and knew as much as Professor Mitchel, I would be willing to study hard."

Why not, my dear boy, emulate the example. Did the barefooted clerk on the countryman's horse, which trudged along the muddy roads two miles an hour, look very much like holding the best minds in New York under the spell of his eloquence? It was the same in Boston, Philadelphia, New Orleans, and St. Louis.

None but the infinite Father can estimate the effect of those unequalled lectures. They awakened an entirely new and profound interest among the people. A host of young persons were led to watch with a delight unknown before the circling constellations, and calm, beauteous planets. The North Star in the handle of the little dipper, the large dipper with its pointers toward that central orb ; magnificent Orion with " his bands " ; the grape-like cluster, Pleiades, about which Job so eloquently discourses ; and Sirius, the dog-star, which was so dazzling when it came like a rising sun before Newton's telescope. he had to withdraw his eyes ; attracted more observers than had gazed upon them at any time since the May Flower was guided by the *cynosure* over the deep.

The excellent use that Professor Mitchel made of the observatory appears in the next published effort of his studious mind; which, if it did not attempt the highest speculations of astronomical science, did perhaps mcre than any other to make it interesting and familiar to all.

And it is delightful to tell you that not only was Mrs. Mitchel an intellectual and pious mother to his children, but "night after night did she sit by his side in his study of the heavens." Her gentle hand assisted at the grand telescope, or wielded for him the pen in writing down his observations.

In 1860 appeared his "Popular Astronomy." The opening lecture is a fine description of the "day-god," worshipped by the Persian pagans ages ago. How clear and sublime the language in which he follows him in his chariot of fire through the heavens, and along the horizon's rim! For you know that, in winter, the blush of sunrise appears far from the place where was seen the richer crimson and gold of midsummer.

"The sun is beyond comparison the grandest of all the celestial orbs of which we have any positive knowledge. The inexhaustible source of the heat which warms and vivifies the earth, and the origin of a perpetual flood of light, which, flying with incredible velocity in all directions, illumines the planets and their satellites, lights up the eccentric comets, and penetrates even to the region of the fixed stars; it is not surprising that, in the early ages of the world, this mighty orb should have been re-garded as the visible emblem of the Omnipotent, and as such should have received divine honors.

" On the approach of the sun to the horizon in the early dawn, his coming is announced by the gray eastern twilight, before whose gradual increase the brightest stars and even the planets fade and disappear. The coming splendor grows and expands, rising higher and yet higher, until, as the first beam of sunlight darts on the world, not a star or planet remains visible in the whole heavens ; and even the moon, under this flood of sunlight, shines only as a faint silver cloud.

" This magnificent spectacle of the *sunrise*, together with the equally imposing scenes which sometimes accom-pany the *setting* sun, must have excited the curiosity of the very first inhabitants of the earth. This curiosity led to a more careful examination of the phenomena attend-ing the rising and setting sun, when it was discovered that the point at which this great orb made his appear-ance was not *fixed*, but was slowly shifting on the horizon, the change being easily detected by the observation of a few days. Hence was discovered, in the primitive ages, THE SUN'S APPARENT MOTION. In case the sun is observed attentively from month to month, it will be found that the point of sunrise on the horizon moves slowly, for a cer-tain length of time, toward the *south*. While this motion continues, the sun, at noon, when culminating on the meridian, reaches each day a point less elevated above the horizon, and the *diurnal arc* or daily path described by the sun grows shorter and shorter. At length a limit is reached; the point of sunrise ceases to advance toward the south, remaining stationary a day or two, and then slowly commences his return toward the north. Thus does the sun appear to vibrate backward and forward between his southern and northern limits, marking to man a period of the highest interest, for within its limits the SPRING, the SUMMER, the AUTUMN, and the WINTER, have run their cycles, and by their union have wrought out the changes of the year."

" And what," asks an inquiring mind, " can you tell us, Professor, of the spots on the sun's face ? "

" To the naked eye the sun's surface presents a blaze of insufferable splendor ; and even when this intense light is reduced by the use of any translucent medium, the entire disk appears evenly shaded, with a slight diminution of light around the circumference, but without visible spot or variation. When, however, the power of vision is increased a hundred or a thousand fold by telescopic aid, and when the intense heat of the sun and his equally intense light are reduced by the help of deeply-colored glasses, the eye recognizes a surface of most wonderful character. Instead of finding the sun everywhere equally brilliant, the telescope shows sometimes on its surface *black spots*, of very irregular figure, jagged and broken in outline

"Besides the mottling of the surface, the telescope detects in the solar orb a variety of brighter streaks, called *faculæ*, whose appearance has been connected, as some believe, with the breaking out of the black spots.

"We are compelled to acknowledge that up to the present time science has rendered no satisfactory account of the origin of the solar light or heat. Whence comes the exhaustless supply, scattered so lavishly into space in every direction, we know not. Neither is it possible to give a satisfactory solution of the solar spots, or of any of the strange phenomena attending their rotation or translation on the sun's surface. The idea that tornadoes and tempests rage in the deep, luminous ocean that surrounds the sun, like those which sometimes agitate the atmosphere of the earth, has no solid foundation. We know the exciting causes of the tornadoes on earth, but why such storms should exist in the solar sphere it is in vain to conjecture at present. Doubtless the time will come when these phenomena will be explained."

Then the professor talks eloquently of Mercury, a planet so near the sun, "that it is said Copernicus himself, during his whole life devoted to the study of the heavens, never once caught sight of this almost invisible world," and yet "it was discovered in the very earliest ages" by the ancients.

"How large is this orb, almost lost in the sun's unquenchable fire, and do people live in that burning splendor?"

The first question only is answered. " Its diameter is but 3,140 miles. In comparison with the vast proportions of the sun, this little planet sinks into absolute insignificance ; for if the sun be divided into a million of equal parts, Mercury would not weigh as much as the half of one of these parts."

Of Venus he says : " The extreme brightness of this planet makes it a very beautiful but difficult object for telescopic observation. Although spots have been seen upon the surface of Venus, I have never been able, at any time, with the powerful refractor of the Cincinnati Observatory, to mark any well-defined differences in the illumination of her surface. If we are to trust to the observations of others, the inequalities which diversify the planet Venus far exceed in grandeur those found upon our earth. It is stated by M. Schroter that, from his own observations, the mountains of Venus reach an altitude five or six times greater than the loftiest mountains of our own globe."

" And what did the most gifted men of the early ages think of our world?" Our astronomer answers :

" The ancients did not reckon the earth as one of the planetary orbs. There seemed to be no analogy between the world which we inhabit, with its dark, opaque, and diversified surface, and those brilliant planets which pursued their mysterious journey among the stars. Sunk as they were, so deep in space, it was very difficult to reach

5*

any correct knowledge of their absolute magnitude. The earth seemed to the senses of man vastly larger than any or all of these revolving worlds. About the earth, as a fixed centre, the whole concave of the heavens, with all its starry constellations, appeared to revolve, producing the alternations of day and night. It was not unnatural, therefore, knowing the central position of the earth with reference to the fixed stars, to assume its central position with reference to the sun, and moon, and planetary worlds."

You have often gazed with wonder at the " Queen of night." You heard in earliest childhood of the " Man in the Moon," that is, the spotted surface somewhat resembling a face. Of this orb he has an interesting sketch :

" Before the power of the telescope had reached its present condition of perfection, the darker spots of the moon were assumed to be seas and oceans ; but the power now applied to the moon demonstrates that there cannot exist at this time any considerable body of water on the hemisphere visible from the earth. And yet we find objects such, that in case we were gazing upon the earth from the moon, possessing our actual knowledge of the earth's lakes and rivers, we should pronounce them, without hesitation, lakes and rivers. There is one such object which I will describe as often seen through the Cincinnati refractor. The outline is nearly circular, with a lofty range of hills on the western and southwestern sides. This range gradually sinks in the east, and a beautiful sloping beach seems to extend down to the level surface of the inclosed lake (as we shall call it, for want of other language). With the highest telescopic power, under the most favorable circumstances, I never could detect the slightest irregularity in the shading of the surface of the lake. Had the cavity been filled with quicksilver and suddenly congealed or covered with solid ice, with a covering of pure snow, the shading could not be more regular than it is. To add, however, to the terrene likeness, into this seeming lake there flows what looks· exactly as a river should at such a distance. That there is an indentation in the surface, exactly like the bed of a river, extending into the country (with numerous islands) for more than a hundred miles, and then forking and separating into two distinct branches, each of which pursues a serpentine course for from thirty to fifty miles beyond the fork, all this is distinctly visible. I may say, indeed, that just before entering the lunar lake, this lunar river is found to disappear from sight, and seems to pass beneath the range of hills which border the lake. The region of country which lies between the forks or branches of this seeming river, is evidently higher, and to the eye appears just as it should do, so as to shed its water into the stream which appears to flow in the valley below. The question may be asked, why is not this a lake and a river? There is no lunar atmosphere on the visible hemisphere of the moon, such as surrounds the earth, and if there were water like ours on the moon, it would be soon evaporated, and would produce a kind of vaporous atmosphere which ought to be seen, but has not been detected.

" What, then, shall we call the objects described? I can only answer that this phenomenon, with many others, presented by the lunar surface, has thus far baffled the most diligent and persevering efforts to explain. Among what are called the volcanic mountains of the moon are found objects of special interest. One of them, named Copernicus, and situated not far from the moon's equator, is so distinctly shown by the telescope, that the sides of it have all the appearance of the action of a crater ejecting immense quantities of lava and molted matter. Can there be, indeed, the overflowing of once active volcanoes? "

Have you not seen in the heavens the red little planet called Mars, the name of the god of war? " Why," perhaps you inquire, " is the fiery Mars so much redder in hue than the other planets? "

" The reddish tint which marks the light of Mars," says the professor, " has been attributed by Sir John Herschel to the prevailing color of the soil. This is all pure conjecture."

How limited the knowledge of the most learned! None can tell whether there be seas or inhabitants on the nearest globes to us. The gigantic planet in our solar system, the genius which often studied its majestic motions, tells us : " Is one of the five revolving worlds discovered in the primitive ages. Its revolution among the fixed stars is slow and majestic, comporting well with its vast dimensions, and the dignity conferred by four tributary worlds. The nocturnal heavens, as seen from this grand orb, must be inexpressibly magnificent. Besides the same glittering constellations which are seen from earth, the sky of Jupiter may be adorned with no less than four moons, with their diverse phases, some waxing or waning, some just rising or setting, some possibly just entering into or emerging from eclipse ; the whole of this splendid celestial exhibition sweeping across the heavens, rising, culminating, and setting in less than five hours of our time. Such are the scenes witnessed by the inhabitants of Jupiter, if such there be."

The splendid planet Saturn with his gorgeous ring, which is scarcely visible when its *edge* is turned toward the observer, Professor Mitchel beautifully traces in its path of light. Of the revolving ring turned edgewise, he says : " The disappearance of the ring which took place in 1848 was watched by the author at Cincinnati Observatory with the powerful refractor of that institution. A minute fibre of light remained clearly visible even when the edge of the ring was turned directly to the eye of the spectator. The delicacy of this line far exceeds any thing ever before witnessed. When compared with the finest spider's web stretched across the field of view, the latter appeared like a cable, so greatly did it surpass in magnitude the filament of light presented in the edge of Saturn's ring. I had the pleasure of witnessing the phenomena so beautifully described by Sir William Herschel, the movements of the satellites along this line of light, ' like golden beads on a wire.' "

We now come to the far-off world, which, until recently, was thought by all astronomers to be the last in the system to which our earth belongs—the *outside* traveller around the sun. Indeed, Sir William Herschel, after whom it was named, supposed it was a comet. The Royal Astronomer at Greenwich, Dr. Markelyne, first declared that it was a neighbor to the globes which before had been known to live in the light of the central luminary

Professor Mitchel watched with intense interest, through his grand telescope, the four moons of the distant Herschel. He assures you that "they are among the most difficult of all the objects revealed to the eye of the telescope. After Sir William Herschel no one for forty years was able to see any of these satellites, his forty-foot reflector having gone into disuse. In 1828, Sir John Herschel, after many unsuccessful attempts, by confining himself in a dark room for many minutes previous to observation, and thus giving to the eye great acuteness, succeeded in detecting two of the satellites. In 1837, Lamont, with the powerful refractor of the Royal Observatory at Munich, managed to follow, with tolerable certainty, the two larger moons, and occasionally obtained glimpses of two others. At this time there were four fine telescopes in the world, capable of showing these four satellites under favorable circumstances. I have frequently seen two of them with the Cincinnati refractor."

Beyond Herschel, by a most astonishing calculation, showing that a planet *ought to be* where it was found by M. Galle, of Berlin, another planet has been added to the solar system, named Neptune. This makes *nine* in the family of planets to which we belong.

You will read with interest the astronomer's account of its discovery :

" The discovery of Neptune is undoubtedly the most remarkable event in the history of astronomical science— an event without a parallel, and rising in grandeur preeminently above all other efforts of human genius ever put forth in the examination of the physical universe.

" The planet Uranus was discovered by the aid of the telescope, not exactly by accident, but still without any expectation on the part of the discoverer that his examination of the fixed stars would result in the addition of a primary planet to the system. Indeed, as we have seen, so little did the astronomical world then anticipate the discovery of a new planet, that the announcement by Sir

William Herschel that he had detected a most remarkable comet was accepted on all hands, and it was only continued observation. that finally compelled astronomers to accept the new object as a planet.   In the case of the discovery of the first asteroid we find a systematic organization of astronomical effort to detect a body whose existence was *conjectured*, on the single ground of the harmony of the universe, or that the law of inter-planetary spaces, interrupted between Mars and Jupiter, could be restored by finding a planet revolving within that vast interval.   Hence a search was commenced, which consisted in examining every star in the region of the ecliptic, to ascertain whether its place was already laid down on any known map or chart of the heavens.   Now it is evident that if it were possible to make a perfect daguerreotype of any region of the celestial sphere, say to-night, and the same could be effected in the following night, the comparison of these two pictures would exhibit to the eye any change which may have occurred in the interval from the one picture to the other ; and hence if a star was found on the second and not on the first picture, this star might fairly be suspected to be a planet, or the same suspicion would attach to a star found on the first, but missing on the second picture.   Now, a map of the heavens, so far as it includes the correct places of the stars, answers our purpose quite as well as the daguerreotype ; and any star found in a region well charted, but not laid down on the map, may be fairly suspected to be a planet. A few hours of examination will show it to be at rest or in motion. If in motion, then its planetary character is decided.

" This method of research has been employed in the discovery of all the asteroids, and there is but one example in which a more powerful and searching examination became necessary. This was in the case of the asteroid Ceres, which, as we have seen, was discovered by Piazzi, at a time when but few observations could be made previous to its being lost in the rays of the sun. For a long time it seemed almost a hopeless task to undertake the rediscovery of the planet, as the telescope would be compelled to grope its way slowly round the heavens, in the region of the ecliptic, comparing every star with its place in the chart. The genius of Gauss succeeded in this herculean task, and when the telescope was pointed to the heavens in the exact place indicated by the daring computor, there, in the field of view, shone the delicate and beautiful light of the long-lost planet.

" The case of the discovery of Neptune is entirely different. Here no planet was known to exist, no telescopic power, however great, had ever seen it. For ages it had revolved round the sun in its vast orbit, far beyond the utmost known verge of the planetary system, unfathomably buried from human gaze and from human knowledge. No sage of antiquity had ever dreamed of its existence. The fertile brain of even Kepler had failed

to imagine its being, and the powerful penetration of Newton's gigantic intellect had failed to pierce to the far-off
region inhabited by this unknown and solitary planet.

" Indeed, with the knowledge which existed prior to
the discovery of Uranus, no human genius, however
mighty, could have passed the tremendous interval which
separates the orbits of Saturn and Neptune from each·
other. The discovery of an intermediate planet was re-
quisite to furnish a firm foothold to him who would adventure to pass a gulf of not less than two thousand
millions of miles at its narrowest place.

" No account, of course, can be given of the mathematical treatment of the problem. It was undertaken at
about the same time by Adams, of England, and by Le
Verrier, of Paris. Each computer, unknown to the other,
reached a result almost identical. Le Verrier communicated his solution to the Academy of Sciences on the
31st August, 1847. M. Galle, of Berlin, directed the telescope to the point in which the French geometer declared
the unknown planet would be found. A star of the eighth
magnitude appeared in the field of view, whose place was
not laid down on any known chart. Suspicion was at
once aroused that this might possibly be the planet of
computation, and yet it seemed incredible that a problem
far surpassing in difficulty any which had ever been attempted by human genius should thus at the first effort
have been solved with such marvellous precision.

" The suspected star was examined with the deepest interest in the hope that it might exhibit a planetary disk. In this, however, the astronomer was unsuccessful, and there remained but one method by which its planetary character might be determined, that of watching sufficiently long to detect its motion. This process, however, must have tried very sorely the patience of the observer, as the motion of the planet at so great a distance as three thousand six hundred millions of miles, was so slow as to require three entire months to pass over a space equal to the apparent diameter of the moon. The position of the suspected star having been accurately determined on the first night of observation, it became evident on the next night that the star had moved by an amount such as was fairly due to the slow motion of so vast an orbit. It could be none other than the unknown planet! A success almost infinitely beyond the expectations of the most sanguine computer had crowned this mighty effort, and the amazing intelligence that the planet was found startled the astronomical world."

And no one can say how long it will be before the world will again be startled by the news of still more sublime discoveries from the heights of observation once occupied by Mitchel, in the years to come.

It is very possible some young reader may yet write his name on the heavens, in the imperishable association of it with the stars.

CHAPTER IX.

EANWHILE, this surveyor of planetary paths,
and of the orbits of flaming suns, had shown
his equally familiar knowledge of *terrestrial*
affairs.   Such great and practical men seldom
appear.

In 1844 he surveyed the Ohio and Mississippi Railroad.   Several years later he crossed the ocean again as
confidential agent of the company, to transact business
for them in Europe.   So well did he manage the concerns
of men who seldom took time to look higher than engines,
iron rails, and the figures of the pen and pencil, that a
few months after his return he was sent again over the
waters.

You will believe me when I tell you that, excepting the waters below and the heavens above, his
interest was quite inferior to the sublime enthusiasm

which led him to Munich.   But he was *no dreamer*.
From the far-off glories of the sky he could come down
to the locomotive, and the profits and losses of running it.
When he returned he was also made president of a por-
tion of that extensive track down the great valley of the
West.

Professor Mitchel also delivered another series of lectures in our large cities on the Astronomy of the Bible.
These were more brilliant than the first.   Did you hear
them?   If not, did father or mother?   If *you* did, you
cannot forget the entranced audience ; wherever you
looked, if your glance was away from the orator for a
moment, the throng seemed carried beyond the stars to
the dazzling throne of the Deity.   Whoever listened will
tell you how like an inspired prophet, or an angel, he sometimes appeared.   God, as creator and governor of the
myriad worlds rolling in the fathomless blue, Law-giver,
Redeemer, and Judge of mankind, whose book and starry
volume agree in every part, was presented in speech more
glowing than ever had issued, till then, from the platform
of a popular assembly.   It reminded the intelligent listener of John Milton, the poet of earth and heaven, *talking* instead of singing the grand cantos.

I shall quote just enough from his glowing pages to
give you specimens of his eloquence, refresh the memory
of those who listened to him, and interest you in the
works he has left for all time behind him.   The motive

which led him to deliver the lectures which he designed evidently to have published, was, first of all, to confirm our faith in the Bible—to show that "the undevout astronomer is mad"—and convince the people of the shallowness of the cavils and scorn of those "scientific men" who try to shake our confidence in the Christian system.

Grandly he did his work. And every thoughtful mind will mourn the death which to us seems premature, that defeated his further purpose to continue these eloquent discourses, and show to the doubting, the Godlike consistency and glory of redemption—of the incarnation and sacrifice of the Creator of the worlds!

He thus begins: " We stand with the philosopher and astronomer on the very apex of that stupendous pyramid which human genius has reared by the protracted labor of six thousand years. We are lifted far above the clouds. We are permitted to examine the

'Thrones, dominions, princedoms, virtues, powers,'

which fill the heavens. Our view sweeps from the humble satellite which acknowledges and obeys the superior power of the earth, through systems, and schemes, and universes, whose vastness no stretch of thought can comprehend, whose numbers no arithmetic can count. *   *

" What hand has launched these flaming orbs in space? Whose eye omniscient has traced out their untrodden paths? What hand omnipotent upholds the stupendous fabric of Nature?

" These are themes of superlative grandeur. No mind can approach their contemplation without an expansion of thought, an uplifting of the powers of the soul, a sensation resembling that which swept across the soul of our great ancestor, when it was whispered, ' Ye shall be as gods'; and then comes a withering sense of our weakness, a consciousness of our utter inability to scale these lofty heights, or penetrate the deep profound which stretches out before us.

" If called upon to discuss these themes in the presence of superior beings, the hierarchs of Heaven, resplendent with exalted wisdom, it would be utter folly to unseal the lip, or move the tongue to the utterance of one solitary thought. But I address not myself to angelic intelligences, but to man, humble, trusting, inquiring, teachable man, conscious of his own weakness, and ever ready to receive with feelings of charitable consideration the humble efforts of those who, like himself, are struggling to discover truth.

" *Does the physical universe proclaim the being of a God?* Should this inquiry be affirmatively answered, we propose to inquire—*If the God thus revealed is the same august and eternal being portrayed in our sacred books?* "

Thus the genius of Mitchel launches out, upborne by

the breath of prayer, and eagle-eyed with the light of faith to roam among the worlds, finding in every part of the dazzling infinity that *God is there*—the God of *the Bible and of all science.*

We must pass without even a reluctant glance at the gems of thought and oratory scattered over these pages, inviting our admiring study, to the closing and impressive words. How fine is the illustration of a "rebel world." After quoting facts in astronomy hinted at in the Bible, and explaining apparent difficulties, he adds:

"We find a remarkable appropriateness in the selections which have been made of the phenomena of the heavens, to illustrate the teachings of prophetic declaration. They were appropriate to the age in which they were written; they have been appropriate in all succeeding ages down to the present time, and science assures us they can now never fail. Can all this have resulted from accident? Can so great a multitude of thoughts, expressions, doctrines, illustrations, and similitudes, have all risen by accident into appropriate use among so many writers, so widely separated in time? If it be argued that after all there is nothing in all this language, in all these expressions, in all these illustrations, and that it is but the perversions of an ingenious fancy which gives to them an appearance of appropriateness, it must still be admitted that it is certainly very wonderful that such a multitude of independent expressions should be capable of being woven into a texture of astonishing harmony and beauty.

" Search the old prophets, the Psalms, the book of Job, even the New Testament, and in all these books, wherever any allusion is made to the physical heavens, it seems to have been written by one possessing the highest intelligence, the most profound knowledge.

" There is but one solitary instance in which an author of any one book in the Bible, was brought face to face with the philosophy of antiquity. This was the celebrated meeting between the great apostle of the Gentiles with the Stoics and Epicureans on Mars Hill, in Athens. As already stated, the Stoics did not admit the power of God to create the material of the universe. He could only arrange and organize what had existed from all eternity. He could banish old Night and subdue the empire of Chaos, but had no creative power. The Epicureans on the other hand were atheists.

" Paul, who was learned in the Hebrew Scriptures, and who had been educated in the law at the feet of Gamaliel, even as a Jew, and much more as a Christian, had imbibed the doctrine so universally taught in the Bible, that all nature is but the offspring of the creative energy of the Divine will.

" Here we find, then, the representatives of the doctrines of the Old and New Testaments, both in philosophy and

6

religion—the two great concerns of humanity—brought
face to face with the philosophers and priests of pagan-
ism, and under circumstances of most extraordinary
grandeur.

"The scene was the Areopagus, on Mars Hill, the
most venerated and revered court of all antiquity. Here,
in seats hewn from the solid rocks, sat the judges, whose
decree fixed not only the fate of individuals, but of empires. On every hand the temples of the pagan divinities
reared their beautiful or majestic forms. Statues of men,
heroes, and gods, in uncounted numbers, filled every niche
and crowned every rock on this lofty eminence. The
sublime form of the colossal statue of Minerva, the tu-
telary divinity of Athens, reared in majestic propositions,
'towering from the rock of the Acropolis.' There were
the shrines of all the divinities, the temples of all the
gods, the sanctuary of the vengeful furies, and, in full
sight, the very gardens where Socrates had poured forth
his lessons of wisdom, where Zeno had organized his
stern stoical school of philosophy, and where Epicurus
had captivated weak humanity with his doctrines of
graceful ease or refined sensuality.

"Such were the circumstances surrounding the repre-
sentative of the philosophy and the religion of the Bible.
Rising, doubtless, under a full sense of the greatness of
his responsibility, Paul uttered that marvellous discourse,
in which he exclaims, 'O Athenians! I perceive that in

all things ye are too superstitious; for as I passed by and
beheld your devotions, I found an altar with this inscription, " To the unknown God." Whom, therefore, ye ignorantly worship, Him declare I unto you. God that made
the world and all things therein, seeing that He is Lord
of Heaven and earth, dwelleth not in temples made with
hands ; neither is worshipped with men's hands, as though
He needed any thing : seeing that He giveth to all life,
and breath, and all things. Forasmuch, then, as we are
the offspring of God, we ought not to think that the God-
head is like unto gold, or silver, or stone, graven by art
and man's devices.' Your philosophy, O Stoics ! is false.
God's creative energy built this magnificent universe, and
God's almighty power guides universal nature. Your
divinity, O Epicureans ! wrapt in sombre abstraction, be-
holding, from afar, with indifference the affairs of men,
is not the divinity of truth ; for we also are the offspring
of the ' unknown God,' and in Him we live and move
and have our being. Your religion, O priests ! is false,
and your shrines and splendid temples, and statues of
marbles and bronze and gold, glittering with precious
stones, graven by art and man's device, are but a mock-
ery ; for this unknown God, who built the heavens and
the earth, and who sustaineth all things by the might of
His power, dwelleth not in temples made with hands.
Turn, then, O priests and philosophers ! from your idolatry and philosophy, to this unknown God whom ye

ignorantly worship; repent, for He hath appointed a day in which He will judge the world in righteousness.

" What response could pagan philosophy or pagan idolatry make to this appeal of the Christian hero; and what response can modern philosophy make this day to the same appeal? God has breathed into our nostrils the breath of life, and man has become a living soul. Say what we may, we are the offspring of God, and as His children we are the heirs of immortality; we may defy the Omnipotent and incur His frown, which withers our very being; or we may bring our hearts and souls in unison with God's holiness, and under His beneficent smile be filled with joy and happiness inexpressible and full of glory?

" God hath given us the power to scan the universe, to detect its laws, to learn its stupendous organization, to lift the soul of man nearer to His divine presence. Where shall the guilty find a refuge? Surely not in the iron—the adamantine laws of physical nature. Suppose it were possible to endow one of these flying worlds —the earth we inhabit—with a will and a rational soul; and the earth, now an independent, thinking, willing being, should rise in rebellion against the laws of God's control, and refuse longer to obey. The rebellious planet exclaims, Let the sun attract me never so much, I care not for his heat, his light, his life; I refuse to reciprocate the attraction: I have a power of will supreme, my destiny is my own! And thus the fatal decision is made. Slowly the rebel world wheels at each revolution, farther and yet farther from the great centre of life and light. In spiral circuit it separates farther and still farther from its wonted path, till finally, cold and darkness and a coming death begin to assert their empire over the misguided world. With a start of horror and a shudder which shakes it to the very centre, it now wakes from its dream of independence and exclaims, I will return! I will return! Alas! the return is impossible. The laws of nature are irrevocable. The sun may yet attract with living power the lost wanderer, but the bond is broken, the equilibrium is forever destroyed, and this rebel planet must become a wandering star, for which is reserved the blackness of darkness forever!

"No, my friends; the analogies of nature, applied to the moral government of God, would crush all hope in the sinful soul. There, for millions of ages, these stern laws have reigned supreme. There is no deviation, no modification, no yielding to the refractory or disobedient. All is harmony, because all is obedience. Close forever, if you will, this strange book, claiming to be God's revelation—blot out forever its lessons of God's creative power, God's superabundant providence, God's fatherhood and loving guardianship to man his erring offspring, and then unseal the leaves of that mighty volume which the finger of God has written in the stars of heaven, and in these flashing letters of light, we read only the dread sentence, ' The soul that sinneth it shall surely die ! ' "

In 1847 the astronomer was appointed Adjutant-General of the State of Ohio, an office he held two years This position placed him on the Governor's staff, and gave him charge of the military business of the State. His education at West Point had fitted him to fill it well. He was also at one time a member of the Board of Visitors annually selected for the examinations at the Military Academy.   He belonged to the Royal Academy of London, and received the honors of other institutions.

During all the years of building, teaching, and travel, the astronomer had also been a brilliant inventor.   His most wonderful invention was the Declinometer.   It would be difficult, until you study astronomy with a good telescope, to make you understand it.   The use of it was to get the position of the stars and number them.   Scientific men affirm, " *that there is no other known method equal to it for rapidity and accuracy in the cataloguing of stars.*" It is a beautiful contrivance.

Another curious invention was nice machinery which made a clock record its beats, or each pendulum swing work the *telegraph,* just as the finger of the operator does in sending a message.   The motions of the mechanism were so delicate that " the assistance of the *spider* was invoked."   His slender web moved a wire cross, which was raised and then dipped into quicksilver once every second for more than *three years!* Much longer might the silken harness have raised the wire sixty times a minute, or *half a million* of times in a year, had it been let alone.

Look at that clock with Professor Mitchel's attachment. Tick, tick, it goes; up and down, the cross held by the web, swings; and dot, dot, on the paper, is the work of a little pointer. The clock keeps time, and works its own telegraph with the precision of the living man over his machine.

Various and extraordinary improvements were added, until the automaton operator became one of the most perfect machines ever created by human skill. It seems as if *a soul* were somewhere in it; such are the wonders of creative genius!

In 1852 he commenced the publication of the *Sidereal Messenger*, the first paper which ever came from the American press devoted to the stars. But there was then too little interest in the bright worlds above our own to sustain the beautiful messenger of his observations—the gathered rays of knowledge which came from the spheres to his mind in the " watches of the night."

CHAPTER X.

N the summer of 1860, the finished professor, engineer, railroad president, and financier, was called to be a *peacemaker* in the cause he loved. General Stephen Van Rensselaer, following the example of Mr. Longworth, offered several acres of highland near the city of Albany for the site of an observatory. Mrs. Blandina Dudley, a wealthy lady there, gave . $13,000 toward a building. Other individuals of means increased the amount to $25,000.

Professor Mitchel furnished the plan of the edifice, which was commenced in 1853. It was completed in less than three years, and named after the principal donor the Dudley Observatory. But the selfish aims and disposition to quarrel, which have ruined the peace of families, churches, and nations, unsettled the management, and threatened the success of the splendid enterprise.

While negotiating with the directors, whose call was urgent, he happened to be in New York May 20th, 1860, when the great mass meeting assembled in Union Square, because rebel cannon had hurled defiance at the Stars and Stripes. Hundreds of boys, with thousands of men, on that signal day, in long processions poured into the ample area, now in the heart of the city. Banners were waved over the throngs, and fluttered from unnumbered windows. Platforms festooned with flags, bands of music, and wildly-beating hearts, were under the shadow of Washington's Equestrian Statue.

Hearken to the eloquent voices that ring out upon the ears of the eager multitude.

The venerable Gardiner Spring, D.D., of the Old Brick Church, made the opening prayer after a few patriotic remarks—the keynote of the grand occasion.

Hon. John A. Dix was chosen president. Among the nearly one hundred vice-presidents were William B. Astor, Esq., W. C. Bryant, the poet-editor, R. B. Minturn, and Henry Grinnell, the merchant princes, with many distinguished citizens from all the professions and business centres of the great metropolis.

The President made an eloquent speech. When he alluded to the gallant defence of Fort Sumter by General Anderson, who was present, and pointed to the tattered flag which waved over the hundred men while several thousand rebels opened upon the fortress, the very statue

6*

of Washington seemed to rock before such a storm of cheering as never went up around it before.

The Hon. Daniel S. Dickinson followed with a thrilling appeal. Of the peculiar and mournful character of the war, he said : " The most brilliant successes that ever attended the field of battle could afford me no pleasure ; because I cannot but reflect that of every one who falls in this unnatural strife, be it on one side or the other, we must in our sober moments exclaim :

> Another sword has laid him low,
>   Another, and another's ;
> And every hand that dealt a blow—
>   Ah, me ! it was *a brother's.*

But we are called upon to act. It is a time when the people should rise in the majesty of their might, and stretch forth their strong arms and silence the angry waves of tumult. It is a question between union and anarchy—between law and disorder. It should be, ' Our country, our whole country, and nothing but the country.'

> " ' 'Tis not the whole of life to live,
>   Nor all of death to die.' "

The next address was a glowing, stirring burst of eloquence by the lamented, brave, noble General Baker of Oregon. He was in the Mexican war at the storming of Cerro Gordo's bloody heights, and fell, you recollect, at Ball's Bluff—a sacrifice to a military blunder. I

will give you a single passage of his impassioned speech,
which moved the vast throng as the tempest bows the
forest before its breath :

"I am not here now to speak timorous words of
peace, but to kindle the spirit of manly, determined war.
I speak in the midst of the Empire State, amid scenes of
past suffering and past glory ; the defences of the Hudson
above me ; the battle-field of Long Island before me ; and
the statue of Washington in my very face ; the battered
and unconquered flag of Sumter waving in his hands,
which I can almost now imagine trembles with the excitement of battle."

The torn banner of Sumter was placed on the statue.

Passing by the speeches of Caleb Lyon, ex-Governor
Hunt, and others, we come to the scene around Professor
Mitchel in front of the Everett House. No speaker could
make all of the immense and excited throng hear his
voice. And at this spot was organized another meeting,
of which ex-Governor Fish was President.

The Rev. Dr. Vinton, of the Episcopal Church, opened
it with an impressive prayer, of which the following words
related especially to the country :

"O God, we have heard with our ears and our fathers
have declared unto us the noble works thou didst in their
days, and in the old time, before them. Let the shield
of thy omnipotent care be extended over the United
States of America, to defend the Constitution, and to

perfect the union of the people. Inspire the people with a spirit to think and to do that which is right. Thou hast proclaimed throughout the land—'Prepare war, wake up the mighty men, let all the men of war draw near, let them come up, beat your ploughshares into swords, and your pruning-hooks into spears—let the weak say I am strong.' A loving patriotism has yielded the pride and treasures of the family to protect the State. May Thy Spirit descend upon the great congregation of Thy people. Inspire the orators to speak the truth in love, and bow our hearts in obedience to duty as Christians and fellow-citizens, as loyalists and patriots, as sinners saved in a common salvation through Jesus Christ, to whom with the Father and the Holy Ghost be praise now and forever. Amen."

The Governor, Hiram Ketcham, and Henry J. Raymond, editor of the *New York Times*, addressed the multitude. An extract from the brilliant oration of the latter contains a fine anecdote of General Anderson:

" I heard an anecdote to-day from Major Anderson (cheers for Anderson) which may interest you, and at the same time illustrate this position. During the attack on Fort Sumter, a report came here that the flag on the morning of the fight was half-mast. I asked him if that was true, and he said there was not a word of truth in the report. He said that during the firing one of the halyards was shot away, and the flag in consequence dropped down a few feet.   The rope caught in the staff, and could not be reached, so that the flag could not be either lowered or hoisted ; and, said the Major, ' God Almighty nailed that flag to the flagmast, and I could not have lowered it if I tried.'   (Immense cheering.)   Yes, fellow-citizens, God Almighty has nailed that resplendent flag to its mast, and if the South dares to march upon Washington, they will find that that cannot be taken down.   No! they will find that that sacred sword which defends and strikes for human rights—that sword which Cromwell wielded, and which our fathers brought into the contest, and which made us a nation—will be taken once more from its scabbard to fight the battle of liberty against rebellion and treason."

No tones of patriotic fervor and stirring oratory awaken a deeper echo, or come from a loftier, purer soul, than those that fell from the lips of Professor Mitchel.   If you did not listen to them, read the burning words that thrilled the populace :

" I know that I am a stranger among you.   (' No, no.')   I have been in your State but a little while ; but I am with you in heart, and soul, and mind, and strength ; and all that I have, and am, belongs to you and our common country, and to nothing else.   I have been announced to you as a citizen of Kentucky.   Once I was, because I was born there.   I love my native State as you love your native State.   I love my adopted State of Ohio as you love your adopted State, if such you have ; but, my friends, I am a citizen now of any State. I owe allegiance to no State, and never did, and, God helping me, I never will. I owe allegiance to the Government of the United States.

"I did not abjure the love of my own State, or of my adopted State ; but over all that rose proudly, triumphant, and predominant, my love for our common country. And now, to-day, that common country is assailed, and alas ! that I am compelled to say it, it is assailed in some sense by my own countrymen. My father and my mother were from old Virginia, and my brothers and sisters from old Kentucky. I love them all ; I love them dearly. I have my brothers and friends down in the South now, united to me by the fondest ties of love and affection. I would take them into my arms to-day with all the love God has put into my heart ; but if I found them in arms, I would be compelled to *smite them down*. (Great cheering.)

"You have found officers of the army who have been educated by the Government, who have drawn their support from the Government for long years, who, when called upon by their country to stand for the Constitution and the right, have basely, ignominiously, and traitorously, either resigned their commissions or deserted to traitors, rebels, and enemies. The traitors and rebels North, and the traitors at the South, we must set aside. They are not our friends. When they come to their senses we will receive them with open arms; but till that time, while they are trailing our glorious banner in the dust, when they scorn it, condemn it, curse it, and trample it under foot, then I must smite.

"My friends, that is the spirit that was in the city yesterday. I was told of an incident which occurred that drew the tears to my eyes, and I am not much used to the melting mood at all. A man in your city had a beloved wife and two children depending upon his personal labor day by day for their support. He met her and said: 'Wife, I feel it my duty to enlist and fight for my country.' Said she, 'That's just what I have been thinking of, too; God bless you! and may you come back without harm! But if you die in the defence of the country, the God of the widow and the fatherless will take care of me and my children.' That same wife came to your city. She knew precisely when her husband was to pass as he marched away. She took her position on the pavement, and, finding a flag, she begged leave just to stand beneath its sacred folds, and take a last fond look on him whom she possibly might never see again. The husband marched down the street; their eyes met; a sympathetic flash went from heart to heart; she gave one shout and fell to the pavement, and there she lay for not less than thirty minutes in a swoon. It seemed to be the departing of her life. But all the sensibility was sealed up. It was all sacrifice. She was willing to meet the tremendous sacri-

fice upon which we have entered. And I trust you all
are ready. Lead me to the conflict. Into that I am
ready to go. I care not where duty calls me, I am
ready. God help me to do my duty. In God's name I
will smite, and as long as I have strength to do it. (Enthusiastic cheering.) Oh listen to me, listen to me! I
know these men; I know their courage; I have been
among them; I have been with them. They have
courage, and do not pretend to think that they have
not. I tell you what it is, it is no child's play you are
entering upon. They will fight with a determination and
a power well nigh irresistible; make up your mind to it.
Let every man put his life in his hand, and say: ' There
is the altar of my country, there I will sacrifice my life.'
(Wildest cheering.) I am ready to fight in the ranks or
out of the ranks. Having been educated at West Point,
having been in the army seven years, having served as a
commander of a volunteer company ten years, and having
served as an adjutant-general, I feel I am ready for something. I only ask to be permitted to act; *and, in God's
name, give me something to do.*"

You cannot well imagine the effect of this glorious
appeal. The throng around the stand waved their hats,
shouted, and not a few wept with the intensity of emotion.
The orator could have led the entire multitude to any field
of conflict at that moment. The stranger went on his
way. Smothering the fire in his soul he repaired to his

watchtower in the capital of the empire State, because *there* was then his post of duty. His patient spirit, which resolved at the beginning of the labors for observatories, *never to get angry*, calmed the strife. Soon the intellectual and moral atmosphere of his presence pervaded the new sphere of his rare abilities. His eagle eye was on the same heavens at night on which he had gazed from the college tower and the heights near Cincinnati. In the Church of God, and everywhere, his influence was benign and cheering as the morning light.

" And what is the real benefit of observatories? What good do they do?" you may ask, reader ; for the question has been asked by men of wealth and influence. Professor Mitchel had to answer it countless times. I will give you *three* great advantages to the people :

They give *accurate time*. The best clocks are kept in them ; and errors, if any, in beating the seconds, are corrected daily by the instruments for the purpose.

In Greenwich, England, there is a curious contrivance to keep the public " posted " on time. On a turret of the Royal Observatory there is a mast, like a large flagstaff. On it slides a ball made of wood and covered with leather *fifteen* feet in circumference. A little before one o'clock each day that ball is raised to the top of the mast. Precisely at one o'clock, by the corrected time, down goes the round signal, and out come the watches, while unnumbered eyes are turned to the clocks of the dwellings and offices of business.   Their pointers are moved, and the people around *agree*, for a moment at least, *in time*.

Nor is this the most wonderful part of the arrangement for the benefit of the public.   A clock inside of the observatory, which indicates exactly the corrections of time, is connected with a galvanic clock at the entrance gate, and also a clock at the terminus of the Southeastern Railway.   It sends galvanic signals every day along the principal railroads which converge in London.   It drops the Greenwich ball, and another in the Telegraph Company's offices on the Strand.   At Deal, the Admiralty have a signal for the benefit of the mariners.

Just think of it.   If the time at the Observatory, measured by the unerring stars, is a minute too fast or too slow, the clockwork tells the fact to the galvanic time-keeper at the gate, and at the great railway station.   And then fleeter than rushing cars, go every day, the signals from one depot to another.   The bright worlds above *telegraph* to the astronomer through his delicate instrument; he touches the mechanism his genius has constructed, and the telegraphic *nerves* in an instant send it over the kingdom.

In Washington, our national capital, the ball drops at twelve o'clock.

Now, my reader, when you reflect on the fact, that a slight error in the sea captain's chronometer may derange his calculations of latitude and longitude, and shipwreck his vessel, how important to *him* is an observatory, and to *you* if, with the travelling thousands, you are on the deep! Then remember that a mistake of a few seconds may bring a collision on the railroad, and kill a score or more of passengers—and how important appears the true time to all the conductors on the iron-paved highway! And similar provisions for safety might be made in every country, state, and province.

Another advantage of observatories, is the *economy* as well as security, of our commerce. Were it not for the labors of astronomers, our ships, as of old, would have to creep along the shores, afraid to traverse the faithless ocean. The shortest routes from one port to another could not be taken; disasters would be increased, and boundless wealth which now comes over the blue main, would remain unsought, unknown.

There is yet another sublime reason for erecting and furnishing on a large scale, and in greater number, astronomical observatories. It is the *education* which they furnish. They benefit the humbler institutions of learning. Wherever there is such a watchtower of the skies, the general intelligence will be increased. The higher learning will *come down* on the lower sphere of culture, and tend to elevate it.

You cannot look up to the observatory without being reminded of the wonders of the firmament, and of Him who bent that arch. Much less can you ascend its stair·

way and look through its telescope, which, with its *harness*, weighs tons, upon the flaming islands floating upon " airy nothing," without purer, wiser thoughts.

The largest telescope in this country is now, I believe, in Cambridge, Mass. The finest in the world was built and is owned by Earl William Parsons Rosse, of Birr Castle, Kings County, Ireland. He erected the Cbservatory on his grounds in 1844. The grand telescope cost *sixty thousand dollars*. The tube is six feet in the opening, and the whole weighs six thousand pounds. It has the most powerful reflector known, prepared by a new method, the invention of Lord Rosse. Several years were required for building the wonderful instrument. It reveals stars—and inequalities in the moon, which can be seen by no other telescope. The noble granite pile which supports it, the tackle for raising and adjusting it, are unsurpassed, and were created from the resources of his own abundant wealth. Should you visit the British empire, and get a view of the blazing orbs through this monster telescope, you would not soon forget the scene.

Before we leave the astronomical career of Professor Mitchel, I must add a few stanzas from a poem suggested by celestial scenery. It is the finest, to my knowledge, in any language. It was appreciated by none more than the devout Mitchel. The author, Derzhaven, was a Russian. He had gazed upon the luminous heavens from his northern home, where they flash and burn as nowhere else so brightly.

The clear cold air gives the stars a singular brightness. The auroral splendor at times seems like a hundred crimson banners bordered and tinged with purple, green, and gold, waving in the sky! The Great Bear, and all the grand constellations circling around the Pole Star, make the dome of the north an object of surpassing grandeur and beauty. It is the inspiration of such a view of the divine power and glory which breathes in the magnificent hymn to

THE DEITY.

O thou Eternal One! whose presence bright
All space doth occupy, all motion guide;
Unchanged through times all devastating flight;
Thou only God! There is no God beside!
Being above all beings! Mighty One!
Whom none can comprehend, and none explore;
Who fill'st existence with thyself alone:
Embracing all—supporting—ruling o'er—
Being whom we call God and know no more!

As sparks mount upward from the fiery blaze,
So suns are born; so worlds spring forth from thee:
And as the spangles in the sunny rays
Shine round the silver snow, the pageantry
Of heav'n's bright armies glitters in thy praise.

A million torches lighted by thy hand,
Wander unwearied through the blue abyss:

They own thy power, accomplish thy command,
All gay with life, all eloquent with bliss.
What shall we call them ?   Piles of crystal light,
A glorious company of golden streams,
Lamps of celestial ether, burning bright,—
Suns lighting systems with their joyous beams ?
But thou, to these, art as the noon to night !

Yes, as a drop of water in the sea,
All this magnificence in thee is lost !
What are ten thousand worlds compared to thee ?
And what am I, then ?   Heav'n's unnumbered host,
Though multiplied by myriads, and arrayed
In all the glory of sublimest thought,
Is but an atom in the balance weight
Against thy greatness—is a cipher brought
Against infinity !   What am I, then ?   Naught !

Naught !   But the affluence of thy light divine,
Pervading worlds, hath reached my bosom too ;
Yes, in my spirit, doth thy Spirit shine,
As shines the sunbeam in a drop of dew.

CHAPTER XI.

EFORE I introduce the splendid astronomer to your admiration under the starry banner of the country which he loved, I will take you back to the scenes which called him from his observatory and charts, dearer to him than all other material objects, excepting the Bible, his family, and the republic. If not a platform reformer, his great heart beat true to God and humanity. From his loving gaze into the star-sown fields of ether, he looked anxiously over the troubled land whose political campaign in the autumn of 1860 had stirred, as no other had, the tides of national feeling. Nor had he forgotten the scenes in Union Square, New York, during the previous May.

For long years the South had been preparing for a conflict with the North. The claim of the former to superior blood, the determination to preserve and extend slavery, and the desire to have a nationality in accordance with these ideas, had for many years been gaining strength and influence in the cotton States. The election of Abraham Lincoln, the "Black Republican," as the majority of the people who elected him were called, because of their hostility to American slavery, was a signal for revolt and revolution.

All the winter succeeding the hour when the people's choice was known, were heard the mutterings of discontent, and seen the preparations for resistance to the incoming administration. Gifted, but evil-minded men in Congress, and even in the President's cabinet, went frowning to and from the national capital. They met in secret council, and with fiery looks and speech talked over a dissolution of the Union—in other words, *death* to the Republic.

The infamous Floyd, Secretary of War, resigned, and the Hon. Joseph Holt took his place, who at once began to look after the defences of Washington. It was then we heard the hypocritical cry, "No coercion! no coercion!" That is to say, let us alone in our treasonable designs.

I shall refresh your memory of a few stirring events of that winter, because they not only thrilled the heart of Professor Mitchel, and suffused his eye with tears of grieving loyalty while fixed on the stars in the field of his telescope, but in their consequences cost him his useful life.

In Charleston harbor, near the city where secession had its birth in formal action, a few months before, stood the forts, Moultrie, on Sullivan's Island, Castle Pinckney, and rising in massive grandeur and mounting one hundred and forty guns, Sumter. Major R. Anderson had been compelled, by the signs of attack, to leave Moultrie for Sumter, a much stronger fortress.

The first thing, after he had entered the fort with his eighty brave soldiers, " Major Anderson assembled the whole of his little force, with the workmen employed on the fort, around the foot of the flagstaff. The national ensign was attached to the cord, and Major Anderson, holding the ends of the lines in his hands, knelt reverently down. The officers, soldiers, and men clustered around, many of them on their knees, all deeply impressed with the solemnity of the scene. The chaplain made an earnest prayer—such an appeal for support, encouragement, and mercy, as one would make who felt that ' man's extremity is God's opportunity.' As the earnest, solemn words of the speaker ceased, and the men responded amen, with a fervency that perhaps they had never before experienced, Major Anderson drew the ' Star Spangled Banner' up to the top of the staff, the band broke out with the national air, ' Hail Columbia,' and loud and exultant cheers, repeated again and again, were given by officers, soldiers, and workmen. If South Carolina had at that moment attacked the fort, there would have been no hesitation

7

upon the part of any man within it about defending that flag."

President Buchanan was perplexed and timid; the rebels in earnest, and fearless. An unarmed steamer, the "Star of the West," went with supplies to Fort Sumter. Upon approaching it, the first guns of the war thundered defiance at the steamer which carried only food for hungry men. This was early on the morning of January 9th, 1861. A wave of indignation swept over the land, and that was all: a cowardly hand was at the helm of the dishonored Ship of State. Government vessels were seized, sometimes surrendered at the mere demand of traitors, whose ordinance of secession had been passed at Charleston three months before. But brightly shone the loyalty of others.

When the "Alabama Navy" commanded Lieutenant Maffit to surrender the Crusader, his noble scorn was expressed in these words: "I may be overpowered, but in that event *what will be left of the Crusader will not be worth taking.*" He got away with his vessel.

Captain Porter was ordered in February to strike his colors to South Carolina. From his ship, the St. Mary's, at Panama Bay, he wrote the following sublimely fearless reply: "All under my command are true and loyal to the 'Stars and Stripes,' and to the Constitution. My duty is plain before me. The constitutional Government of the United States has entrusted me with the command of this beautiful ship, and before I will permit any other flag than the 'Stars and Stripes' to fly at her peak, I will fire a pistol into her magazine and blow her up. This is my answer to the infamous proposition."

February 11th, Abraham Lincoln gave his fellow-citizens at the railroad depot, Springfield, Illinois, the following impressive farewell, worthy of the newly-elected ruler of a great nation threatened by rebellion :

" My friends ! No one not in my position can appreciate the sadness I feel at this parting. To this people I owe all that I am. Here I have lived more than a quarter of a century. Here my children were born, and here one of them lies buried. I know not how soon I shall see you again. A duty devolves on me which is perhaps greater than that which has been devolved upon any other man since the days of Washington. *He* would never have succeeded except for the aid of Divine Providence, upon which he at all times relied. I feel that I cannot succeed without the same divine aid which sustained him. In the same Almighty Being I place my reliance for support, and I hope you, my friends, will pray that I may receive that divine assistance, without which I cannot succeed, but with which success is certain. Again I bid you all an affectionate farewell."

At Indianapolis, Cincinnati, Columbus, and other cities along his route, echoing bells, booming cannon, and other demonstrations of enthusiastic joy, greeted him.

At Buffalo, he passed under the flag of the Young Men's Christian Association bearing the inscription, "We *will* pray for you." After similar receptions at Albany, New York, and Philadelphia, he reached Harrisburg.

Here it became evident, beyond a reasonable doubt, that a conspiracy existed to assassinate Mr. Lincoln, and to prevent his inauguration. The plot was ripened in Baltimore. An Italian, a barber, it was afterward reported and believed, was to pluck the fruit. He was to see that the fatal blow was given amid the confusion of the riot, when the train in which the President-elect was expected, arrived. A railroad official promptly planned an escape from the peril. The few friends who were in the secret approved of it. A carriage was ordered, Mr. Lincoln stepped into it with his unofficial escort ; and with an order given to the driver to cast no backward look, he was carried to another point of departure, reaching Baltimore by way of Philadelphia before the arrival of the cars he had intended to take. The conspirators were not looking for him, and of course were foiled in their fiendish purpose. The object of their hate passed on safely to Washington. Saturday, February 23d, when the train bearing Mrs. Lincoln without her husband reached Baltimore, the mob in a rage were compelled to give up the search for their victim.

This fact, with others which I shall narrate, were related by Adjutant-General Thomas, who has so nobly carried out the President's proclamation of freedom to the enslaved. He has for many years been the superintendent of a Sabbath-school in Georgetown, near Washington, and speaks of it with more interest than of his military honors.

General Scott was at the head of the United States Army, and General Thomas was then his adjutant. Standing by the side of the chief, it was his responsibility to act under him in preparing for the next attempt to put Mr. Lincoln out of the way, which was to be at the inauguration. It is not the place to tell you all this quiet work of the hours before the 4th of March, 1861. How the armed men were drilled, and assigned their positions; the cannon placed at the commanding points around the capitol, and "shotted;" and then, when the congressional halls were filled, how, putting off his military dress for a plain citizen's apparel, General Thomas went among the people there to feel the excited pulse, and learn, if possible, what to expect.

But you know that the day wore away peacefully. The President's oath was taken; silence wrapped the late night in Washington with no tragedy to mar its peace. Soon came the scenes of Forts Moultrie and Sumter; the uprising of the people; and the murder of Massachusetts soldiers in Baltimore April 19th, the anniversary of the first blood-shedding in the Revolutionary struggle eighty-five years before, in Lexington, Massachusetts. Unless you recollect the state of feeling then, you cannot imagine the depth and intense excitement of the national indignation. It reminded one of the story of a Scotch nobleman who drew long iron bars across a deep mountain gorge to make a harp for the storm. The morning and evening breeze passed over those gigantic strings with no answering sound. But when the tempest swept down from the mountains and darkened the heavens, then the metallic chords vibrated to the wild strokes of the storm, and filled all the region with strange, wild music.

The nation's heart is not easily moved; but when that terrible outburst of treasonable passion reached it, the loud and thrilling tones of patriotism went over the land, ringing back upon the traitorous throng the death-notes of a doom which has made a graveyard of the South. We will add a strain or two of the free North's battle songs:

> " The streets our soldier-fathers trod
>   Blushed with their children's gore ;
> We saw the craven ruler's nod,
> And dip in blood the civic rod—
> Shall such things be, O righteous God,
>   In Baltimore ?

> " Bow down, in haste, thy guilty head !
>   God's wrath is swift and sure !
> The sky with gathering bolts is red—
> Cleanse from thy skirts the slaughter-red—
> - Or make thyself an ashen bed—
>   Oh ! Baltimore !

CHAPTER XII.

HE summer spread its harvest glories over the earth—and our national anniversary passed with sobered rejoicing. Then the terrible battle of Bull Run, July 21st, thrilled afresh the popular heart, when God vindicated his Sabbath law in our defeat, who opened the engagement.

In August the successful bombardment of Forts Hatteras and Clark by General Butler of the land forces, and Commodore Stringham of the navy, cheered our despondency. The late summer season found the professor's purpose matured of entering the arena of conflict. He had read, and thought, and prayed, till the pure orbs above, to his eye, were hidden behind the darkening war-cloud, bidding him to go where its bolts were falling upon his countrymen in arms. He offered his services to the Gov-

ernment, feeling, with General Grant, that his military
education at West Point had created a special claim to
them, and given him the peculiar advantage of preparation
for the field. The commission of brigadier-general of
volunteers was dated August 9th, 1861.

This is *loyalty*—preferring to suffer with the country
for its redemption, than enjoy in peaceful employments
the blessings it confers. How base and wicked, in contrast, appears the disloyalty of the fault-finding lovers of
ease, and friends of the oppressor !

By a singular, perhaps a designed coincidence, the
general was placed in command of the Department of the
Ohio, with his headquarters at Cincinnati, the theatre
of his first great scientific achievements. It was no common struggle of feeling when he turned from the home
which was ever his earthly paradise, and the tower of
celestial observations, to the distant latitude of his former
brilliant career in the walks of science and business, soon
to make the solitary tent and the battle-plain his abode
and circle of activity. The farewell words were spoken ;
the strong Christian heart beat tenderly, but firmly ; and
away he hastened to the banks of the Ohio. The world
did not know the greatness of the sacrifice made by one
large and loving heart. When Mrs. Mitchel gave him
up, she gave all, and soon laid down herself to die.

The professor returned to the very shadow of his
Observatory, to assume the chieftain's post of duty for

the same country of his love and labors.   How different
now his employment !   Riding from one side of the city to
another, he carefully surveys all the approaches to the
beautiful town lying on- the banks of the Ohio, with the
green rich slopes of terraced hills behind it.   There was
no city in the Union which he would have so fondly
watched as this.   It was endeared to him by the external
loveliness of its position and proportions, the rewarded
toils of the past, and the residences of munificent " merchant princes," who had generously aided him in his
struggles.   Redoubts went up under his vigilant hand,
and lines of defence were laid out to meet any raid of the
enemy, who threatened all the important points within
striking distance of their arms.   This forethought, and
the readiness to meet any assault, which it secured,
strengthened the mutual affection between him and the
intelligent, appreciative people of the western metropolis,
and had much to do with warding off the blow which the
foe desired, but feared to give.

You will recollect that a few weeks before General
Mitchel was ordered to the West, General Grant was
placed in command of Cairo and the district extending
from Cape Girardeau to New Madrid; and that, finding the assumed and absurd as well as wicked neutrality
of Kentucky broken by the rebel occupation of Columbus and Bowling Green, he sent a few of the " boys "
to Paducah, at the mouth of the Tennessee, and also to
7*

Smithland, at the mouth of the Cumberland, blockading those rivers. Still it was not certain which side in the civil war the State would take. The prospect was that the secession frenzy would seize the majority of the people, and hurl it into the chaos of revolt.

It was at this crisis that General Mitchel looked over the field into which he had entered, and resolved to make an effort to save Kentucky and Tennessee to the Union. This result was desirable on many accounts. One was a border State, naturally allied to the North; and the resources both furnished for the support of our army, were considerable. The attachment to slavery in the former was not so intense as in the cotton States, and it was washed by the rivers of the great West.

General Mitchel therefore ardently engaged in the enlistment and organization of troops for the Kentucky shore. Could you have seen him in the " Queen City," where he had stirred the popular heart with his eloquent flights among the stars, and toiled with brain, heart, and frame, to secure an observatory for the benefit of the people; and the honor of the State on whose soil it was to stand, you would have wondered at his industry and success in labors so different.

Now talking with officers, and then with the citizens who could aid him, appealing to the patriotism of the young men, and superintending the mustering of the volunteers, he was the busiest worker in all the stirring city

and on the Kentucky border.   Here they gathered on the
soil of the undecided State, until the force was large
enough to move with hope of success.   His wisdom and
comprehensive oversight, his vigor and transparent integrity, attracted the admiration of the intelligent observers
about him, and of the Government.   General Mitchel
then asked leave to take them to the field of greatest
promise for the uncertain prize.   The prompt, earnest,
heroic man is ready to confront the armies of treason.
His fine eye is aglow with enthusiasm, and nothing
clouds the open intellectual expression of his face but the
shadow of suspense.   One day, with no messenger or telegram to announce his coming, the Secretary of War suddenly appeared on the ground, to see what this general
was doing.   There is excitement in the camp, and the
cheerful aspect of relief in the bearing of General
Mitchel.   Watch him walking or riding by the Secretary's side during the hours of that visit, with animation
giving the details of his work and his plans, pure and sim-
ple-hearted as a child in his unhesitating and modest communications.   Then, turning with dignified and appealing
earnestness to Mr. Cameron, he said: " Mr. Secretary,
I should not have been able to raise these troops and prepare them for the field by saying, ' Go boys.'   But I have
used the language, ' Come, and I will lead you.'   Now I
desire to keep my promise to my troops.   And I solicit
permission to march at the head of these troops upon

Cumberland Gap, and push through, if possible, to Knox-ville, and liberate East Tennessce." The privilege was denied him, because the petty ambition of superior officers created opposition. The country must suffer loss, and the war be prolonged, rather than permit a bold and gifted commander to cross the lines of their departments. The Government spared no effort for conciliation and har-mony. It is fearful to think of the sacrifices of life, and aggravations of the war every way, by well-intended, but undeserved kindness to rebels, and shameful *indulgence of friends.*

A few weeks later the departments of the Ohio and Cumberland were united under General Buell. He was distinguished for bravery in the Mexican war, and hith-erto had sustained the character of a true soldier in the regular army. But he was unlike General Mitchel in natural qualities, early education, and habits. Though born in Ohio, he was *southern* in his sentiments and selfish in his ambition; ready to resign his place under the flag which had *honored* him, rather than render unconditional loyalty to it. General Mitchel was assigned a command under him in charge of a camp of rendezvous, with his headquarters at Bacon Creek, near Louisville, Kentucky.

The very bearing of General Mitchel won respect and regard. The unmistakable manliness and goodness of character, the stamp of genius on his brow and in his ex-pressive eye, made their impression upon the western "boys" who gathered about him. And then the entire absence of tinsel and " red tape" in his official appearance, and the thoroughly practical energy of his earnest work of preparation for service, awakened the enthusiasm of his troops. You will not forget that, truly in his career, the child was father of the man. The errand duties, getting astride the leader of the countrymen's team, and pushing his way to West Point, were the outworking of the same "sleepless soul" that later in life built railroads and astronomical observatories, and has now girded on the sword for his native land.

There was a still higher source of power over men. He was a *Christian hero*. Unselfish in his aims, he was blameless in his example. You have heard, it may be, gay persons speak of religion as a weakness ; a sad resort of those who are superstitious and afraid to die. How pitiful is such blindness ! Think of Washington, Foote, and Mitchel, with a host of gifted men living and dead. It was the sincere piety of the astronomer and commander that *fused* together in a well nigh perfect, and a lofty character, the native elements which lay in the heart, taking from them the dross of selfishness.

The soldiers are fond of pet names for their officers, expressive of their estimate of the commanders. And the *professor's* fame was established, while his martial deeds were yet to be won. Natural enough, in the admiration and growing confidence felt toward him, his brilliant achievements in celestial studies, furnished the familiar title.   General Mitchell had not long been among the troops before brave lips said something about "Old Stars."   It went like a fire in one of the prairies not far distant, among the ranks.   "Old Stars" was on every tongue.   He had lived in thought and study among the stars, and would soon show himself equally able to gaze undazzled upon the stars of military glory, and also worthy to wear them.   These were not his aim, for he was serving under a King who held over his head a crown of unfading stars!   Before Him, how mean were the honors of a day!

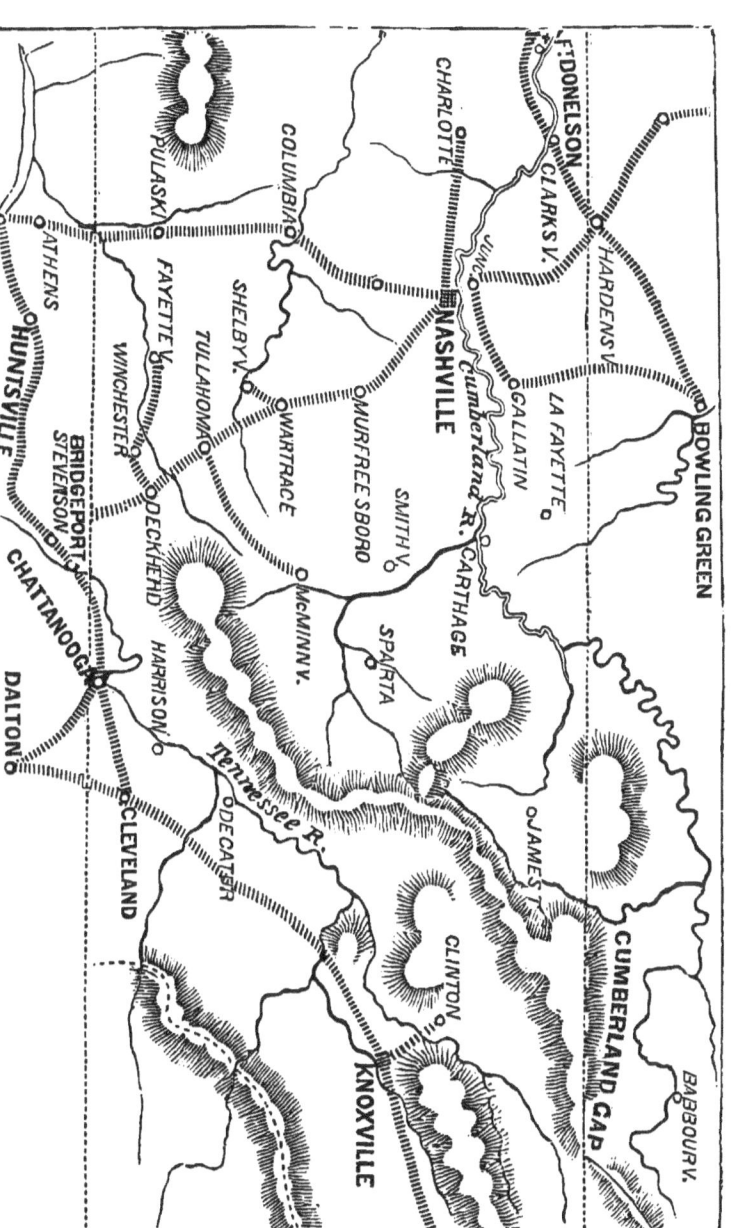

MAP OF GENERAL MITCHEL'S CAMPAIGN, p. 158.

CHAPTER XIII.

HE battalions under the discipline of General Mitchel were called the Third Division of the Army of Ohio. His headquarters were at Bacon Creek, Kentucky. The genius of the commander was devoted to the thorough training of the troops for military duty. There was nothing done for show simply, but all for the attainment of the highest degree of martial culture for the field. The men caught the enthusiasm of their leader. They saw the lofty motive, and aimed at the ideal before his comprehensive mind.

He had learned to do *well* whatever he deemed worthy of his attention; to make the most of himself and his opportunities. His thoroughness and mastery of tactics moulded the troops into a united, solid body, wielded by his single will. The proud and heroic ranks have been compared to the Old Guard of Napoleon. And perhaps nowhere in the army was there a finer example of perfect and merited command. It was like the hand of a skilful engineer on a finished locomotive; moving to the slightest motion of the hand, with no friction or jar in its movements. The difference was great, however, in this : it was the supremacy of a splendid mind over admiring and loving hearts.

Could you have walked through the camp, or met miles from it a soldier of that gallant host, and inquired of him where he belonged, he would immediately have answered, " I belong to the Third Division." It was honor enough to be under the command of " Old Stars." All inferior authority, however cheerfully obeyed, was forgotten under the sway of a master genius, regulated by a large and benevolent heart. The chief and his trained legions were ready and impatient for the smoke of battle. The camp could do no more for them, excepting to weaken their manly strength, at its highest point of preparation for the red field on which they desired to test it.

Did you ever see the encampment of an army? If not, you cannot get a perfectly correct idea of it by pictures or description. But I will take you to that of the Potomac Army as I saw it in the winter of 1863 and '64. Get with me into the cars at Washington and cross the Long Bridge over the Potomac, across which have marched our volunteers by thousands. At Alexandria you begin to see the *war*. Right by the track we read in large letters on one side, "Soldier's Retreat;" on the other we see, as far as the eye can reach, the rows of *soldiers' graves*. Then for about sixty miles we ride in the "U. S." train, for no others pass over the road, through a desert, though on the "sacred soil" of Virginia. Fences are gone, buildings burned, and the blackened chimneys standing—graves, dead horses, and mules, and regiments of soldiers with their camps, to guard the road, arrest the eye; and over all, myriads of crows make up the scene, till we get to "Brandy Station," a few miles from rebel pickets. Soldiers line the platform as we get out. Near by is a building, and around it a group of tents. One of them is the office of the Christian Commission, the grandest enterprise that ever softened the savage aspect of war, and cared for body and soul with motherly tenderness and watchfulness. We start, satchel in hand, for the headquarters of the army, a mile away over the hill, which is scarred with wheels and hoofs, and barren as the ocean beach.

The first man that passes us is a chaplain on horseback, with a polite salutation. The next is an aged negro, who inquires, "Do you think the soldiers will get sixteen miles below? I have a wife there in slavery." We tell him *yes*, and pass on. The first tent, as we approach the pines over the crest of the hill, is that of a *daguerrean*.

Then we come to a semicircular row and groups of tents half a mile at least in extent. The *hamlet* nearest, as we advance, is the provost-marshal-general's department. There is his tent, at the end of a lane cut through the pine trees, and fenced in with boughs; and on the left are the tents of his staff in a row. Let us knock at General M. R. Patrick's tent. "Come in!" rings out from the lips of the hero of Mexico and Florida, the patriot and Christian, who can give a splendid lecture on Hebrew poetry, or attend to the details of his immense department, with its post office for two hundred thousand men, prison for rebels, hospital, &c.

We pass on to General Meade's headquarters, about midway in the curved line of tents. He is absent; but there sits the gallant, lion-hearted Sedgwick. We look upon his pleasant face and hear him speculate upon the war, but do not know that in a few weeks a sharpshooter's bullet will pierce his noble face. Apart and back of this centre of command lie the batteries, dark and silent, and apparently all harmless.

In another direction are the supply wagons, the field for the horses, and other appliances for army support and movements. Sentinels keep their round day and night. The drum beats tattoo at night, and the bugle sounds sweetly on the morning and evening air.

Two, four, six miles, in different directions, are similar encampments, subordinate, like planets to the sun, to this.

Such is the outline of life during the intervals of active field service. And when the order flies along the telegraph wires connecting the headquarters of the major-generals, to prepare to advance, what a magnificent sight it is, as from one to two hundred thousand soldiers strike their tents, and in lines of cavalry and columns of infantry sweep over the country!

This reminds me of another part of army movements, which you may not have even seen or noticed at all; I mean the Signal Corps. Do you ask what it does? Then I will here answer the inquiry:

" Probably no class of men employed in the army are more useful than those engaged in the duty of sending army despatches from one point to another, by means of signal flags. These flags are of different colors—white, black, or red, to suit different circumstances. They are either four feet or six feet square, fastened to jointed poles, the length of which can be increased or diminished as required. The officers in charge of a station are furnished with field glasses and powerful telescopes, by means of which they can read the signals from twelve to eighteen, or twenty miles distant. For night work torches are used. The operation of transmitting signals is performed in this manner: The message is sent to the signal station, which is generally located in the highest tree, upon the loftiest mountain or hill top. The officer in charge arranges his ' key' upon a circular pasteboard instrument, marked with numerals. When all is ready, by the turning of this disc the proper numbers appear and are called off to the flagman. This flagman, on hearing the number, immediately places the flag in the position indicated. Thus, waving the flag according to a number requiring it to move from right to left, will mean a certain word. The flag is then straightened up, and another number called, which may raise the flag above the bearer's head, or drop it toward the ground. Again, some number called out, causes the flagman to make a motion with the flag that conveys a whole sentence of information to a distant station where another signal officer has been reading off, through his telescope, the numbers previously sent. The reader of the 'despatch' sits looking through his glass, calling off the numbers to his assistant, who notes them down upon the 'field-book.' When the entire message has been received the numbers are transmitted to the next station, and so on until it reaches the general to whom it is sent. The whole time occupied in sending a despatch of thirty lines is generally less than as many minutes. The flagman, by constant practice, works rapidly, and the reader calls the numbers with equal speed; and where there are two or more officers, or flagmen, at a station, the message is passed on to the next as fast as it is received. When the numbers reach the last station, the 'key' signal is sent over, and being properly adjusted, the officer at the receiving station can then write out for, or read the message to, his commanding general. These 'keys' are constantly changed. A combination of 'keys' is arranged between two commanding generals in a manner that insures their despatches against any chance of being read by even the officers making the signal, and of course, if the rebels saw them, they would be unable to decipher them. For instance, General Sherman has arranged with General Howard that the 'key' to his despatches shall be sent under cover of a particular word. Accordingly, when that word is received, General Howard has the 'key' that unlocks the remainder of the dispatch. On Monday morning General Sherman may make use of a 'key' that he discards in the afternoon. The afternoon 'key' is known to General Howard by the 'word' that accompanies the message. If General Sherman desires to 'speak with' General Logan, who may be stationed miles away, his arrangement of 'key words' may be totally different from those used in communicating with Howard. Signal officers, by long practice, are often able to abbreviate messages, especially when they know that the station beyond is commanded by an officer familiar with the abbreviations. A bystander looking on, when a message is being sent, will see the flags in the hands of the man near him waving rapidly, and strain his eyes in every direction to see where the persons are who are taking 'notes.' He will see no one, unless favored by a sight through the telescope at the station. The great

merit of this system of signalling consists in the secrecy
with which messages may be sent, and answers returned,
although it is equally advantageous in an engagement,
when secret messages are not required, and orders are
rapidly conveyed from one part of the field to another.
It is at this time that the signal officers and men are in
the greatest danger. The rebels have an offensive way
of intercepting despatches, with Minié bullets, sent by the
rifle of some sharpshooter, detailed to pick off the flagmen
and others engaged at the signal station."

No order to take the field came to the gallantly
impatient leader and his restless troops. He could
no longer wait. Approaching his superior in command, General Buell, he addressed him in these brave
words :

" General, we must now either be permitted to go into
the field and meet the foe, or we must degenerate and go
backwards. It is utterly impossible for me to carry my
division any further in my drill of discipline. The men
have learned every thing they can learn, and from this
moment we must commence to decline unless we are sent
into actual service."

General Buell made but little reply, only intimating a
grand movement soon. The rebel force was strong at
Bowling Green.

General Grant had moved upon Forts Donelson and
Henry, and planted the national banners on their walls.

General B. F. Butler, the wisest, boldest, and most successful commander then in the field, with Commodore Farragut, called the "Old Salamander," with his naval force, were preparing to advance on New Orleans. Ship Island, a narrow strip of sandy land several miles in length, and a few hours' sail from the mouth of the Mississippi, was to be the place of rendezvous and starting.

General Grant was on his way to Nashville, followed by the victorious flotilla.

General Buell decided to make an expedition from his department toward Bowling Green at that time, the strongest point in the enemy's western army movements. You will recollect it was one of the first places fortified when the rebels invaded *neutral* Kentucky. General Mitchel intensely desired to try the metal of his "boys" in the seizure of a prize worthy of their arms. He asked the privilege of striking boldly then. A wide-awake and far-seeing chieftain, he also "kept his own counsels."

Monday, February 10th—for the general avoided working, when possible, on the Sabbath—he issued in the evening, the order to his troops to be ready for marching the next morning at six o'clock. That night was a busy one in camp. See the tents come down, the knapsacks packed, the horses caparisoned, and the thousands of impatient volunteers waiting the command to march in the first beams of morning.

"Forward!" and Bacon Creek, Kentucky, received the farewell look of the departing troops, whose canvas city had disappeared like frostwork in the rising sun. They swept along toward Green River, giving no intimations of approach. The clear eye that traced the paths of the nightly host with unrivalled accuracy, surveyed carefully the whole field before him.

There can be no more gallantly patriotic and sublime spectacle in the field of martial exploits than the progress of General Mitchel from Bacon Creek to Bowling Green. Scouts, that is, horsemen to discover danger or search for the enemy, were sent forward toward the town. Silence reigned in forest and field. No sign of alarm appeared. How unlike the campaigns in the army generally! Somehow, the rebels have learned when and where our troops were in motion, and have been prepared to meet them. In one instance a large and splendid host were marching in several divisions on a secret expedition to surprise "the flower of the rebel army." A prominent general was to leave a certain point at half-past seven o'clock in the morning, and another pass that place at nine o'clock. When the latter arrived, the other, who should have been an hour and a half on the march, was just eating his breakfast. Whether, as many believe, he was made stupid by strong drink the night before, or not, it deranged the whole plan of the attack, and gave the enemy all the notice he desired of the hostile visit. Of course with the slaughter and wounding of many brave fellows, the well-planned and hopeful enterprise failed. '

Not so with the Third Division. Prayerful, sober, far-seeing and vigilant, the general stole upon the foe along a track of forced marches, like the Angel of Death upon the camp of Senacherib. The cavalcade dashed onward ten miles ; and being tired, because they had been so long idle, and also then delayed by repairing a bridge, they halted a mile beyond Green River. Their place of rendezvous was called Camp Madison. Here they rested on Wednesday. At night the picket-guard were out, and the order issued to be off again at four o'clock the next morning.

With scarcely a streak of day upon the eastern sky, the refreshed and cheerful troops move rapidly toward Bowling Green, forty-two miles distant. As the light deepens, they discern in the ponds scattered over the country heaps of dead cattle, mules, and horses, thrown into them by the foe, for the Upas shadow of war has been there. There are no signs of human life. Pause under that tree by the deserted home. Hearken amid the stillness whose music is the sound of flowing streams, and the noise of insects in the air. What a thunder of hoofs and heavy tramp of armed men breaks on the ear ! Nearer and nearer the strange echoes rise. Another moment and

8

the long procession rushes past with banners, and gleaming steel, and grim-mouthed cannon.

The morning kindles on the hills, and onward sweep
the battalions over plain, through forest, and across cur-
rents which catch the spreading light brightly, as though
no tumult of war had hushed the hum of the little dwellers
in the branches on the banks. Tramp, clatter, rumble,
go troops, feet, and wheels, toward Bowling Green, with
a secrecy and celerity unsurpassed, if ever equalled.

The secession stragglers who catch a glimpse of the
hurrying caravan of war's legions, fly from the path of
their march. Jokes and laughter enliven the long hours
of the advance toward the unsuspecting enemy. Many
think soberly, and some sadly, of home, the anxious hearts
there, and the possibility of sudden death and a burial
among strangers. Bravely, and with elastic step, the
troops follow a leader who has won affectionate confidence unrivalled in the army.

"Halt!" What is it that brings the battalions to a
sudden pause in the forest path? Like an abatis before
a fortress, lie the fallen trees across the way, heaped there
by the enemy. Almost before the word of command can
reach them, the two companies of engineers and mechanics advance. How bravely the axes swing! The implements for "casting up a highway" move with the rapidity
of sabre-strokes, and in *fifteen minutes* the formidable
obstruction is brushed aside, and "forward!" rings on

the air just now echoing to the hundred blows or more, of manly arms. No groans of the dying, no shouts of conquest mingle in the bloodless strife. Nature "makes no sign" of suffering when the glittering steel falls upon the subjects of her domain.

CHAPTER XIV.

OWLING Green is on Barren River, a branch
of the Green River. General Mitchel heard
that the bridge over it leading to the town was
destroyed, and that the rebels would meet them
on this side of the stream. To be ready for
them, Colonel Turchin takes the cavalry and Loomis' battery, and dashes off at a rapid pace. It is a fine sight.
Did you ever behold a similar spectacle? I shall not
soon forget the contrast between peaceful parades on the
park or green, and these scenes on "the front"—the
bugle notes that *mean sober work*, the prancing steeds,
the long and waving lines of soldiers, the plumes and
banners, the cannon with their carriages and caissons,
and all moving over fenceless fields, scarred and scathed

with the tread of war, toward the plain of slaughter.
Such was the scene between Glasgow Junction, near
which the last halt was made, and Bowling Green, on
the morning of February 13th, about the hour my reader
was entering the quiet school-room, or college hall.   The
columns that press on behind hear, about ten o'clock, the
booming of the artillery echoing from the banks of Barren River.

Oh! how the heroes start—eyes flash—and a general
movement is visible.   The steps are quickened, but the
knapsacks in the forced march of forty-two miles in
thirty-seven hours, have grown heavy.   A new idea is suggested by the burdens.   There comes a *secession* wagon.
" Stop there, driver !   Just take these knapsacks along."
In a minute, under guard, the " team " drags the Yankee
freight toward Bowling Green.

A few miles further another teamster is hailed ; the
tired troops are relieved, and almost run for the goal of
conflict.   The advance find no foe in battle array, and no
bridge across the deep, broad current.   Colonel Turchin
sends a signal shell over it into the town.   What a sudden excitement among the soldiers and citizens !   Three
regiments " are seen scampering to the cars, and putting
off with what they had."   The Texas Rangers start,
torches in hand, for the public buildings.   It is sad to
watch the flames curling, in magnificent waves of ruin,
over the beauty and pride of the town.

The victories of General Grant and Commodore Foote, and the progress of the dreaded gunboats up the Cumberland River, had awakened apprehensions before the messenger of death startled the traitors.   They were getting ready to leave.

Look along the railroad toward Nashville, and you will see immense trains of loaded cars.   The rebels are *moving* to that city.   Not dreaming of danger from any quarter besides the base of General Grant's operations, they "packed up;" and perceiving no necessity of great haste, they had been waiting unconsciously for General Mitchel.   That shell over the coldly flowing river is like a note of doom from the clear heavens.

Another, and then another globe of imprisoned fire, makes its graceful curve above the dividing stream. What "hurrying to and fro," and cries of terror !

" Shall we set fire to the trains?"

" Yes," shouts an officer.

" No ! the Yankees are too near for that."

And through the streets soldiers and citizens rush in the gloom of the night, whose stars are reflected from the surging waters.   The snow had whitened the earth, and the cold wind sweeps around the shivering volunteers.   Fires soon blaze on the river bank, and near them some almost benumbed declare they "would rather be shot than frozen."   They lie down " snugly tucked in their blankets," to snatch a brief slumber.   Scarcely are they asleep before

" the assembly beats to arms, and the brigade is again in ranks."

Upon them falls yet no herald-rays of the morning. It is gloomy and chilling. The engineer companies have repaired an old wherry or kind of flatboat, running a rope across the dismal flood of Barren River. Quickly as the spider builds her nightly suspension bridges, had the army *athletes* spanned the bridgeless stream, and now the brigades begin by small detachments to cross over.

Mournful spectacle is that which meets the vision in the dawn of day ! Mansions are in ruins—relics of flight strew the forsaken streets. Comic scenes, too, are there. A poor sutler had run away in such haste that all his good things for army speculation were left for our hungry " boys." They do not wait for a spread table or knives and forks. They snatch the eatables, and are on the march again. Then they enter the ruins of a storehouse of arms which the rebels had burned. And such a medley of weapons ! Old musket and pistol barrels, bowie knives, " hangers," savage blades, butcher knives, and every imaginable tool for murdering and mangling men are there. But much plunder is saved. Half a million of dollars is an unexaggerated estimate of its value to the Union cause. We give you the despatches to the general-in-chief, McClellan, and the congratulations on the victories :

LOUISVILLE, *February* 15, 1862.

To Major-General McClellan:

Mitchel's division, by a forced march, reached the river at Bowling Green to-day, making a bridge to cross. The enemy burned the bridge at one o'clock in the morning, and were evacuating the place when he arrived.

D. C. BUELL,
Brigadier-General Commanding.

The following is a general order, issued by General Buell to the troops of General Mitchel's division, after their advance upon Bowling Green :

HEADQUARTERS, THIRD DIVISION, CAMP JOHN Q. ADAMS, }
BOWLING GREEN, *February* 19, 1862. }

SOLDIERS OF THE THIRD DIVISION: You have executed a march of forty miles in twenty-eight hours and a half. The fallen timber and other obstructions, opposed by the enemy to your movements, have been swept from your path. The fire of your artillery, and the bursting of your shells, announced your arrival. Surprised and ignorant of the force that had thus precipitated itself upon them, they fled in consternation.

In the night time, over a frozen, rocky, precipitous pathway, down rude steps for fifty feet, you have passed the advance guard, cavalry and infantry, and before the dawn of day you have entered in triumph a position of extraordinary natural strength, and by your enemy proudly denominated the Gibraltar of Kentucky.

With your own hands, through deep mud, in drenching rains, and up rocky pathways, next to impassable, and across a footpath of your own construction, built upon the ruins of the railway bridge destroyed for their protection by a retreating and panic-stricken foe, you have transported upon your own shoulders your baggage and camp equipage.

The general commanding the department, on receiving my report announcing these facts, requests me to make to the officers and soldiers under my command, the following communication :

" Soldiers who by resolution and energy overcome great natural difficulties, have nothing to fear in battle, where their energy and prowess are taxed to a far less extent. Your command have exhibited the high qualities of resolution and energy, in a degree which leaves no limit to my confidence in their future movements.

" By order of   Brigadier-General Buell,
        " *Commanding Department of the Ohio.*"

Soldiers ! I feel a perfect confidence that the high estimate placed upon your power, endurance, energy, and heroism, is just. Your aim and mine has been to deserve the approbation of our commanding officer, and of our Government and our country.

8*

I trust you feel precisely as does your commanding general, that nothing is done while any thing remains to be done. By order of

       Brig.-Gen'l O. M. MITCHEL, Commanding.

Bowling Green was occupied, and nothing saved the rebel army which fled from it but the necessity which General Mitchel felt of making sure his communications. Otherwise he might be surprised, his retreat cut off, and his command taken prisoners, or at best, badly " cut up."

Ferry-boats were constructed, and such defences planned as promised the greatest possible security to the troops, and success to the bold expedition.

In the midst of these labors, his unselfish heart throbbing with love to the land of his birth, and the high ambition to hasten its deliverance from mad misrule, General Buell suddenly appeared in camp. His less ardent and less comprehensive mind was disturbed by General Mitchel's daring movements.

General Mitchel encounters here a new trial of his noble nature. It will be among the saddest records of the war, that officers like General Don Carlos Buell allowed political or military aspirations, or half-hearted loyalty, or, at best, great blunders, to sacrifice thousands of lives, and imperil, more than all other dangers, our national honor and existence. General Mitchel spread out his plans.

" We must move cautiously ; do nothing to exasperate *our Southern brethren;*" seemed to be the settled policy of the chief of the Cumberland army.

" We must move rapidly, strike boldly, and follow up every advantage to subdue the traitors," was the tone of each word added by the commander of the Third Division.

The result of the discussion was, permission under certain conditions for General Mitchel to go forward with his campaign. He was a free man *dragging a chain.* The weight was a hindrance, and it might be made fast at any moment ; the finishing blow of a selfish policy, which at length came. The locomotives which stood puffing on the track when the shell crossed the river, drew the Union forces toward Nashville.

It is Sunday evening. War does not respect the holy hours of the Lord's day. There had been no signs of its advent in that excited town. Armed men, citizens in groups, or hurrying through its streets, and scornful wo-men on balconies and in the doors of the mansions, are the scenes of February 23d, 1862.

The city authorities gather to the appointed spot of meeting the commander of the Union troops and his staff. Colonel Kennett has been selected to receive, in behalf of General Mitchel, the possession of the town. It was a bitter necessity to many ; a most welcome transition to others who had not ceased to love the old flag.

Nashville deserves a brief description, which will interest you. It is on the left bank of the Cumberland, two hundred miles from its mouth, and six hundred and eighty-four from Washington. The capitol stands on an elevation one hundred and seventy feet above the river, commanding a glorious landscape. It is built of lime-stone, costing a million of dollars, and is one of the most magnificent structures of the kind in the country. The private residences are elegant, many of them palatial—rich in material, surroundings, and furniture. A suspension bridge spans the stream there. The city is the terminus of the Nashville and Chattanooga Railroad.

General Mitchel called, in company with other officers, upon the widow of President James K. Polk, as did General Grant while there. During the interview, the dignified lady, addressing him, said: " General, I trust this war will speedily terminate by the acknowledgment of Southern independence."

This direct appeal to his loyalty turned all eyes to him. The silence which followed was brief. Calmly and firmly he spoke from the fulness of his earnest heart, with equal dignity, and great impressiveness :

" Madam, the man whose name you bear was once President of the United States. He was an honest man and true patriot. He administered the laws of this Gov-ernment with equal justice to all. We know of no inde-pendence of one section of our country which does not belong to all others ; and judging by the past, if the mute lips of the honored dead who lies near us could speak, they would express the hope that the war might never cease, if that cessation were purchased by a dissolution of the union of the States over which he once presided."

The fair traitor was silenced, and loyal hearts deeply moved.

CHAPTER XV.

ND now we come to the first great opportunity to
show the splendid qualities of our hero in daring
and difficult military movements, the very martial ability peculiar to Napoleon Bonaparte.
You will find on the map, a little southeast of
Nashville, and one hundred and sixteen miles from it,
Huntsville, Alabama. It is a handsomely-situated town.
The capital of Madison County, it has a finely-built court-
house, which cost forty-five thousand dollars. The population is four thousand. Though an important centre of
business for the region, the great attraction to General
Mitchel was its *situation*. It is on the Memphis and
Charleston Railroad, which, with intersecting tracks,
poured into the depots of the southeastern rebel army

the men, munitions of war, and the supplies of the West. See how the network of iron paths in Kentucky, Tennessee, and Mississippi, connect with this grand central thoroughfare of trade and travel. General Mitchel determined to march his comparatively small army a hundred and thirty miles through the enemy's country to Huntsville, and cut that great artery of life to the Confederacy.

The value of this road to the rebel army you will learn from a secession paper published at Florence, which lies upon it, between Huntsville and Corinth. The news of Grant's progress southward from Fort Donelson had reached the place. The *Gazette* of March 12, 1862, had the following very significant article :

" We learned yesterday that the Unionists had landed a very large force at Savannah, Tenn. We suppose they are making preparations to get possession of the Memphis and Charleston Railroad. They must never be allowed to get this great thoroughfare in their possession, for then we would indeed be crippled. The labor and untiring industry of too many faithful and energetic men have been expended on this road to bring it up to its present state of usefulness, to let it fall into the hands of the enemy to be used against us. It must be protected. We, as a people, are able to protect and save it. If unavoidable, let them have our river ; but we hope it is the united sentiment of our people, *that we will have our railroad.*"

General Mitchel carefully counted the perils and the cost of the bold adventure. The possibility of being caught by the rebels away from the centres of our military strength, he knew. Libby prison for those who were not killed in the fight, or the hospitalities of any other place of Southern incarceration, were not pleasant to contemplate. On the other hand, he had learned that, without a risk, a resolute attempt to overcome obstacles, nothing worthy of a man, and especially of a Christian, was ever accomplished. Providence was his trust; and He honors a faith that depends on His interposition to give success, if that aid may be intelligently expected.

General Mitchel, with a bounding heart of hope and pure ambition to do what he felt able and called to perform for the republic, advanced from Nashville to Murfreesboro' early in March. His superior officer had other work enough to fill his hands, which left our commander for awhile unembarrassed.

Movements were made pointing to the hastening conflict at Shiloh, by the hostile armies of the western field. General Buell commenced his march over the country toward the Tennessee River. General Grant, whose enlarged command was now the "Department of the Mississippi," had moved his battalions already in the vicinity of Pittsburg Landing. The rebel army of the Southwest was intrenched at Corinth, a few miles distant in a southwesterly direction, on the Memphis and Charleston Railroad.

The splendid victories of Grant and Foote in the northern part of the Mississippi valley, and of Butler and Farragut near the mouth of the Father of Waters, had alarmed the traitors. The ghostly thought, that the "Yankees" *might* "hew their way" through that magnificent valley, and cut their revolted territory in two, began to haunt their proud dreams of conquest. Beauregard was the chief of the concentrated forces prepared to dispute the advance of the Union troops.

It was at this crisis of affairs that General Mitchel was at Murfreesboro'. You recollect his engineering on the railways while at Cincinnati nearly twenty years before. Now this practical knowledge was just the thing for his raid, as it may be termed. The rebels, in their late retreat, had destroyed all the bridges on the route. General Mitchel, in ten days, had twelve hundred feet of these demolished structures rebuilt and ready for the advance.

It is the sixth of April, the Sabbath-day. Listen, with the ear turned toward Pittsburg Landing or Shiloh —the latter name being that of a church near—and you can almost catch the thunder of terrible battle. General Grant has been unexpectedly attacked at that point, instead of meeting the enemy as anticipated at Corinth.

Generals Albert Sidney Johnson and Beauregard have

made a bold push forward. Like a long spectral caravan, their splendid army swept through the forest in the morning twilight, to fall upon General Prentiss' division. Oh! what carnage, consecrated with the blood of patriots, that day of the Lord! And how strangely tragedy and comedy are mingled sometimes in war!

On the rebel side of the field a commander gathered around him his brigade, and in the hearing of our men, whose battery was concealed by a forest, he commenced his address in these words: " Sons of the South! We are here to defend our homes, our wives and daughters, against the horde of vandals who have come here to possess the first and violate the last. Here, upon this sacred soil, we have assembled to drive back the Northern invaders—drive them into Tennessee. Will you follow me? Is there a man so base among those who hear me as to retreat before the contemptible foe before us? I will never blanch before their fire, nor——" Just then a strange screaming sound in the air, and *six shells* dropped around the orator. With the dust, he and his audience in a hurry cleared away. The speech is doubtless unfinished to this hour.

And where is Mitchel, who longed for the smoke of conflict which rolled in dense clouds over Shiloh? He is sweeping like the wind toward Shelbyville, on his way to Huntsville. Meanwhile his depot of supplies was removed to within fifty miles of Huntsville. You know

the food for an army, including horses and mules, requires the greatest forethought and care. Let thousands
of soldiers, with the necessary animals, be caught without
subsistence in an enemy's country, and starvation or surrender must soon follow. To prevent this, *headquarters*
for the supplies, as well as for the commanding general,
must be secured with the advance of the army from one
centre of operations to another. Long trains of cars, or
of wagons, convey these means of sustaining the immense
cavalcade of the moving battalions to a convenient distance from the troops.

To give you an idea of army trains, I will add a description of one of these. An army corps of 30,000 infantry has about 700 wagons, drawn by 4,200 mules.
Including the horses of officers and of the artillery, about
7,000 animals have to be provided for. On the march,
it is calculated that each wagon will occupy eighty feet,
in bad roads much more; so that a train of 700 wagons
will cover 56,000 feet, or over ten miles; the ambulances
will occupy about a mile, and batteries about three miles;
30,000 troops need six miles to march in if they form one
column; the total length of the marching column of a
corps is, therefore, *twenty miles*, without including the
cattle herds and trains of bridge materials. Impatient
critics of army movements would often be more lenient
were they to familiarize themselves with the details of

the immense difficulty of organizing and moving large trains and artillery.

The bitter spirit of the rebels in the country which General Mitchel traversed, was shown whenever an opportunity occurred. A member of his staff told me that all manner of sport was made of the movements and soldiers of the army. Mimickry, ridicule, and curses, were the salutations continually. Men, women, and children, vied with each other in the effort to annoy the troops, and display their demoniac enmity toward the "Yankees." No clearer evidence of a bad cause could be given. The consciousness of a righteous and worthy enterprise will lift those engaged in it to rational and decent conduct: the old proverb, "murder will out," has forcible application here.

The worst effect of slavery, perhaps, is the tyrannical, irritable, and selfish disposition it cultivates. To make property of another race—to be relieved from all labor by those who are at the mercy of their owners—nurtures the basest passions. Embodied in political action, and then military force, the motto has been and is, "*Rule or ruin*."

While at Shelbyville General Mitchel received, under flag of truce, a rebel officer. The returning captive was taken sick. He was nursed for many days in his pain and weakness. No stranger would have guessed, from the kindest attention and medical aid, that he was a faithful soldier of Jeff. Davis. When he recovered, the flag of truce was borne by an escort of the officer toward Corinth, where the troops of Beauregard held their strong position.

The sad news from our army of the first day's battle at Shiloh, had reached the towns on the route. At Fayetteville, which you will observe is on the curve made by the course of travel, twenty miles from Shelbyville, the exulting people excelled the forest savages in their inhumanity. A flag of truce, the world over, is regarded sacred. Without such respect, there could be no intercourse between hostile armies. It is the flag whose meaning is just the opposite of the *black flag*, which signifies no mercy. But at Fayetteville it was scorned. The barbarians were so sure of sweeping the Union legions from their soil, they could meanly, basely, insult the peaceful banner over the head of an officer from their army. The life of the escort was in danger. A ruffian took him by the hand and rudely pulled it, saying, with an oath I will not repeat: "You infernal Yankee, what are you doing here?"

It reminds us of the stories of Indian captivity, in the early history of our country, when a prisoner became the object of cruel pastime till death released the victim. The officer and his lieutenant sat up all night to watch over the life of the truce-flag bearer. The returned rebel wrote to General Mitchel, deeply regretting the injury,

and making all the apology in his power for the outrage
And to illustrate the spirit of the women, I must add an
extract from a letter addressed to

"Dearest Aunt: If there is an hereafter, a heaven or
hell, I pray to go to perdition ere my soul would be joined or rest in heaven with the fiendish foe.   Heaven would
not be the place described to us were it filled with spirits
so foul, so hellish (excuse the expression).   Words are
too weak, too trite, too feeble to convey even the slightest
idea of feeling with which our refined, elegant, high-toned,
principled, chivalrous people look upon such an offcast,
degenerate set. . . . Oh! the thought is too painful, to
see our men, the choicest, the most refined specimens of
God's work, destroyed and even forced to take up arms
against the dregs of creation ; for every man they lose is
a blessing, a godsend to humanity and society.

" ANNA."

Such was the welcome of the citizens, for the most
part, to General Mitchel, pushing with sublime daring
into the heart of the treasonable South.   You will read
with admiring interest his eloquent " declaration of sentiments," in respect to his own conduct amid such provoca-
tions :

"In my treatment of the people I adopted a very
simple policy at the outset.   I have studied the great
platform of the rebellion to the best of my ability, and

made up my mind that no cause existed for the South
raising its hand against the United States—not the
slightest; that it was a rebellion, a downright piece of
treason all the way through; and that every individual
in that country who was either in arms, or who aided
and abetted those in arms, was my personal enemy, and
that I would never break bread, or eat salt, with any enemy of my country, no matter who he might be; and I
have never done it up to this day. In the next place, I
determined I would show them I was honest, and had an
object in view; and while I treated them with the most
perfect justice, I determined to make every individual
feel that there was a terrible pressure of war upon him,
which would finally destroy him and grind him to pow-
der, if he did not give up his rebellion."

Words more just, patriotic, unselfish, and appropriate,
no lips have uttered since the Declaration of Independence proclaimed the birth of the Republic! They were
the keynote of that peculiar and fascinating earnestness,
which not often lends its glow to fine intellect and high
culture. There was so much *soul* in all he did. I do not
mean merely enthusiasm, which may be very *shallow*. It
was depth of feeling, moved like the tides by the sun and
moon, when any object worthy of his powers engaged
them. It gained for him a privileged place in the Academy, built observatories, captivated the *élite* of the land
while he discoursed of the stars, and made him a leader

on the battle-field, second to none in promise of grandest success. How unlike the compromising, hesitating policy of many distinguished generals in our Union army, from the beginning of the war! And how unlike the terrible earnestness of the foe!

You have heard of the guerrillas? And you may have seen the anecdote of a man who confounded the name with *gorilla*, a powerful and savage animal resembling the orang-outang—not a very bad mistake either; for the guerrillas are a band of lawless robbers, who prowl over the country, plundering and murdering the Union people without mercy.

General Mitchel learned that they had driven the inhabitants of Franklin and Marion Counties, in East Tennessee, to the mountains, away from their homes, crops, and all their comforts. Thousands of peaceable citizens, because they loved the Republic, were thus, like the Christian martyrs under the pagan and papal kings, "wandering in the dens and caves of the earth." White and black alike were hunted down by the rebel bandits—pillaged, insulted, outraged.

General Mitchel sent General Negley, a brave officer of the stamp of his commander, to look after these ruffians; and after he had administered justice from the mouths of rifles, and from sabre-tongues, to make a call at Chattanooga. There, was a strong position of the enemy. On the cavalry flew, toward Winchester, by forced marches,

to surprise General Adams, near Jasper.   How splendidly
those troopers climbed the steep declivities, and moved
like a huge anaconda over the mountain crests, and along
the rugged slopes !   Twenty miles of this gallop were left
behind, when the Union force struck the pickets of Adams' battalions, and captured them by the most adroit attack.   Soon General Negley met the main force, which
fled up a narrow lane.   Hotly pursued, the enemy crowded
the unfrequented road toward Jasper, until compelled to
turn and fight.

Now comes one of the severest " hand-to-hand fights "
of the war.   Gallantly dash Taggard and Wyncoop's
cavalry upon the desperate rebels.   Spur, carbine, and
sabre do their work well !   The burnished blades wave
and cross, and go down to drink blood in the electric air
of that fierce battle.   See that fine-looking guerrilla, his
face half buried in whiskers and mustache, lifting his
blade with defiant swing !   Down it goes, with sudden,
aimless curve, toward the ground.   The proud head
droops—the blood gurgles from a mortal wound !   That
dying officer is Major Adams, brother of the commanding
general.

And then the reins are drawn on the steeds, and their
heads turned toward Jasper.   In the town an effort is
made to rally the terrified fugitives, but, cursing Adams
and ill luck, on they sweep toward Chattanooga.   For
miles the road is strewn with weapons, knapsacks, and

9

all the relics of a flying host, leaving a score or more dead in their wake.

General Adams finds rest in Chattanooga, to the very gates of which General Negley follows him. Colonel Sill advances to Shell Mound, on the river. Meanwhile, from the mountain passes of the Cumberland Range, the overjoyed exiles come streaming into Jasper, haggard, weary, and hungry. Oh! 'tis touching to see strong men weep with grief and gratitude, and vainly endeavor to express their thanks for the deliverance wrought by General Mitchel and his heroes.

Despatches pass back and forth between Generals Negley and Mitchel, breathing victory and congratulations. The cobwebs are swept from long-forsaken homes, and lights at evening again burn by their altars.

Upon one occasion an officer, with whom General Mitchel had business of great importance to transact, reported himself at a later moment than he had appointed for the interview. When the officer came into the general's presence, with no thought of any allusion to a little delay, his commander said promptly :

" Sir, you are late."

" Only a few seconds," replied the officer.

" Sir," replied General Mitchel, " I have been in the habit of computing the value of the hundredth part of a second."

The rebuke was felt and borne in silence. The astronomer had learned the importance of the fraction of a second in the measurement and motions of the heavenly bodies, which may be equally precious in the movements of armies and destinies of men.

Look away toward that wild summit, around which lies a rugged and romantic landscape, bathed in the morning light of the Sabbath! Tents dot the slopes, and over them waves, in the refreshing breeze, the " Star Spangled Banner." Excepting the track of the Union army, and its encampments, heights and valley are hostile soil.

The Ninth Ohio Brigade have gathered to the bugle-call for religious service. The brave " Buckeye " volunteers stand with uncovered heads, while the chaplain's prayer ascends to the God of battles. Then the sacred song rises and swells upon the mountain air, floating away to the eagle's nest, and blending with the wild bird's notes of praise to Him " who hears the young ravens when they cry." The sermon follows. When the preacher leaves his platform General Mitchel mounts a rock, and modestly, earnestly addresses the troops. His clear voice and eloquent words held in breathless attention every hearer.

He begins by assuring the vast audience that he does not " appear before them as the general commanding, but in a higher capacity; that he shall address them as a man speaking to his fellow men—as one striving for the

same eternal rest offered to all in this probationary life."
He urges the duty of the soldier to be a Christian; that
religion heightens every enjoyment, and prepares him to
discharge better every obligation

For half an hour the scholar, general, and orator, presents in glowing light the transcendent excellence of
Christian character, the ingratitude and ruin of an irre-
ligious life.

Seldom, if ever, has the war-field presented so sublime
and impressive a scene. The Sabbath-sky arched the
mountain top, glittering with arms and uniform, from
whose rocky eyrie for the first, and doubtless last time,
worship ascended to the "King of kings." And when the
sun went down in glory over the guardian heights of East
Tennessee, brave hearts were touched with the memories
of that appeal—tears glistened while its magic power sent
the thoughts away to Christian homes and temples, perhaps to be seen no more. Snatches of sacred melody
from scattered tents died on the bosom of night—the
mountain vespers of freedom's advancing host!

CHAPTER XVI.

A daring Adventure under General Mitchel—The leader of the band detailed to conduct it—Perilous Travelling—Partial Success—The Flight for Life—Arrest of the "Engine Thieves."

E come now to a wild episode in General Mitchel's campaign; an adventure, the like of which, I think, was never known before. To understand it, you must recollect that the rebels had been driven by General Grant from their great frontier posts, and had fallen back on shorter lines of defence—that is, placed their troops around a smaller territory.

The railroad which General Mitchel was after, was the western artery of supplies to the enemy. The map will show you on the easterly side of a vast parallelogram of railways from Memphis to Chattanooga, thence to Atlanta and Jackson, and round again to Memphis, forming the life-enclosure of the hostile field, the *Georgia State road.*

If along with success in the magnificent enterprise of General Mitchel, this important line could be destroyed or even crippled, East Tennessee, then poorly defended, would be at the mercy of our General Morgan lying before Cumberland Gap, ready to spring like a lion from his lair, whenever the prey was within reach.

Mr. J. J. Andrews, a secret agent of the United States, who had often been through nearly every part of the South, matured a very bold plan of cutting off communication by this route. It was a military expedition of small proportions, but attended with a courageous fearlessness, and with perils surpassing any other deed of artifice, and defiance of suffering and death, in the annals of war.

A score of men were to penetrate to the enemy's country, seize the trains on the track from Atlanta to Huntsville, and burn the bridges behind them; thus interrupting communication, till a decisive blow could be laid upon the almost isolated foe. The proposition was first made to General Buell, who referred Andrews to General Mitchel. With him the bold raiders were successful. The audacious design just suited the enthusiasm and energy of the chief. The greatest caution and secrecy was to attend every movement of the pretended friends of the Confederate Administration while under its protection. Among them was a young man named William Pittinger, an Ohio farmer's boy, only twenty-two years of age. Like his general, he was early fond of astronomical studies. When only seventeen years of age he constructed a telescope of considerable power, "which his friends from near and far came to see and gaze through, at the wonderful worlds unthought of before." An intelligent, yet imaginative youth, he asked as a special favor that he might be permitted to join the expedition. He has since published an account of the wild, exciting, and tragical adventures of that select company, who were all from Ohio excepting the leader Andrews, and William Campbell, both of whom were from Kentucky. Several of the fearless band of twenty-four, who were gathered from four different regiments and eight companies, made short excursions to the enemy's lines, and came near being captured at Chattanooga. They had gone in citizen's dress from that place to Atlanta, intending there to seize a Georgia engineer, take his train, burn the bridges behind them, and run through to our lines. But he had been pressed into Beauregard's service, then mustering his forces at Corinth, and thus escaped.

At length all was ready for the grand dash into the heart of "rebeldom." The little camp was pitched above Shelbyville, where General Mitchel's battalions lay. April 6th, the Sabbath-day, smiled brightly on the scene. Writes young Pittinger: "The earliness of the clime made the birds sing, and the fields bloom with more than the brilliancy of May in our own northern land

Deeply is the quiet of that Sabbath with the green beauty of the warm spring landscape pictured on my mind. An impression, I know not what, made me devote the day to writing letters to my friends. It was well I did so, for long and weary months passed ere I was permitted to write to them again."

Monday morning, Andrews reported to General Mitchel that he had been along the line of the Georgia State Railroad, and the "scheme was still feasible, and would be of more advantage than ever."

The leader of the band was a noble specimen of Kentucky manhood. He was "nearly six feet in height, of powerful frame, black hair, long, black, and silken beard; Roman features; a high and expansive forehead; and a voice fine and soft as a woman's, with the most cool and dauntless courage," and great refinement of feeling. He had a single defect of character, it would seem, from the history of the expedition. While, as a secret agent, he was always deliberate in action, his very habit of acting *alone*, unfitted him in some degree to act for others, in a startling surprise, when "*instant* action is the only chance of safety." Still a braver, manlier spirit, never staked every thing in a desperate adventure, than this loyal son of Kentucky.

At four o'clock on that Monday afternoon, the sunbeams fell unclouded upon the gallant company striking their tents, and leaving camp in the bracing air of the

closing day. They hastened to Shelbyville, to bid adieu
to old comrades and their brave officers. The eyes of
scarred heroes were suffused with tears while they grasped
hands, in a parting which appeared to those who remained
behind, a final one. Alas! it proved to be so to more
than a third of the number.

The orders were, to proceed in separate squads along
the road toward Chattanooga, and halting two or three
miles from Shelbyville, meet in consultation, and arrange
the programme of dangerous advance into hostile territory.

Now look into that thicket of shrubbery and old fallen
trees, opening into the fields and road; a partial concealment, and yet affording a glimpse of the approaches to
prevent a surprise by straggling foes. The silent stars
flash above the ambush, and the dry leaves rustle in
the night wind, while Andrews in subdued and earnest
tones reveals the plan of action. The band are to travel
in companies of three or four toward Chattanooga, avoid-
ing suspicion by such stories of their adventures as might
be suggested by the occasion. They are to reach the
stronghold, one hundred and three miles distant, on
Thursday evening. The road is hard, and every step
under the shadow of danger. With nightfall comes a ter
rific storm, and rayless darkness wraps the lonely path
of travel. But onward, falling into swollen gutters and
sinking into mire, Pittinger and his comrades go toward

9*

their unrelenting enemies. At midnight they find shelter in a loghouse. The owner, alarmed at the unseasonable call, begins to question the "boys."

They reply: "We are Kentuckians, disgusted with the Lincoln Government, and are seeking an asylum in the free and independent South."

"Oh, you have come on a bootless errand," he adds; "and you had better go home, for I have no doubt the whole of the South will soon be as much under Lincoln as Kentucky is."

"Never! we will fight till we die first."

This deceives the Union settler, and chuckling over his own contrary belief, he says:

"Well, we'll see; we'll see."

The adventurers do not dare disclose their real character, and the quiet loyalist entertains the supposed chivalry, promising not to inform the Union pickets of their refuge.

We do not justify such a resort to falsehood, but war sets aside the rules of peaceful life. The next morning they pushed on through the storm again, which soon beat upon them with pitiless fury. At Manchester, entirely beyond our lines, they found intense excitement over the rumor of an approaching force of Yankee cavalry. Hastening, with the peculiar emotions of loyal hearts, to the public square, from which, it was stated, the invaders were visible, they saw the dreaded troopers rising over the crest of a hill. How suddenly the delusion vanished! For lo! a company of negroes General Mitchel had frightened from the coal-mining works he had just destroyed, were hurrying into town. The chagrined chivalry dispersed, cursing the "sons of Ham," on whose unrequited toil they flourished, and for which they had opened the sluices of human blood in the land. The dinner hour found them hungry, and near a "Sand-hiller's" solitary and humble drelling.

"What are "Sand-hillers"? asks a young reader.

The name is applied to the poor whites of the South, who feel almost as crushingly the curse of slavery as do those who are bought and sold. They own no land, but have their cabins on the poorest soil of the planters, and with a corn-patch, live as they can by the fish-hook and gun—a miserably ignorant, squalid, servile class, who are merely the tools of the aristocracy. They are also called "clay-eaters."

A good appetite made even the coarse corn bread, half baked, and tainted meat relish—the only repast the raiders could have that dark day. At night they were sheltered by a bitter secessionist, with whom they discussed the tyranny of the Republican Administration. The morning of Thursday dawned on the weary and jaded company, still a long distance from Chattanooga, determined to force their way on to the appointed place of meeting, when Andrews concluded to defer the final dash a single day—as it proved, a strangely fatal delay.

A few hours later they were in Jasper, hearing and seeing what they could ; apparently as good rebels as any of the villagers. You will know more of this town in General Mitchel's movements. Here, news of the battle of Shiloh were just received—it was said, exultingly, that thousands of Yankees were killed, and one man affirmed that *five hundred gunboats* were sunk. After all sorts of adventures—getting lost among the Cumberland Mountains, and perils among foes—they followed a valley to the river-bank, opposite Chattanooga. In an hour or two the cars would pass on the opposite side, in which they *must* be passengers. Between them and that track was a ferry, swept by a gale of wind. The unsuspecting ferryman tried to cross, but his boat was beaten back, like a nautilus-shell in a storm at sea. After repeated efforts, the hazardous passage was accomplished.

The next barrier, which was the most dreaded, was the guard. But the arrival of General Mitchel at Huntsville had so alarmed the people that they evidently forgot the ferry in looking toward that centre of terrible interest —the armed watchmen were gone. With a sense of relief, the little band hastened to the mountain-environed town, near the rushing Tennessee. A peak, seven hundred feet high, frowns in singular grandeur over it, from which lookout four States are visible. To the depot they hur

ried, and bought their tickets, when, just as the sun
stooped to bathe lovingly, with farewell smiles,

> "——Earth's gigantic sentinels,
> Discoursing in the skies!"

the train came thundering along. In another moment
the raiders were safely seated in the cars, and gliding
along those smooth metallic lines, gleaming in the golden
flame of the west, toward Marietta. Sleep overcame the
exhausted travellers, until the conductor's call, at midnight, "Marietta!" startled them to realize that the goal
was won—they "were in the centre of the Confederacy."
They walked, with rapid step and quickened pulse, to
the Tremont House. With strange, sobered thoughts,
they went to their last *bed* for many eventful, memorable
months.

The leader, Andrews, who stopped at another hotel,
had given orders to start in the four o'clock train the next
morning. The waiter awakened the unsuspected "boys"
at that hour. Big Shanty, eight miles from Marietta,
where the train stopped for breakfast, was selected for the
daring attempt to seize the engine, and drive it in hot
haste for our lines.

The early morning air and the vernal bloom softened
even the savage aspect of war along the route, bordered
with encampments, and scarred with the hoofs and wheels
of their locomotion. And here I shall let young Pittinger tell his own story:

"As soon as we arrived, the engineer, conductor, and many of the passengers went over to the eating-house. Now was our opportunity! Andrews and one or two others, went forward and examined the track to see if every thing was in readiness for a rapid start. Oh! what a thrilling moment was that! Our hearts throbbed thick and fast with emotions we dared not manifest to those who were loafing indifferently around. In a minute, which seemed an hour, Andrews came back, opened the door, and said very quietly and carelessly, 'Let us go, now, boys.' Just as quietly and carelessly we arose and followed him. The passengers, who were lazily waiting for the train to move on and carry them to their destination, saw nothing in this transaction to excite their suspicions.

"Leisurely we moved forward—reached the head of the train—then Andrews, Brown, our engineer, and Knight, who also could run an engine, leaped on the locomotive; Alfred Wilson took the cars as brakesman, and the remainder of us clambered into the foremost baggage car, which, with two others, had previously been uncoupled from the hinder part of the train. For one moment of most intense suspense all was still—then a pull—a jar—a clang—and we were flying away on our perilous journey.

"There are times in the life of man when whole years of intensest enjoyment seem condensed into a single moment. It was so with me then. My heart throbbed with delight and gladness that words labor in vain to express. A sense of ethereal lightness ran through all my veins, and I seemed to be ascending higher—higher—into realms of inexpressible bliss, with each pulsation of the engine. It was a moment of triumphant joy that will never return again. Not a dream of failure now shadowed my rapture. All had told us that the greatest difficulty was to reach and take possession of the engine, and after that success was certain. *It would have been* but for unforeseen contingencies. Away we scoured, passing field, and village, and woodland. At each leap of the engine our hearts rose higher, and we talked merrily of the welcome that would greet us when into Huntsville a few hours later—our enterprise done, and the brightest laurels of the guerrilla Morgan far eclipsed!

" But the telegraph ran by our side, and was able, by flashing a single lightning message ahead, to arrest our progress and dissipate all our fondest hopes. To obviate all danger on this point, we stopped, after running some four miles, to cut the wire. John Scott, an active young man, climbed the pole, and with his hand knocked off the insulated box, and swung down on the wire. Fortunately there was a small saw on the engine, with which the wire was soon severed. While this was being done, another party took up a rail, and put it into the car to carry off with us. This did not long check our pursuers, but we had the satisfaction of learning that it threw them down the embankment.

"When the engine first stopped Andrews jumped off, clasped our hands in ecstacy, congratulating us that our difficulties were now all over; that we had the enemy at such a disadvantage that he could not harm us, and exhibited every sign of joy.

"'Only one train more,' said he, 'to pass, and then we will put our engine at full speed, burn the bridges after us, dash through Chattanooga, and on to Mitchel at Huntsville.'"

Alas for the boasted wisdom and security of human plans! The expected train came rushing on—the plea that Beauregard ordered the strange haste gave them an unchallenged flight still onward, but a *red flag* on the last car told of another coming engine—it swept by, and also hung out the flaming *signal*. The *whistle of the pursuing engine* now shrieked on their ears!

The steam was crowded—the ponderous wheels went round like a spinning-top, and struck fire on the sounding rail—the car bounded and rocked, tossing the raiders about, as "peas rattle in a gourd;" but on the exasperated rebels rushed. Such a war-scene was never witnessed before. Nearly a mile a minute, the pursued and pursuers flew past villages, hamlets, and houses, from which the astonished people gazed with terror, till within fifteen miles of Chattanooga. The alarm had called out the military

force there—cannon were planted ready to fire on the imaginary host—trees were felled across the track to oppose
the advance—for the telegraph had helped the enemy
in spite of early success in cutting it.   Wood and water
were now low, and the hunters in sight !

Andrews seemed bewildered.   Instead of holding together his band, and striking across the woods for the
Tennessee River, only about a dozen miles distant, he
shouted :

" Leave the train—disperse—and each man save himself as best he can."

A moment more and the " boys " were scattered
among the spurs of the Cumberland Mountains.   Soon as
the first shock of the unexpected and stunning blow had
passed away, and the rebels found that the " engine-
thieves " were in the wilderness, the great " man-hunt "
began.

We cannot follow them through their wanderings and
hiding-places, with hunger, and thirst, and bruises, added
to the continual fears of discovery which haunted the fugitives.   But one after another they were chased down,
and carried into Chattanooga.   Here they were thrown
into an old negro prison, with its dark subterranean dun-
geon, where, through a trap-door, the captives were hurried in a suffocating air and oppressive gloom.   Daily, at
the same opening, the jailer let down in a bucket the small
pieces of bread and meat for their meals.

CHAPTER XVII.

T Ringgold, Robinson and young Parrott were
taken. The captors determined to make Parrott betray his companions, especially Andrews. He nobly *declined* to do so. Then they
stripped him, laid him on a rock, and a lieutenant gave him a *hundred lashes*. He bore them without a
murmur or wavering in his purpose. The " heroic boy "
was then chained and conveyed to the prison, where all
were handcuffed and bound together, by twos and threes,
around the neck.

One day light broke into that horrible place, which
kindled a smile upon the haggard faces of the prisoners,
and made them feel like shouting—it was the tidings that
Bridgeport was taken by General Mitchel. This splendid
victory is recorded in another place. After the capture,
one of two who did not awaken in the morning, at Mari-

etta, to go with their companions, succeeded in reaching our lines from a rebel battery which they had been compelled to join. This created a suspicion in regard to the other, who was also put in the "black hole" of Chattanooga.

The inmates were all suddenly removed to Atlanta, Georgia, under the startling apprehension that General Mitchel would visit Chattanooga in his mysterious and rapid movements.

A few days later, when the fear of immediate danger had subsided, the prisoners were returned to Chattanooga, and thence to Knoxville, Tennessee, for trial. Here they found, in frightful want and suffering, many Union men who refused to acknowledge the Confederacy. The higher class of captives—the *prison aristocracy*—were confined in *iron cages*. There were five of these in the fine and antiquated old building used for a military prison. A part of the company of " engine thieves," as they were called throughout the South, were put into the very one in which Parson Brownlow was caged and shot at by his guards ; the bullet marks were still upon it.

Such are the tender mercies of professedly civilized men, engaged in a cause which fires the base passions nourished by slavery under the surface-dressing of society.

While the court-martial was in session, several weeks later, when number seven in the list was called, there was a pause. A strange sound was in the air. They listened—it was a shell! General Mitchel, whose magnificent dash through rebel States was troubling the subjects of Jeff. Davis all along his route, was opposite Chattanooga, and sending his heralds over the river. Never did a court break up more suddenly, and away for Atlanta again the prisoners went—Atlanta! the splendid prize of the unrivalled Sherman two years later. ·

The barbarities of the rebels, who have always, you know, talked of mercy, and complained of Yankee cruelty, are illustrated in two other instances I will add. One man, by the name of Whan, who assisted in burning bridges, was put in a barrel *filled with spikes*, rolled down a hill, and then taken out bleeding, and *hung*. Andrews when swung off from the gallows, among the first caught, touched the ground; so the murderers *dug the earth* from under his feet, to save repeating the execution.

" *How* was he caught?" you ask.

He was pursued with the rest, and overtaken. With a comrade he escaped, with blankets tied together, from the prison in Chattanooga. Crossing the river, he reached an island. But his hunters, with bloodhounds, came there. Nearly naked, and bleeding, he ran from one side of the island to the other, and through the water, to elude the dogs, and at length climbed a tree of thick foliage. After the rebels had given up the search in despair of finding him, two children, who had followed from mere curiosity, saw a *bunch* on the tree. Carefully looking at it, they called out, "It is a *man!*" The alarm was sounded ;—poor Andrews, faint and disheartened, dropped from the tree, seized a log in the water, and paddled out ; but a skiff with men in it was near, and he had to surrender. He was taken back, and soon after hung, as already described.

And thus ended the career of a young man of intellect, energy, and culture, who, like Major Andre, the British spy, a finished gentleman, was a felon-victim of war ; that is to say, died a criminal's death. And yet it is the *character*, and not the mode of dying, that makes the event important.

Hearing that a son of General Mitchel was captured, it raised the hope in the hearts of the survivors of an exchange, which proved an illusion. Passing over further details of this tragic and romantic history, we will look in upon Atlanta jail, while General Mitchel was spreading terror along his path of conquest, sad, with a host around him, at the failure of the almost recklessly daring adventure, and the fate of his brave men. You shall again hear the noble young Pittinger tell the tale of sorrow and joy most affectingly mingled :

"One day while we were very merry, amusing ourselves with games and stories, we saw a squadron of cavalry approaching. This did not at first excite any attention, for it was a common thing to see bodies of horsemen in the streets; but soon we observed them halt at our gate and surround the prison. What could this mean?

"A moment after, the clink of the officers' swords was heard, as they ascended the stairway, and we knew that something unusual was about to take place. They paused at our door, threw it open, and called the names of our seven companions. With throbbing hearts we asked one another the meaning of these strange proceedings. Some supposed they were to receive their sentence; others, still more sanguine, believed they were taken out of the room to be paroled, preparatory to an exchange. I was sick, but rose to my feet, oppressed with a nameless fear.

"A moment after, the door opened, and George D. Wilson entered, his step firm and his form erect, but his countenance pale as death. Some one asked a solution of the dreadful mystery, in a whisper, for his face silenced us all.

"'We are to be executed immediately!' was the awful reply, whispered with thrilling distinctness. The others came in all tied, ready for the scaffold. Then came the farewells—farewells, with no hope of meeting again in this world! It was a moment that seemed an age of measureless sorrow. Our comrades were brave; they were soldiers, and had often looked death in the face on the battle-field. They were ready, if need be, to die for their country; but to die on the scaffold—to die as mur-

derers die—seemed almost too hard for human nature to
bear.   Then, too, the prospect of a future world, into
which they were thus to be hurried, without a moment's
preparation, was black and appalling.   Most of them had
been careless, and had no hope beyond the grave,   Wilson was a professed infidel, and many a time had argued
the truth of the Christian religion with me for half a day
at a single discussion ; but in this awful hour he said to
me :

   " ' Pittinger, I believe you are right now !   Oh ! try
to be better prepared when you come to die than I am.'

   " Then, laying his hand on my head, with a muttered
' God bless you,' we parted.

   " Shadrack was profane and reckless, but good-heart-
ed and merry.   Now turning to us, with a voice the
forced calmness of which was more affecting than a wail
of agony, he said :

   " ' Boys, I am not prepared to meet Jesus ! '

   " When asked by some of us, in tears, to think of
heaven, he answered, still in tones of thrilling calmness,
' I'll try ! I'll try ! but I *know* I am not prepared ! '

   " Slavens, who was a man of immense strength and
iron resolution, turned to his friend Buffum, and could
only articulate ' Wife—children—tell— ' when utterance
failed.

   " Scott was married only three days before he came
to the army, and the thought of his young wife nearly

drove him to despair. He could only clasp his hands in silent agony.

" Ross was the firmest of all. His eyes beamed with unnatural light, and there was not a tremor in his voice as he said :

" ' Tell them at home, if any of you escape, that I died for my country, and did not regret it.'

" All this transpired in a moment, and even the Marshal and other officers standing by him in the door exclaimed : ' Hurry up, there ! Come on ! we can't wait ! '

" In this manner my poor comrades were hurried off. Robinson, who was too sick to walk, was dragged away with them. They asked leave to bid farewell to our other boys, who were confined in the adjoining room, but it was sternly refused ! Thus we parted. We saw the death cart containing our comrades drive off, surrounded by cavalry. In about an hour it came back empty. The tragedy was complete ! "

Wilson asked permission to speak on the scaffold, which was granted, doubtless anticipating something which might excuse the murder. Instead of this he made to his savage audience a calm, earnest, manly Union speech. He assured them that the South was wrong, and that the flag of our country would again wave over the very soil *beneath his scaffold*. The excited crowd evidently felt the appeal, but did their work of death.

Let us return to the prison and the group still within its walls. Adds Pittinger:

" There were tears from eyes that shrank from no danger. But I could not shed a tear. A cloud of burning heat rushed to my head that seemed to scorch through every vein. Slowly and silently the moments wore on, and no one ventured to whisper of hope. At last some voice suggested that we should seek relief in prayer. The very idea seemed to convey consolation, and was eagerly accepted. Soon we knelt around the bare walls of our strange sanctuary, and, with bleeding hearts, drew near the throne of God. Captain Fry first led us, mingled with sobs and strong supplications. Then each followed in turn, with one or two exceptions, and even these were kneeling with the rest. As the twilight deepened, our devotional exercises grew more solemn. In the lonely shadow of coming night, with eternity then opening tangibly before us, and standing on its very brink, we prayed with a fervor that those who dwell in safety can scarcely conceive. It was a holy hour; and if the angels above ever bend from their bright mansions to comfort human sorrow, I do believe that they were then hovering near. From that hour I date the birth of an immortal hope; and believe that many of my companions, also, in looking back, will realize that they passed from death to life in that dreary prison-room ! "

Young Pittinger was released after long months of
10

captivity, and became a minister of the Gospel which he embraced in that Atlanta jail, over which waves the Star-spangled Banner !

I need not tell you that no blame attached to General Mitchel, either because of the hazardous nature of the expedition, or its failure.   He did not suggest it ; and if he had done so, it was only one of those great risks some-times taken, which, if successful, would have been a splendidly heroic affair ; but which, in this melancholy result, excites but little interest.   Still it was a subor-dinate move in the grand marches of General Mitchel, deserving a record that shall immortalize the patriotic band who staked their lives upon its high design.

CHAPTER XVIII.

HEN General Mitchel started from Shelbyville the railroad *raiders* were lost from view. He had heard the rebel account of the so-called defeat of General Grant at Shiloh. The possibility of darkest disaster there flung a dismal shadow on his path; but his chosen goal was before him. Cautiously, rapidly, he moved over the twenty miles to Fayetteville. This town is on Elk River, nearly south of the former, on Duck River. Here General Mitchel prepared to lead the Third Division forward to Huntsville; the entire force was to act with the leader in the division in advance. April 10th he was at Fayetteville. Then commenced another forced march unsurpassed in modern warfare.

You will learn what the " boys " thought of Fayetteville by an extract from a letter written just after they left it : " The order to march from Fayetteville was received with pleasure—a pleasure which was slightly annoyed with regret that we had not destroyed the town It is a miserable little secession hole ; and the shameful insult that had been offered to our flag of truce, with the threatening and scowling and searching looks of the inhabitants whenever they showed themselves at the windows of their houses, to which General Mitchel had ordered them, had pretty thoroughly angered us against them. Nothing would have pleased the boys better than to have given the rascals a lesson which would never have departed from their memory, provided, after the lesson, they had any memory left."

How gently in those days we did deal with foes who scoffed and cursed in return ! It was well intended, but sadly-mistaken kindness ; quite as much so as indulgence of a wilful and rebellious child, whose greatest need is a thorough whipping. It was not according to our hero's views of the warfare.

When the troops crossed the boundary of Alabama they found quite a number of Union men. Meeting a venerable planter, he was questioned closely : " It seemed like tearing out my heart to give up the old Union," he said ; " but when Alabama voted to separate, I thought it my duty to sustain her."

" But Alabama, in attempting to break up the nation, did what she had no right to do," replied the volunteer.

" Ah ! " responded the aged gentleman, " passion and prejudice blinded our eyes to that truth."

" Are you willing, then, to see the authority of the national Government restored? " was the next inquiry.

" Yes," said the planter, " and to pray from this time forth that all her people may be willing to return to their allegiance."

And then the heroes went " marching on," in doubt whether the old slaveholder, after all, didn't mean to go with Alabama whatever her course. Soon after the troops moved along the line of the rebel General L. P. Walker's plantation, an immense estate, extending for miles beside the road. The stately mansion was deserted, and the furniture gone. Instead of " fair women and brave men," it poured forth negroes in a throng, who came to see the northern invaders. They laughed hysterically, they sang, they danced in their childlike glee.

" By golly," exclaimed an athletic, intelligent young negro, " I'se a great notion to go along with dis crowd. What do you say, massa? "

" My poor friend," was the reply, " if you do you will probably be turned out of our lines the first place we encamp. Somebody who claims you will come and take you back ; and besides being severely punished for running away, you will in every respect be worse off than before."

"It is very hard, massa," he resumed. His voice trembled, the tears were gathering in his eyes, and the volunteer confesses he had to ride away to hide his own. But such was our "*policy*" then. One of General Walker's plantation houses was in flames, but how it was fired no one seemed to know.

The next striking incident along the march was meeting a negro of the same plantation, with a heavy iron ring and bolt fastened to his leg.

"How long have you worn that?" asked a cavalryman.

"Three months, massa," answered the slave.

The trooper slid from his horse, knocked off the fetters, fastened them to his saddle, and rode off, muttering: "I would forfeit a year's pay for the privilege of transferring them to the leg of the rascal who put them on that man." *That is slavery.*

It must have been a splendid sight—those columns, like a solid mass, moved by a single genius, rushing forward to surprise the enemy, hour after hour, over field, through forest, and across streams, as if unconscious of fatigue. If a rebel is caught he is sent to the rear, so that he may give no intelligence to his friends.

On—on—the troops, inspired with their chieftain's ardor, press. The bayonets gleam, the artillery thunders along, the horses seem to prance with sympathetic haste, and jokes pass from rank to rank to cheer the brave hearts on the way. Broad plantations, verdant woods, flashing waters recede in the distance, as the battalions march toward the unsuspecting enemy. The sun goes down on the scene, reflected from gold, silver, and steel, with no sign of faltering in the "boys." Suddenly they came to a stream wide and deep. There were no boats, no bridges. That night they must cross to reach the goal in the morning. The pause is brief. In the gloom General Mitchel flies on his steed along the lines, and says : " My boys, there is but one chance for us. Will you plunge in with me?" A hurrah—and in they dash. The waters surge around them in the shadows, vexed, as never before, . by an armed host, darkening all the flood. Emerging from the baptism for the next day's stern and perilous work, they built their camp-fires and prepared for sleep. While General Mitchel was sitting by his crackling flame, with no other mark of a chieftain's headquarters, a soldier leading a negro came into its glare, the first *prisoner* of the raid. The astonished captive stood in mute suspense before the commander, who said mildly to him :

" Well, what have you to say ? "

" Massa, dey going to eat you up down dare in Huntsville. Dey got five thousand troops down there, sir."

" How do you know that ? "

" I heard my massa say so at supper table to-night. I've come out of Huntsville, and am sure of it. De trains come in, locomotives whistle, five of 'em. Each of 'em brought a thousand soldiers. Many beside dare before ; and dey 'stroy you certain, sir."

It was likely enough to be true so far as troops were concerned. On their way to Corinth they might, be ready to welcome the bold adventurers with their fresh and superior force. No matter ; the die was cast. No thought of retreat or hesitation stole over a single mind. Then nature yielded to the demand for repose. · Soundly slept the wet heroes till two o'clock in the morning.

General Mitchel, awaking from brief slumber, went through the camp with the muffled voice and step of a spirit from the dark depths of the forest. No drum beat, no signal gun disturbed the silence. The whispered words were few. But the legions rose as if by magic in line of march, waiting for the word of command to dash forward. To each regiment, while moving past him to receive his final orders of advance, he said : " Now, boys, perfect silence ; not a word to be uttered. Move straight forward, and let not the enemy know that you are advancing by any sound whatever."

Never was a chieftain's command more faithfully obeyed. A more spectral march of living men was never seen. The well-drilled thousands swept along with no sound but the faint echoes of hoof and wheel in the gloom of waning night.

Impressive, marvellous scene ! That fragment of the national army, separated by more than a hundred miles of hostile land from the rest of it, fearlessly, noiselessly threading unknown paths in twilight shadow, to strike at a vital point the unsuspecting traitors. So still is that march that the columns go through a small town five miles from Huntsville without waking a sleeper. The whole force defile through the streets, brushing the very threshold of dwellings ; and when the sun shines on the risen inhabitants, not one of them knows that the brave host have been there. Scarcely an hour after that hamlet of unmolested rebels is passed in the reddening dawn, an advance force of a hundred and fifty cavalry, together with a part of Captain Simonson's battery, assisted by Lieutenant M. Allen, the whole under the charge of Colonel Kennett, first catch a glimpse of Huntsville and the beautiful cedars surrounding it. They *want* to shout ; but not a sound breaks in upon the death-like stillness.

There lies the prize of long, sometimes wet and weary marching. No herald has apprised the unsuspecting inhabitants of the danger near. The morning faintly kindles, as hitherto, upon the hills and roofs of fancied security. The iron track gleams in the morning light; workmen, in their humble dwellings along its line, as unconscious as itself of the advent of new managers and hands *tc run the road*. But the decisive blow will be no martial pastime. The troops understand the game and the stake. To seize the great path of transportation and travelling, cutting the communication between the rich

10*

and boundless West, and the blockaded, war-ravaged East, might be no very difficult move. To apply the torch to the extensive machine shops running day and night for the Confederacy, and make a bonfire of the depots piled with army supplies of material, might not cost much conflict or time. But General Mitchel knew his perilous ground, even with this accomplished.

Nearly east was the stronghold of Chattanooga, where the defiant foe challenged the strength of the Union army. A little further west was Corinth, whose fortunes for the few days of his swift march had been changing, he knew not how. The report was that they were greatly improved by our defeat. Instead of such disaster, the country was wild with excitement over the enemy's repulse.

General Grant had stemmed the overwhelming tide of rebellion, and, reënforced by General Buell, had rolled it back toward Corinth. Congress paused to hear and cheer over the telegram, and a salute of a hundred guns thundered forth the jubilant joy from the national capital. General Mitchel had no signal of the victory.

CHAPTER XIX.

THE advance dashed forward on double-quick, when two locomotives came puffing toward them. A flash, and the first artillery thunder broke the stillness, and was the *order to stop*. One of the engineers tried to escape, when another command from the brazen orator of freedom brought him to a halt. In a twinkling away dashed the first engine and train, and the cavalry after it; a hundred and fifty Gilpins chasing the iron horse *ten miles,* with the speed of the wind. The whole force now came up. Troops are suddenly seen moving toward the right, and stealing toward the railroad. Another swept away to the left. Both were armed with the roughest implements of war, iron bar and "pick," to destroy not human, but *business life.* Their attack was to be directed to the unoffending metal and wood. See yonder another body of soldiers moving toward the town—and *there*, another. Why is this division of strength? It is not the bloody encounter they expect or seek, but the capture, without a gun or shot, of depot, telegraph office, and every other valuable public building of the city. Quietly they advance ; no sign of expectation of the visit appears. The brightening sky bends over a slumbering people.

The word of command to move on Huntsville is passed along the lines. General Mitchel leads the troops into the startled town. Like the lightning flash the alarm flies over the city. The first notes of terror are the screams of locomotives, making haste to escape with their trains. But they soon find the *end* of the track— the iron bar and pickaxe have been there before them. East and west the puffing engines stop. The operator hastens to the telegraph office to announce to friends who may come to the rescue, the advent of the " Yankees ; " but a new occupant is there. The depot master and others rush to the storehouse of supplies to destroy, but armed men have the needed freight under bayonet *charge*.

But look ! Over that excited population, from a slender flagstaff on a private mansion, the national ensign is floating in the breeze. What can it mean? for it was there when the " Third Division " reached the city. A brave patriot lives under those starry folds.

The Hon. Judge Lane accepted the appointment to the

judicial bench from President Lincoln, soon after his inauguration. He knew the dangers of the position. The South
had entered upon the mad work of resistance to the lawful
Administration, hurling denunciation upon those who approved it. But Judge Lane was a man of resolute will
and courage. He told his angry fellow-citizens that he
intended to perform, according to his ability, the duties
of his office regardless of their displeasure. The infu-
riated mob surged around his dwelling, and threatened
both it and himself.

" Resign! resign!" was the loud demand.

" I am ready to die," he replied, " for my country, if
necessary; but I am a loyal man to my Government, and
shall remain so till death."

To leave no shadow of doubt on the minds of the astonished traitors, he seized a flag of the Union, and bore
it to the top of his house, saying, that " whoever dared
attempt to tear it down, would have to pass over his
dead body."

This sublime moral courage and defiance, seemed
to awe the exasperated haters of the old flag, and they
did not venture on further violence.

Are you not reminded of the gallant Ellsworth? He
died tearing down the banner of treason; and we cannot
help feeling that his heroism had in it a *dash* of rashness—
that his valuable life might, without *that*, have been spared.

Judge Lane's safety, on the contrary, depended on

fearlessness ; and the cause he loved, called for the manly scorn of the treasonable throng.   He was one of the few in the Cotton States, who continued unseduced and un-moved amid the bribery and threats of the lawless con-spirators against the Republic.   The citizens of Hunts-ville were unarmed, and many of them *undressed*, when the footsteps of the gallant invaders echoed through the streets.   It was too evident that no defence could be made successfully to attempt it, and the town surrendered to the abhorred defenders of the starry flag of the Union.

Sixteen locomotives, and a hundred cars, fell into our hands.   Indeed, all the resources of the important place came under the new administration without injury, the surprise was so complete and admirably conducted. General Mitchel ascertained in an hour, through his proper officer, the exact condition and availability of the railroad.   The means of transportation were sufficient for moving his forces to any desired point on its track. If you turn again to the map, you will notice that the Tennessee River in its southerly course bends into Ala-bama, and is crossed eastwardly from Huntsville at Bridgeport by the railway, and westwardly at Decatur, which is south of Nashville.

General Mitchel decided at once to send an expedi-tion to each, and burn the noble structures, to cut off the approach of enemies.   He commanded the one toward Chattanooga ; Colonel Turchin the one in the direction of

Corinth. General Mitchel stopped at Stevenson, a town at the junction of the Nashville and Chattanooga Railroad with the Memphis and Charleston Railroad, on which Huntsville stands, to secure whatever was valuable to him at that important connection. He then went on, and applied the torch to the Bridgeport bridges. He was now secure from an attack by an advance from either direction by the railroad. On Saturday he reached Huntsville again. The work of destruction for safety was all done.

The Sabbath dawned. General Mitchel loved this sacred pause in the world's busy life. Could he have acted with his feelings, the day would have been given up to devout thanksgiving, and entire rest from military movements, and even plans. But war has *no holy* time ; and without a mutual agreement by the hostile armies, it would be impossible to keep the day. And even then, it would be extremely difficult to regulate the marches and battles with regard to its observance. On that morning, when, all over the loyal States, the sound of the church bells floated over the peaceful homes, the cars were conveying General Mitchel to Decatur.

What a Sabbath it was there, and beyond! The enemy was flying in terror, the excited imagination magnifying the number of the Union troops, and creating an unreal fear of their nearness. The smoke of burning bridges left in the wake of retreat, rose here and there, the offering to Mars from those plains of slavery.

General Mitchel hastened forward his troops in hot pursuit. The chase was continued to Tuscumbia, about half way to Corinth, and opposite Florence, on the other bank of the river. It is in Franklin County, Alabama, a mile from the Tennessee River. There is here a curiosity. From a fissure in the solid limestone rock, a living spring gushes forth, discharging from the smooth, pure mouth, twenty thousand cubic feet of water every minute. What a blessing such a fountain will be if ever a large city supplants with northern enterprise the quiet village! It is sixty-seven miles from Huntsville.

Here he communicated with the "Department of the Mississippi," where General Grant was getting ready to move on Corinth. His despatches to General Buell, dated at Tuscumbia, gave an account of his brilliant successes in modest language. This very cautious officer, superior only in command, read them with surprise, if not regret. The comparatively new general had made a clear track for the Union troops, *one hundred and fifty miles* across the rebel State of Alabama. The brief period, the unsurpassed boldness and heroism of the achievement, startled and gladdened loyal hearts all over the land. Think of it—in two days from the morning he came like a whirlwind upon Huntsville, that entire distance had changed hands; dilapidated locomotives were completely repaired, and every thing pertaining to the road was in running order. The shops rang with the sound of "Yankee" blows, the engineers had on their caps the " U. S," and the whole was guarded by northern volunteers. Meanwhile, a new time-table was prepared and printed, to guide the conductors, who, had they been caught there unarmed and with *no evil design*, three days before, would have ridden on quite a different rail. You can imagine the amazement, alarm, and rage, which made all this seem like a horrid dream to the inhabitants. And you will be interested in General Mitchel's spirited congratulations to his troops, in which he sums up the brilliant exploits of the few days before.

HEADQUARTERS, THIRD DIVISION. ⎫
CAMP TAYLOR, HUNTSVILLE, *April* 16, 1862. ⎬

Soldiers : Your march upon Bowling Green won the thanks and confidence of our commanding general. With engines and cars captured from the enemy, our advanced guard precipitated itself upon Nashville. It was now made your duty to seize and destroy the Memphis and Charleston Railway, the great military road of the enemy. With a supply-train only sufficient to feed you at a distance of two days' march from your depot, you undertook the herculean task of rebuilding twelve hundred feet of heavy bridging, which, by your untiring energy, was accomplished in ten days. Thus, by a railway of your own construction, your depot of supplies was removed from Nashville to Shelbyville, nearly sixty miles in the direction of the object of your attack. The blow now became practicable. Marching with a celerity such as to outstrip any messenger who might have attempted to announce your coming, you fell upon Huntsville, taking your enemy completely by surprise, and capturing not only his great military road, but all his machine-shops and rolling stock. Thus providing yourselves with ample transportation, you have struck blow after blow with a rapidity unparalleled. Stevenson fell, sixty miles to the east of Huntsville. Decatur and Tuscumbia have been in like manner seized, and are now occupied. In three days you have extended your front of operations more than one hundred and twenty miles, and your morning gun at Tuscumbia may now be heard by your comrades on the battle field made glorious by the victory before Corinth. A communication of these facts to headquarters has not only now the thanks of our commanding general, but those of the Department of War, which I announce to you with proud satisfaction. Accept the thanks of your commander, and let your future deeds demonstrate that you can surpass yourselves. By order of

Gen. O. M. MITCHEL.

Having determined to attack the enemy at Bridgeport on the 29th, General Mitchel was within three miles of the town, after a rapid and most difficult march. Here he encountered the enemy's pickets. " Crack ! crack ! " sound the rifles, and away they fly. The valorous chief hurries on to the railway bridge which he had burned, and by a feint of general attack there, makes the rebels believe the trial of strength has come. Meanwhile, forming with the artillery in the centre, the Thirty-third and Second Ohio on the right, and the Tenth and Twenty-first Ohio on the left, he sweeps round *between two divisions* of the foe, toward the crest of a hill overlooking his entrenchments. Daring stroke of strategy! He is between two mill-stones—if they discern the move, and can *grind them together* before he is able to defeat them, he will be hopelessly crushed. But with superhuman energy he presses across the ground, and up the slope. Now look! There in battle array stands Mitchel's brigade, almost under it are the enemy's works. The first alarm had startled the troops to arms, but their fears had subsided in the lull of his advance over the country, the very cause of greatest alarm had they known it. The Sabbath sun is sinking in the west. His farewell beams fall in dazzling splendor on the stacked arms of the regiments, who have coolly gone to supper.

Major Loomis, a brave officer, steps forward to the very edge of the summit, and gazes down upon the rebels, counting their number. Then falling back, he gives the command to fire. Oh! watch those shells and balls crushing through the lines of men at the table of the evening repast. Blood and fragments of flesh are the quick response. Then a rush to arms, another discharge

of our artillery, and the rebels retreat, firing the noble
bridge for the public travel as they go.   General Mitchel
hastens forward to save it.   It rested on an island, and
he rescues from the flames the main structure extending
from this natural abutment.

The general, anticipating a reënforcement by the
other division of the enemy upon the railroad, hastened to that part of the field.   Soon the fresh troops came
dashing down the line in splendid style—the body of cavalry making an imposing and martial appearance, which
drew forth the spontaneous admiration of our men.   The
Union artillery opened, cutting a gap in a moment through
the chivalrous ranks.   The deadly greeting was repeated,
and then the horses' heads were turned for flight—"the
red field was won."

CHAPTER XX.

EVERAL questions now tried the wisdom and ability of General Mitchel. The first was, how to hold the conquered territory in the midst of enemies. From Nashville to Decatur the road was open, and it was not difficult to get sufficient food for the troops. But the poor horses—their racks and mangers were empty, or scantily supplied. These " un-armed heroes" must starve unless forage is obtained from the country around them. General Mitchel's comprehensive and practical genius is equal to the emergency. A good man is always merciful to the brute. No surer evidence of a narrow or base mind, than cruelty to the dependent animal, can be given. Not only was humanity a conspicuous quality of General Mitchel's character, but horses and mules are as needful as men in war ; that is to say, they are indispensable, and they must be fed.

The sagacious commander set his *scribes* to work. These were Union men whose principles had been tried, like Judge Lane's, almost in the flames of martyrdom. It was easy to complete this roll of honor—the list of the faithful amid treachery.

My reader, it is impossible for you to realize the trial of loyalty in the Border and Cotton States. No ordeal excepting the inquisition, and manifold tortures of Papal persecutions in the centuries past, compares with it. Demons abroad could have done no more to vex and ruin. For no other crime than loyalty to the old flag, unoffending citizens were taken from their place of business, or on the highway, and shot or hung. Dwellings were burned, and helpless women and children left roofless in the dead of night and winter. I knew a widow who was living in that region of rebel power, who, because her husband had joined the Union army, when he was at home on a short furlough was visited by a band of rebels. He was demanded, but she refused to tell them where he was. Searching they found him, and fired upon him, wounding him. He fled to the yard, when several bullets soon finished the work of death. Reëntering the house, they asked for the rest of the family. She had hidden a son in the chimney. They then made preparations to burn the dwelling before the tearful face of the mother, taking the last blanket from a sick child. When she asked for her husband, " Oh," the fiends replied, "you'll find him in the yard." "You haven't murdered him!" With a wife's frantic affection she flew to the lawn, and there beneath the watchful stars lay the pierced and bleeding body. But she was a *mother* too, and hastened again to plead for her children. Destitute and bereaved, the traitors left her at length, hurling back curses on the midnight air.

The tragical incident is an illustration of common scenes, varying in the degree of atrocity, belting the broad land from the Carolinas to the Western territories.

General Mitchel soon obtained from the tried loyalists the long list of open, determined rebels. He had also the names of the smaller number of the once loyal, who, yielding to the terrible sweep of the current of secession, were borne on its angry bosom. When the enrollment of the citizens was completed, General Mitchel sent an order to the undisguised enemies of the Union, demanding a correct statement of the contents of their granaries. The hay and grain, with supplies of every kind, were to be truthfully stated. The number of their horses and mules was included in the required memoranda; for the commanding general intended to provide for, and if wanted, *use* them. Any concealment or treachery in the transaction, if suspected, would be thoroughly searched out, and receive the merited punishment. General Mitchel was just, but no trifler with rebellion. The enemy saw that he meant all he said, and made correct returns.

Excepting a sufficient allowance for the plantations, nothing could be used, nothing sold or given away, without
his permission.

It was a principle with him, and in that regard he
was in advance of a majority of the Union officers, and
even statesmen, to spare no rebel interest which sustained
the revolt, and employ whatever resources of success in
subduing it, he found on hostile soil. The rebellion was
"evil and only evil, and that continually" in his view.
No affectation of charity for our "misguided brethren"
lightened the pressure of his hand on the foes of his
country. In this respect he resembled the pioneer in
right opinions and action, General Butler. No king ever
ruled with more unquestioned power, and more *nobly*,
for the cause of freedom and the Union, than he did in
New Orleans. General Mitchel comprehended likewise
the real issue, and the people we had to deal with, in
saving the nation.

When the census was finished, he directed his quartermaster to go the traitors, and demand a tenth of their
possessions which were useful to his army. Watch the
officer at the door of that elegant mansion, in which the
proud planter stands.

" We have called with an order from the general to
get supplies," quietly says the officer. .

The planter growls, wants to resist, but yields, and
directs his slave to "load up." This scene is repeated

till the desired quantity is received. The rebels then present their bills, which are promptly paid.

By this means General Mitchel supplies his army, and robbed no man. His severity was the severity of justice. The foe had to support the military visitors with a hospitality compelled by the sword, and bribed by the price in " greenbacks." And who furnished the " greenbacks"? The *rebels*, indirectly, as you will see. And in the way it was done, you have another fine illustration of the general's engineering ability and energy. Like Grant, he was practical, on the alert, and thorough in his work. Marching along, one day, he came in sight of what appeared to be a fort. It was a huge pile, in spots white as the snow. Advancing, he saw near it the ruins of a bridge he wanted, which the enemy had burned. In a few moments more it was all plain enough. The rebels had made a defensive work of cotton, to guard the bridge before the torch was applied. Five hundred bales of it were piled there, and either because in too great haste, or not apprehending its capture, they had not made of it a bonfire. Of course it was lawful plunder.

This was taken from Decatur to Stevenson, where he wished to cross the river. The deep current rolled along in a channel some three hundred yards wide, between his troops and the opposite shore. About

11

seventy of the oblong squares are rolled out; crowbars are used to pry up the ropes that bind them, and rails are run under the cordage. The bales held together by the rails are ten feet apart. You will understand at once, that in this way he made pontoons, or floating abutments, which, one by one, were launched upon the bosom of the river, and fastened to each other by the same method.

The next thing in the novel building of the structure, is to lay planks over the gaps between the bales. Now look! from shore to shore stretches a cotton and wooden bridge, under which the unobstructed current flows. Before the day is gone, the command is given, "Forward!" Three thousand men, horses, and cannon, move upon the pathway over the waters, till the last foot and wheel strikes the solid earth beyond. A genius equal to any command, only, could have performed the feat of skill and despatch. Napoleon himself would have been proud of it.

But General Mitchel is not done with the cotton. The bridge is unharnessed, the bales released from the fastenings, and conveyed to the railroad. It reaches Huntsville, and there readily finds market, for the handsome sum of *thirty thousand dollars*. Add to this, ten thousand dollars more received for transportation by army-wagons and cars to its destination, and we have forty thousand dollars in the treasury of the United States, the amount paid for the supplies and forage he had bought. Was not the management a shrewd and capital way of making the rebels pay the expenses of the Third Division, after helping the battalions safely over the river?

Another question besides the maintenance of his army on an enemy's soil, gave General Mitchel anxious thought; and that was *slavery*. What shall be done with master and slave so far as they come in direct contact with the army, was the great problem. The bondsman would flee to the camps, and the master follow him, to demand his property, according to the unrepealed law of the land.

The Government, when the war began, tried, as always before, to have nothing to do with slavery. The conflict was for the old order of things, with system of human bondage included. General Mitchel was both conservative and radical in the true signification of the words. He would *preserve* the Constitution and the Republic entire, and *uproot* American slavery as necessary to the successful termination of the war—to the very preservation of the State. But he was under a superior officer who thought otherwise, and the national councils then urged indulgence toward the master, and a war apart from the cause of the war. It is sad and humiliating to think of the nation's folly in this regard.

It is a singular fact, that the hero of New Orleans, General Butler, a democrat of the old school, or Buchanan stamp, and a politician, should have been the leader in the

great work of emancipation. When he went to Fortress
Monroe, General Mitchel was superintendent of Dudley
Observatory, in Albany. With the large majority of the
people the astronomer did not then intend to " mix up the
question " with the civil strife, but simply beat down the
mad rebellion.

A commander in the navy told me at that very time,
that " the moment emancipation had any connection with
the contest, *he would change sides.*" But General Butler
had a singular insight and foresight on the subject. Colonel Mallory, a rebel, sent to him, under flag of truce, to
demand those slaves who had come into our lines. The
Colonel and General Butler had belonged to the same
political party. He said to his former partisan:

" I have come, general, to claim my servants."

" You hold, do you not," replied General Butler, " that
negro slaves are property ; and that Virginia is no longer
a part of the United States?"

" I do, sir."

" You are a lawyer," continued Butler, " and I ask
you if the Fugitive Slave Law is binding on a *foreign nation?* and if a foreign nation employs this kind of property
to destroy the lives and property of the United States, if
it ought not to be regarded as *contraband?*"

The enraged colonel disappeared ; and a new word
was added to our vocabulary, so far as its application to
negroes is concerned. " Contraband" in this connection,

is a term for which we are indebted to General Butler and the war.

The "contrabands" continued to come in, and were set to work on the fortifications. Though General Mitchel's opinions changed less rapidly, he desired to know and do his duty.

General Buell had issued an order, that no protection should be extended to slaves who appeared within the lines. This was just what the masters desired. You may recollect the case of the poor fugitive, who, under such a cruel rule, after having shown the commanding officer where arms were hidden by the rebels, was given up to the master; by him dragged after his horse with a rope round the fugitive's neck, and then whipped to death.

General Mitchel made his earnest protest against the order. His policy was to allow neither master nor slave in his camp. This, indeed, was the best compromise in the circumstances he could make. But according to the principle of action already alluded to, of crushing, in all possible and right ways, the rebellion, he used the negroes when he could, and gave them protection for the service. Hear his noble words to Mr. Abbott:

"I organized these negroes into watchful guards, throughout the entire portion of the territory of my command. They watched the Tennessee River, from Chattanooga entirely down to Tuscumbia and Florence. To every negro who gave me information of the movements of the enemy, who acted as guide to me, or who piloted my troops correctly through that unknown country, I promised the protection of the Government of the United States; and that they should never be returned to their masters. I found them extremely useful. I found them *perfectly reliable*, so far as their intention was concerned; not always accurate in detail, but always meaning to be perfectly truthful."

This is the testimony of all candid and humane officers. It was with great reluctance the Government allowed them to fight for our country, and *their own;* and yet braver troops we have not in the army. At Port Hudson, when an officer was lying wounded under the fire of the rebels, the commander of the forces, among whom were colored soldiers, asked for men to go into the storm of shells and bullets, to bring away the fallen, bleeding form. Immediately four negroes stepped forth, and were sent over the plain of death. They lifted the body, and turned toward our lines; soon three of the four dropped before the bullets of the exasperated foe. Again the call for help was made. Four more of the dark-browed heroes promptly came out of the ranks. With firm, elastic step, they started where their comrades fell, for the Union lines. Two of the new volunteers were struck, and their grasp relaxed. Once more the demand for bearers of the wounded warrior is responded to, and the brave fellows lay down their burden within the protection of our ranks.

Such is the unselfish kindness of a proscribed race, whose patient endurance of injustice is a most wonderful thing. Everybody expected insurrections when the war began—that the opportunity afforded by the political convulsion, would be embraced by the slaves. Instead of this, they have prayed, and waited for God to open the way of deliverance to them, whose *crime* is " a color unlike our own," given them by a common Father! How abhorrent to *Him*, the scorn and injury to them! The magnanimous spirit of General Mitchel felt this, whatever difficulties he encountered in the exercise of his humanity and religion, created by the law of the land, or commands of a superior officer.

CHAPTER XXI.

ENERAL MITCHEL'S abhorrence of the slave-
system increased with the progress of the war.
You know it is not the slave alone who suffers,
but all who have the least taint of African blood.
Both North and South they have been, are yet
persecuted. He may be free, educated, religious—it is
all the same, if he is connected with the enslaved race.

We quote a forcible illustration given by an author
before quoted, because he had the stirring narrative,
as you will notice, from the witness of a part of the
scenes narrated. About the time the war opened its
awful tragedy, he was travelling from Washington to
Philadelphia. A gentleman came into the cars and sat
down by him. The conversation naturally turned upon
secession and war, when the gentleman said:

"A very painful event is this day transpiring in my own town in Delaware. There were two gentlemen in business in Maryland. They owned several slaves. After a time they dissolved partnership, and one of the firm moved from Maryland to Delaware. One of the slaves, a light mulatto, probably the son of one of the partners, certainly the son of a white man, fell to the Maryland master.

"Charles, as the slave was called, was very intelligent. He was very useful to the firm, and by his integrity and energy secured the respect of his master. The indulgent owner, who was probably his father, upon his dying bed gave Charles his freedom.

"Charles bought a small farm. He became a prosperous man, built a neat house, owned a horse, a yoke of oxen, two or three cows, and fifty dollars' worth of poultry. From the product of this little farm he carried supplies to the market in Baltimore. He had a wife and four children. Charles was a Christian. The voice of morning and evening prayer was ever heard in his dwelling. On the Sabbath, in accordance with the usages of the Methodist persuasion, to which he belonged, he was in the habit of preaching to the colored people in his own vicinity.

"One day a vigilance committee in Maryland called upon Charles, and told him that he was too enlightened and thrifty a 'nigger' to be allowed to live in the State;
11*

that his intelligence and prosperity made the slaves dis-contented. Charles, in dismay, asked if he had said or done any thing which was wrong, or could excite sus-picion.

" ' No,' was the reply, ' but it is not safe for us to have in the midst of our slaves a free " nigger," as rich and knowing as you. And you must leave this State within a fortnight, or you will fare badly.'

" This unoffending Christian man, whose rights were thus horribly outraged, was in despair. What to do he did not know. Where to go he did not know. It was mid-winter. The crops were in his barn. How to dis-pose of his farm, his stock, and his crops, at such a short notice, he did not know. He consulted friends, they shook their heads and said :

" ' Poor fellow, we are sorry for you, but cannot help you. Your living here makes the servants discontented, and you must go.'

" Perplexed and alarmed, Charles stayed about his premises till the day before the one on which he was warned to leave arrived. The vigilance committee called again, and said in tones of menace, which almost froze the blood in the veins of the helpless man :

" ' Charles, if we find you here to-morrow morning, as sure as you are alive we will hang you to the limb of that tree.'

" In his terror, Charles abandoned every thing, his

house, his fields, his crops, his cows, his oxen, his poultry, and taking his wife and four little children in his wagon, fled. His alarm often made him cast a look behind him to see if his enemies were in pursuit. Not knowing where else to go, he turned his steps into Delaware, that he might seek protection of his former master, the partner once of him who gave Charles his freedom. It was twelve o'clock at night when the poor fugitive, wearied, with his terror-smitten exhausted family, reached the Delaware planter's home. He rapped at the door. His former owner opened his eyes in utter astonishment, and exclaimed:

" ' For heaven's sake, Charles, what brought you here ?'

" He soon told his own story.

" ' But why did you come here?' exclaimed the man. ' You cannot stay here. The laws of Delaware will not allow free negroes to come into the State. If you stay here you must be arrested.'

" 'My God! my God !' gasped Charles, folding his hands in anguish, and the tears rolling down his cheeks, ' what shall I do? They threatened to hang me if I stay in Maryland. You tell me I cannot stay here. Where shall I go?'

" ' Well,' replied the man, ' it is a clear case that you cannot remain here in Delaware. You are liable at any moment to be arrested. But there is no help now. You must stay here until morning.'

"Such.was the state of the case when I left this morning."

We may never know in this world the fate of that hunted family. Very plainly has God brought us to the battle plain, to suffer His righteous retribution for our impious abuse of both the black and the red races ; for "lo, the poor Indian !" he has fared no better in proportion to the power over him in the hands of unprincipled men.

It is not strange that Pierpont sung :

"The fratracidal war,
Grows on the poisonous tree,
Which God and man abhor,
Accursed slavery.
And God ordains that we
Shall eat this deadly fruit,
Till we dig up the tree,
And burn its very root."

General Mitchel was convinced that the axe of emancipation must be laid at the root of this tree.

Another method of weakening the rebellion he embraced, and was left free to try. He knew that the leaders of it would never yield, until compelled to do so, either by our arms or the voice of their own people. It was clear to him then, as to us all now, that the traitors who had for long years matured their infamous conspiracy, would be the very last to quit the field of conflict. They staked every thing when the homicidal hands were raised against the Republic; their motto was truly the reverse of our own:

"Divided *we stand*, united we fall."

But many of the people who were opposed to secession in the South thought not with our noble commander They said: " We can do nothing at all. We must wait for our rulers to negotiate peace, and in some way bring this war to a close."

General Mitchel replied:

" Gentlemen, this is impossible. The war can never be ended in that way. There was a time before this war broke out when your Government sent their representatives to Washington; but they could not be received, and cannot be received now. The thing cannot be done. You, the people, must rise and say to your rulers, ' The war shall not go on any longer; we refuse to support your army.' Do that and the war must cease, and the old flag again wave over the country."

My reader, we of the North have, from the beginning of the war, been sadly mistaken in our expectations. This has led to awful waste of life and treasure. We thought the rebels would soon get tired of the conflict, and, like disobedient schoolboys well punished, come back to loyalty and love. A few *knew* better; among them some plain, uneducated, sensible men. I recollect one whom I met on the coast of Cape Cod a few weeks after the struggle commenced, in 1861. He was a stranger to me—an old "coaster" or fisherman, I judged him to be.

"What's the news from the war?" he inquired.

"We are making slow progress," I answered; "moving too cautiously, I fear."

"Yes, yes," responded this singular specimen of humanity—singular in dress and appearance—"'tis no use to carry on a *genteel* war with the South."

No wars are so cruel and costly in the end as *genteel wars*. If men will fight, the motto should be, *fight*. The rebels have been our teachers in this simple truth.

General Mitchel believed in this, while he hoped, with multitudes, that the masses in the seceded States would see the treasonable ambition of their leaders, and save themselves the heavy blows he intended, and desired all in command to deal upon them while disloyal, by deserting Jeff. Davis and his associates in revolt. Therefore he did not compel the people in quiet life to swear allegiance to the United States. There were, however, exceptions. A rebel soldier had left his army and came within our lines. After a while he asked permission to return to his home.

"No, sir," replied General Mitchel; "never until you take the oath of allegiance to the United States to nullify the oath you took to the Confederate Government."

The guerillas continued to hover around the army,

and also distress the inhabitants. General Mitchel wanted to get the people enlisted in the suppression of these law-less bands. So he said to them : " You must denounce this murderous warfare, or sign a pledge to have nothing to do with it, and give intelligence of any attack intended by them known to you."

This was reasonable and just. Whoever signed the paper could come and go about their business unmolested. The rest were closely watched. Guards were on the alert. The vigilance of the Union troops became so very un-comfortable, that the majority of the people *signed the pledge.*

The next thing was to have courts of justice. There was soon established a court-martial for military offences ; then followed a court of examination to inquire into the case of prisoners brought into camp ; and a third organ-ized, was a military court for the trial of criminal offences. These courts were for the conquered territory, and kept always in session.

Brave, victorious General Mitchel ! In every march and measure in his department, shone the Christian hero and gentleman.

But up to this time in our country, success, if gained by " hard blows," that is to say, if the rebels were treated as such, the clamor of complaint soon rose from half-hearted and timid patriots, which was echoed by dis guised secessionists. Especially did the newspaper correspondents mislead often the public, and influence un-justly the Government.

The arrows of detraction were even aimed at this pure and splendid officer, until he demanded investigation.

Reader, never worry or despond because you are slandered, if consciously innocent of the charge. The best of men have had this experience. Do not chase a false report; if self-respect, and a proper regard for your reputation, demand attention to the maligner, then make thorough work of the investigation, and a dignified defence.

General Mitchel was, unfortunately for his success and peace, superior in intellect and greatness of character to other and ambitious officers, and in advance of the slowly-ripening popular estimate of the real nature of the war. Besides, he was honest and frank. He did not disguise his bold designs. So he must be sacrificed;—one of the costliest offerings of the war. No patriotic mind able to appreciate General Mitchel, can think of it without a pang of bitterest regret, and a thrill of deepest indignation. The lofty spirit of him who could call the stars by name, disdained the grovelling policy of aspiring commanders and tricky politicians.

In the midst of his usefulness—when planning grander campaigns, and making the traitors of Tennessee and Alabama tremble—an order came from the Secretary of

War requiring his presence at once in Washington. Always obedient to lawful commands, he turned from the troops he loved, and who loved him, with surprise and sadness, and hastened to the national capital.

CHAPTER XXII.

HE second day of July he received the order, and on the the fifth he was in Washington. The Secretary of War, Mr. Stanton, had no words of condemnation for the heroic, patriotic, conscientious, and upright Mitchel. He had displayed only the highest qualities of a noble manhood and true generalship. Their interviews, and those held by them with the President, only increased the confidence in our gallant chief. The best evidence of this is seen in the proposal made to him to command an enterprise of great importance. After carefully studying the plan and object, he decided to accept the responsibility: it was tc sweep down and open the mighty valley of the West—the very work assigned afterward to our honored Lieutenant-General. Mr. Lincoln then suggested that the bold design be delayed till General Halleck, next to the Executive in command, who was absent, returned. He was opposed to the appointment for reasons not known to the public, and which, it is difficult to believe, were just and sound, and advised an "indefinite postponement." So the splendid Mitchel must be laid aside with the scheme just suited to his daring spirit.

The months pass, and the terrible war grows threatening, while a giant in power to smite the rebellion, is *doing nothing.* Our President is honest—God's gift in times when *that* quality is indispensable in the attempt to hold the people together at all; for genius without integrity, cannot steady the popular will, when the skies are dark and sacrifices are demanded. There must be a ground of faith—a reflection, to some extent, of the Divine government in the human authority.

But at Washington and in the army, dishonest men, disloyal parasites, and vacillating, narrow minds, have done mischief which God's judgment day alone can disclose.

The sad inquiry went over the North, "Where is General Mitchel?" Like the sun setting at noon, he had disappeared, and no one could tell *why.* While he was in the city of New York, the order came, with the advent of autumn, to repair to Hilton Head, South Carolina, to take command of the Tenth Army Corps, whose headquarters were there. He reported at Washington September 5th;

he started for his Southern Department on the 12th, and was at his post on the 16th. Before we follow his brief career, I will give you a glimpse of the history of Port Royal before he landed there.

Just after George B. McClellan succeeded General Scott to the command of the army, the navy began to move in earnest in the war. A grand expedition was fitted out, and the ships gathered in Hampton Roads, under the protecting guns of Fortress Monroe. Only those who planned the enterprise knew where the magnificent fleet was going, which carried and attended the troops. Commodore Dupont commanded the naval squadron of eighteen men-of-war, and thirty-eight transports, or passenger and supply vessels. This, as yet, the greatest naval force of the war, sailed majestically out of Hampton Roads October 29th, 1861. On the 30th, the heavens gathered blackness, and the wild winds blew.

Did you ever see a storm at sea? I have witnessed one, and it is the awfulest, grandest sight on land or water. The billows, crested with foam, toss like a plaything the ship, and sweep the deck—the cordage rattles, and makes a dismal harp of the winds. The whole scene is terrific and sublime.

Think of the power and peril of the gale, which so scattered that fleet of fifty-six vessels, that next morning from the dripping deck of the noble Wabash but a single sail was visible. But soon the stray canvas wings began to whiten the sobbing ocean; and two days later, twenty-five ships came to anchor off Port Royal, a fine harbor fifty miles from Charleston. A glance at the map will show its locality. The dispersed fleet continued to come in, excepting the few vessels lost. Two days more passed while the commodore was *feeling his way* around the rebel forts, and getting ready to open the grim and silent ordnance upon them. At length fifteen of the battle leviathans are ready for the fight. They form in an elliptic circle.

The enemy's forts lay at the extremities of the circular path. At each sweep of the ships, fifty shot and shells *every minute* were rained upon the batteries of treason. In the annals of warfare there are few spectacles of such beauty and grandeur, as this affair at Port Royal. The lovely bay, sunlit and calm, the imposing march of the men-of-war in the ellipse about two miles by one, the thunder of cannon shaking the land and deep like an earthquake, the smoke rolling upward and spreading like a pall over the work of death, the scream and crash of shells—all combined to make the scene memorable in the history of this and all other wars.

The boasted Gibraltar had to strike colors in the resistless tempest of iron and unimprisoned fire. It was told after the victory that a master said to his slave, profanely:

"The forts at Hilton Head cannot be taken. I tell you that God Almighty could not take those forts!"

" Yes, massa," replied the negro, with a significant shake of his head, " but suppose the Yankees come with God Almighty?"

The Lord was on our side, we may believe, and gave us a brilliant victory. Then came the landing of troops, the finding of treasures left in the hasty flight of the rebels, and the general rejoicing. . I shall go a little further in the story of Port Royal, which was to be, in less than a year, the command and the *graveyard* of General Mitchel. The people he especially cared for, early after this battle showed themselves to our troops. The slaves declared that they had been long waiting for the Yankees. Said one of them :

" Bress dè Lord, massa, we'se prayed and prayed de good Lord to send de Yankees, and we'se knowed you'se a comin'."

" How did you know?" asked a soldier, " you cannot read the papers?"

" No, massa, we can't read, but we can *listen.* Master and missus used sometimes to read loud, and then we used to listen so," touching his ear and stooping as if listening at a key-hole ; " I'se listened, an' Jim, an' we put de bits togedder, and we knowed you's a comin, bres de Lord !"

Another, who having heard the common and profane epithet, " damned Yankees," whenever Northern men were mentioned, supposed, in his simplicity, it was a necessary appellation—the proper one. And in a religious meeting he prayed, in these words: "O God, we thank thee thou has sent dese kind soldiers to be de friends of the de poor slaves. Like Jesus, dey have come with good tidings of great joy." He then asked God's blessing on the Yankees, using the very expression with which he had always been familiar.

I could relate many touching scenes among the poor contrabands, of families reunited after a long separation—of services rendered to our army, and of beautiful religious faith. Soon the "contrabands" increased to a thousand, sheltered by four buildings two hundred and fifty feet long and thirty wide, erected expressly for them. Thus Port Royal became the first great depot of emancipated slaves. It was to this post of duty in a limited field of action, because not designed for the arena of great deeds, and therefore not furnished with troops and other resources for extensive operations, that General Mitchel cheerfully went; still he felt that he had been misrepresented and misunderstood.

He was sure he understood the rebellion, and how to treat it. Yet, with confidence in the President's honesty and aims, he bore the burden of "wounded spirit" in silence. No sooner had he surveyed the theatre of achievement, than his unresting soul sought for labor and peril in his country's behalf.

CHAPTER XXIII.

THE fine impression which the arrival and prompt action of the new commander made upon the army and people, was given by a correspondent of *The Independent*, who was there : " The afternoon of the 15th of September, on which the Arago came up our magnificent bay, with the American ensign at her fore, while the thirteen guns from the fort, echoed by the same salute from the Wabash, proclaimed a major-general, ushered in an epoch in the Department. Before the end of that week, General Mitchel had visited all the camps on Hilton Head, at Beaufort, and at Fort Pulaski, and had addressed all the regiments except such as chanced to be absent on picket duty. In another week the expedition to St. John's Bluff was matured, though its execution was twice deferred by storms.

" The week in which that expedition sailed witnessed an expedition that burned the extensive salt works, a quarter of a mile long, at Blufton, and a reconnoissance up Savannah River, proceeding further and achieving more than any previous reconnoissance had done. And before these lines reach you, other projects will have become history.

" And all this activity while his predecessors were forever complaining that they could do nothing with the limited number of troops in the Department ; and yet more, when shortly before his coming here some eight regiments were transferred to Virginia !

" His clear sight saw that the negroes were an important element in the condition of the Department, and he immediately began to occupy himself with plans for their becoming a source of happiness to themselves, and of strength and prosperity to the Government. He found some six or seven hundred negroes hived in three wooden buildings within the stockade, near to the camps, and all their demoralizing influences. He set the negroes at work building log-houses for themselves, out in the country remote from the camps. He appointed a teacher, who has begun a school among them. Last Sunday he attended the morning service of the colored church, when their new house of worship was dedicated, and addressed them in counsels of singular appropriateness and wisdom. His leading idea was, ' White men can do nothing for you ex-

12

cept to give you a chance. You must do for yourselves.
You must raise yourselves. You must for yourselves re-
fute the unfriendly predictions of your enemies.' Though
not a professed abolitionist, yet General Mitchel is a better, wiser friend of this people than either of his predecessors has been.

" He understands, as real generals have always done,
the need of having his soldiers in sympathy with him.
He says a cheering, inspiring word to a knot of men as
he rides through a camp; it is passed from man to man
till the regiment feels the thrill. As a specimen of the
brief, pithy, unpremeditated talks by which he kindles the
men, this afternoon he passed the camp of the Seventh
Connecticut, just as they were on battalion drill. He
stopped and watched their drill, and being asked to address them, he consented. So they were formed on close
column by divisions, and he said : 'Officers and soldiers
of the Seventh Connecticut, I thank you for what you did
last week in Florida. You did all that could be asked of
you. Now I have another job for you. In a few days
the word will be *March !* I don't want any man who
cannot stand a march. Your first business now is to be
well. The skies are bright. The people of the North are
looking to the South. Soon large reënforcements will be
on their way here. But let us first show them what we
can do without reënforcements.'

" More, and better than all, General Mitchel is a

Christian, who makes a conscience of his work, and whose trust is in the Lord God of Hosts.

" Finding there were large numbers of contrabands at Hilton Head, subject to ill treatment and often abuse from the prejudiced whites, his first work (almost) was to see to their comfort. Very soon a number of houses were erected for them, just beyond the village of Hilton Head (for it is now grown into a village), and quite out of the way of the camps, where they could be comfortably lodged and sheltered. A church has been erected for them, and at its dedication General Mitchel addressed them as a kind father would speak to his children. On another occasion he did the same. And to a friend he afterwards said: 'I have addressed large audiences, of the most literary and scientific men and women, in all the great cities of the United States, and I say to you *I never was so moved before in my life* as when standing before that multitude of the poor, the humble, and the wronged, who have but now come out of bondage into a hoped for freedom.'

" O craven hearts of the North! here was a man, loaded with wealth, honors, and privilege, yet he spurned not the poor, nor feared to stand in his place before them and speak words of hope and consolation to their stricken and trembling hearts. To all those engaged in teaching or otherwise in the mission, with whom he conversed, he promised his hearty coöperation in every practicable effort."

His fertile brain and adventurous spirit began to push out on every hand in plans to embarrass the enemy. On St. John's River was a fort of considerable strength, and in another direction the Bluffton Salt Works, of great value to the enemy. He sent successful expeditions to both, and also drew Beauregard out of Savannah with twenty-five thousand men.

The next bold movement of General Mitchel was a repetition of the gallant exploits in Alabama. Take the map and you will notice smaller streams flowing into Broad River, and just west of them, making a broad curve, the Charleston and Savannah Railroad. Though furnished with much smaller force than he needed, General Mitchel was resolved to use it well, and deal the heaviest blows upon the merciless enemy that could be given by it. It was to be his last earthly work. The only reason why it did not accomplish all that he intended, was the want of sufficient means to secure the highest results—painful it is to know it. War at best is *waste;* but when military or political ambition and mistakes, which will enter always more or less into all war, especially in a Republic, throw away noble, lives it is enough to break the heart of patriotism, and kindle the quenchless fire of indignation upon its altars.

Wrote an eye-witness of this daring and brilliant

movement, true to the promise that he made his troops, of giving them active employment on assuming command of the Department of the South :

"General Mitchel has just prosecuted a third expedition, of greater magnitude and of more important aim, which, while yielding fresh lustre to our arms, I grieve to say has only partially achieved its object, and so adds another long list to the names of martyrs in the Union cause.

"The especial design of this enterprise was to destroy the trestle-work bridges of the Charleston and Savannah Railroad, crossing the Pocotaligo, Tullifiny, and Coosahatchie. These streams are all tributaries of the Broad River ; and to approach them it was determined, after a careful study of the map of this peculiarly impracticable and most difficult country for military operations, to make a landing at Mackay's Point, at the junction of the Broad and Pocotaligo Rivers, a distance of twenty-five miles from Hilton Head, where our troops could be debarked under cover of gunboats, and a march of eleven miles would take them to the village of Pocotaligo, at which place it was supposed the enemy would make a stand. The attack was intended as a surprise ; and while our main force was to advance, as stated, a smaller body of troops, commanded by Colonel Barton, of the Forty-eighth New-York volunteers, was to create a diversion by penetrating to the Coosahatchie bridge in the steamer Planter, convoyed by the gunboat Patroon ; but with imperative orders

to retire should they encounter a superior force. By cutting the railroad in the manner proposed, communication
between the cities of Savannah and Charleston would be
destroyed, and the way opened for a sudden blow upon
one or both of these places, at the discretion of the commanding general.

" The plan of this expedition was skilfully conceived,
and every precaution adopted to render it successful.
Few can imagine the perplexities attendant upon the
movement of troops and artillery by water. It was necessary to construct flat-boats for the transporation of field-
batteries ; to concentrate all the light-draught boats ; to gain
such knowledge as might be gained imperfectly through
scouts, of the character of the country to be traversed ; to
decide upon the possibility of debarking at the point selected ; arriving at proper tides ; providing for the subsistence of the troops, and a hundred other details regarding
prudence and sagacious foresight, and which after all were
susceptible of disarrangement. Considering all these circumstances, and the fact that so many persons are employed in the organization of an expedition of this kind, it
is not to be wondered at that information of the projected
attack passed our lines, and the enemy consequently was
ready to receive us.

" The army transports of light draught were not sufficient for the transportation of the number of men required
for this service ; and in the emergency, Commodore Godon,

of the navy, was applied to by General Mitchel for assistance. Commodore Godon promptly agreed to take troops on the gunboats, and the soldiers were assigned as follows :

"Gunboat Paul Jones, Captain Charles Steedman, commanding naval forces, towing Wabash launches. Transport Ben Deford, with six hundred of the Forty-seventh Pennsylvania volunteers, and four hundred of the Fifty-fifth Pennsylvania volunteers. Gunboat Connemaugh, with three hundred and fifty of the Fourth New Hampshire volunteers. Gunboat Wissahickon, with two hundred and fifty of the Fourth New Hampshire volunteers. Transport Boston, with five hundred of the Seventh Connecticut volunteers, and three hundred and eighty of the Third New Hampshire volunteers. Gunboat Patroon, with fifty of the Third New Hampshire volunteers. Gunboat Uncas, with fifty of the Third New Hampshire volunteers. Transport Darlington, with three hundred of the Sixth Connecticut volunteers. The Relief and schooner, with two hundred of the Sixth Connecticut volunteers. Gunboat Marblehead, with two hundred and thirty of the Third Rhode Island volunteers. Gunboat Vixen, with seventy of the Third Rhode Island volunteers. Steamer Florida, with three hundred of the Seventy-sixth Pennsylvania volunteers. Gunboat Water Witch, with one hundred and thirty of the Seventy-sixth Pennsylvania volunteers. Army gunboat George Washington, with two hundred and fifty of the New York Volunteer Engineers.   Steamer Planter, with three hundred of the Forty-eighth New York volunteers.   The Ben Deford towed a flat boat having on board a section of Lieutenant Henry's battery First United States artillery, and the Boston another flat boat carrying a section of company E, Third United States artillery.   The entire land forces were composed of portions of the first and second brigades of the Tenth army corps, respectively commanded by Brigadier-Generals J. M. Brannan and A. H. Terry, the former being senior officer, and therefore commanding the expedition.

" At nightfall of Tuesday, the twenty-first, the expedition was ready for departure, but did not leave until midnight, as nothing could be accomplished by reaching its destination before daybreak.   The vessels left in the order above designated, but the night was misty, and one or two of them ran aground, delaying their arrival at the rendezvous for some hours beyond the time which had been fixed.

" Meanwhile the tug Starlight was despatched with some boats of the Paul Jones and a small company of soldiers of the Seventh Connecticut, under Captain Gray, to capture the rebel pickets at Mackay's Point and at a plantation on the Pocotaligo River, a few miles distant. This project was only partially successful.   At the plantation, Lieutenant Banks, of the enemy's picket, and three men, were made prisoners, but through the incompetency of a negro guide, the guard at the point escaped, giving warning of our approach. From the rebel officer who was taken, General Brannan learned that our attack had been apprehended by the enemy, and for several days they had been preparing for the encounter.

"The tedious process of putting the men ashore in small boats was commenced soon after six o'clock A. M., on Wednesday, and by ten o'clock, men, horses, and guns were landed, excepting the detachment of the Third Rhode Island volunteers, who were on the gunboat Marblehead, which was aground all day some miles down the river.

"The line of march was taken up soon after ten, the section of Lieutenant Henry's battery being at the head of the column with skirmishers of the Forty-seventh Pennsylvania regiment. Advancing slowly over an admirable road for seven miles, we failed, during the march, of encountering the enemy, who had prudently recoiled from a meeting until it should take place beyond range of our gunboats, although the nature of the ground over which we passed afforded many excellent positions for defence.

"The road alternated through dense woods and through marshes, only passable over a narrow causeway, save at one or two points. Choosing a position at the opposite end of this causeway, the enemy opened a furious fire of shell and canister on our advancing column, which was promptly met by the battery under Lieutenant Henry.

12*

Immediately the order was given by General Brannan for his brigade to form line of battle, the centre resting on the causeway. After a brisk fire of both musketry and artillery the rebels retired to the dense woods in their rear, tearing up the causeway-bridge, which delayed the advance of our artillery until it could be repaired.

Meanwhile, the First Brigade pressed on to the woods, which they penetrated, driving the enemy before them, and closely followed by the Second Brigade, under General Terry, who came up with a cheer, and were quickly in the engagement. Here the fight, it may be said, fairly commenced—the enemy's sharpshooters picking off our men rapidly. The artillery fire from our side was not slackened while the bridge was being repaired, and it was not long before the batteries went forward to the work in support of the infantry.

" This action began between twelve and one, and lasted about an hour, ending in the retreat of the rebels to another position at Frampton's plantation, which lies two miles beyond. The enemy were closely followed, and after a fight more hotly contested than the first, our troops were again victorious, the second time driving the rebels from their well-chosen position, and two miles beyond, which brought them up to Pocotaligo bridge (not the railroad bridge), over which they crossed, taking shelter behind earthworks on the farthest side. To this point our troops nearly approached, but found further progress impossible, as the bridge had been cut by the enemy on his retreat. This fact we construe into a clear acknowledgment of his defeat.

"Although these events are thus briefly noted, it required upward of five hours of impetuous and gallant fighting to accomplish them. At no one time was the entire field of combat in view from a given point, and I therefore find it impossible to speak in detail of the operations of my own regiment. Both brigades participated in the action, and both Generals Brannan and Terry were constantly under fire, leading and directing the movements of their men, awakening enthusiasm by their personal bravery and the skilful manner in which they manœuvred their commands. Frequently, while the fight was progressing, we heard the whistles of the railroad trains, notifying us of reënforcements for the rebels, both from Charleston and Savannah; and even if we had had facilities for crossing the river, it would have been unwise to have made the attempt in view of these circumstances. General Brannan therefore ordered a retreat, which was conducted in a most orderly manner, the regiments retiring in successive lines, carrying off their dead and wounded, and leaving no arms or ammunition on the field.

"Of the exact force of the rebels, of course we know nothing, although General Brannan was of the opinion that it equalled our own. Certainly their artillery ex ceeded ours by four or five pieces, and this we have from the seven prisoners taken, one of whom, William Judd, belonged to Company B, Second South Carolina cavalry, whose horse was also captured. The prisoners informed us that General Beauregard commanded in person.

"While these events were taking place between the main forces on either side, Colonel Barton, of the Forty-eighth New York, with three hundred of his own men and fifty of the Third Rhode Island regiment, under command of Captain J. H. Gould, went up the Coosahatchie River, convoyed by the Patroon, to within two miles of the town of the same name. Landing this force here, a march was made to the village through which runs the railroad. Arrived there, they commenced tearing up the rails, but had scarcely engaged in the work when a long train of cars came from the direction of Savannah, filled with troops. This train was fired into by our party, killing the engineer and a number of others. Several soldiers jumped from the cars while they were in motion, and were wounded. One was taken prisoner—thirty muskets were captured, and colors of the Whippy Swamp Guards taken from the color-bearer, who was killed by our fire. The work of tearing up the rails was not accomplished in time to prevent the onward progress of the train, and our men afterward completed the job—also cutting the telegraph, and bringing away a portion of the wire with them.

" Colonel Barton next attempted to reach the railroad bridge, for the purpose of firing it, but was unable, as it was protected by a battery of three guns. Fearing that his retreat might be cut off by the enemy's cavalry, he gave the order to retire to the steamboat, which was done successfully. His men had nearly all embarked when the cavalry boldly came directly under the guns of the Planter and Patroon, and fired upon both steamers. A few rounds of canister dispersed them, and the only damage which they inflicted was the serious wounding of Lieutenant J. M. Blanding, of the Third Rhode Island artillery.

" Nearly all Wednesday night was passed in bringing the wounded from the battle-field and placing them upon the transports. This humane work was personally superintended by General Terry and Brigade Quartermaster Coryell, of General Brannan's staff. As fast as the boats were filled they returned to Hilton Head, and by Thursday night the whole force had reëmbarked. Before our last regiment left Mackay's Point the enemy's pickets had reappeared, but not in sufficient force to molest us.

" Scarcely five minutes after the first engagement began, wounded men were brought to the rear. Surgeon Bailey, the Medical Director at Beaufort, who accompanied the expedition, established a hospital almost under fire, by the roadside, beneath the shade of the stately pine woods, with Surgeons Merritt, of the Fifty-fifth Pennsyl-

vania, and McClellan, of the Sixth Connecticut, and these
gentlemen soon had their energies taxed to the uttermost.
It was a spectacle to make one shudder as the poor fellows, wounded and dying, were emptied from the ambulances upon the green sward.

" A striking instance of heroism came under my observation. During the thickest of the fight, Artificer Zincks,
of Henry's battery, seized a shell which had fallen into
our ammunition-box, and threw it into a ditch, where it
exploded, seriously wounding him. Had it not been for
his bravery and presence of mind, the most serious consequences might have ensued. Lieutenant Henry's horse
was shot under him, and the shell that killed the animal
also killed one man and wounded five others. It is a singular fact that Lieutenant Gettings, of the Third United
States artillery, whose section also did good service in the
fight, also lost one man killed and five wounded by the
explosion of a single shell. Lieutenant Gettings himself
was wounded in the ankle.

" Three howitzers from the Wabash, under command
of Lieutenant Phœnix and Ensigns Wallace and Larned,
accompanied the land forces, and won a great deal of
praise for gallantry and effective firing. Young Wallace
was sent by General Terry to cover the retreat from
Pocotaligo bridge, which he handsomely accomplished
He had delivered two rounds of grape into the enemy's
ranks, when a shower of rifle-balls were sent against him,

wounding three of his men and perforating his own clothes. The-heroic young fellow was then ordered to retire, which he reluctantly did, after vainly asking permission to fire another round.

" The rebels left fifteen or twenty of their dead on the field, and the inference is that their loss must have been severe, or they would have had time to remove all in their successive retreats. Two caissons filled with ammunition were captured from the enemy during the second battle. Our own supply of ammunition at this time having been well-nigh exhausted, this proved very opportune.

" Although the main object of the expedition failed of success, yet the benefits conferred were not of trifling value. We have made a thorough reconnoissance of the heretofore unknown Broad River and its tributaries, and ascertained the character of the country, which is knowledge of immense importance, in view of future movements in that direction. We have also demonstrated the necessity of heavy reënforcements if the Government desire General Mitchel to strike heavily in his department."

But in nothing was his Christian philanthropy and patriotism more conspicuous than in his attention to the great work of taking care of the " contrabands ", gathered by thousands within his department. Their physical wants were supplied, their education provided for, and religious instruction furnished them. He knew the affectionate regard of these _simple-hearted refugees from slavery, which has been recently warmly expressed in naming a new settlement and headquarters of operations in their behalf, *Mitchelville*—in memory of the generous ·and benevolent chief of the department, whose loss they will never cease to mourn.

A careful observer of passing events at Beaufort, already quoted, added the following testimony respecting the emancipated slaves, whose prospects so deeply interested the departed chief:

" Yesterday completed a year since the flashing broadsides of the Wabash and the gunboats were echoed from the fortifications guarding either side of the bay. The recurrence of the day leads me to review the results of the past year in this department.

" Even those most hopeful for the future of the Africans have not been able to repress a fear that when they were released from the immediate pressure of the lash, a motive to industry would be wanting, and that indolence, dependence, misery, and degradation would result on a scale unparalleled in history. The past year of the department has gone far to solve the problem. The negroes have been placed under circumstances the most unfavorable. Their industry has been interrupted by removals and evacuations. They have by no means been secure of having the avails of their labor. Not unfrequently their crops have been pillaged by lawless soldiers. And yet under all these disadvantages, the negroes working on their plantations and in the quartermaster's department have shown a readiness, an activity, an efficiency, varying indeed with the skill, energy, and adaptation possessed by the persons appointed to oversee their labor, yet on the whole affording much encouragement. Under the wise arrangement made by General Mitchel, all of the work of getting out the timber and constructing the buildings of the new negro quarters was done by the negroes themselves. It was a most gratifying spectacle to see them, morning and evening, going to their toil or returning home, with the saw and the axe and the spade upon their shoulders. Many of the difficulties which must attend the passage of a people from bondage to freedom are being met and removed, and suggestions are furnished as to the best method of procedure in future.

"One of the superintendents, who unites with this office that of a pastor among the negroes, told me lately that, finding that the great body of the people had never been married, he had been marrying not only couples newly joined, but those who for years had been just "living together." Also finding that many of the people had of their own will dissolved their former ties, he had represented to General Saxton the need of having a regular tribunal to act in cases of this kind, and to decree or refuse divorces as it deemed best. Accordingly the General, acting as Governor, has instituted a Commission for this purpose. Thus, one by one, the questions which must hereafter arise upon a vast scale are met, considered, adjudicated, within the narrow limits of this department. And whenever the time shall come (may God hasten it!) that the millions of Africans shall be raised into enfranchisement, then the rulers, the philanthropists, to whom the honorable but herculean task shall be committed of molding their new-born liberty into the forms of life, will find their safest, most invaluable guidance in the history of the enfranchised people of Port Royal.

" Lately, a new question, much disputed, has advanced toward a solution among us—the question of the possibility of making soldiers of the negroes. The expedition by the Darlington returned, having, without any loss, accomplished all its objects successfully, and bringing away sixty contrabands. Of course, the most important result achieved was the proof afforded of the capacity of the negro race for warlike exploits, and the encouragement given to themselves. Their courage was put beyond a peradventure. When ordered to take to the boats, for the purpose of effecting a landing, they would leap into them with an alacrity which nothing could exceed. When engaged in the skirmishes with the enemy, they could with difficulty be kept under cover of the stockade erected around the boat. They would stand out on the spar-deck, loading and firing, till ordered by their officers to go in.

" The captain of the gunboat Potomska, who accompanied the expedition, has written a letter paying the strongest tribute to the soldierly qualities displayed by them.

"THE NEGRO IS OUR INVALUABLE AND OUR NATURAL ALLY.

" It was a negro who saved the expedition from utter failure, and the troops from probable ruin. On reaching the mouth of the St. John's River, it appears that there was no way for the troops to get in the rear of the battery on the Bluff, except by marching for forty miles around the head of Pablo and Mount Pleasant Creeks. They must carry their rations, and the sick or weary must be left by the roadside to be murdered by the guerrillas of the enemy. The troops would reach the scene of action utterly exhausted, and if defeated, would be likely to be annihilated. Yet there was no alternative, and the order for the desperate march was given.

" But about midnight, a negro came from shore and told the general of a point of land where the troops might land with ease and safety, and by a march of some eight or ten miles would reach a spot where they could cover the landing of cavalry and artillery, and from thence by a march of four miles could reach the battery from the rear. He described the roads, and gave all needful information as to the topography of the region with perfect clearness and absolute accuracy. His advice was adopted; the enemy found themselves assailed from a side where they had not dreamed of attack, and fled precipitately.

We owe the bloodless victory of St. John's Bluff, and the opening of St. John's River, to the bravery and intelligence of a negro (no longer, thank God, a slave).

"And they are our natural, unbought allies. They know by instinct that there is friendship between us, and that the rebels are their enemies. For example: I was walking through one of the streets of Jacksonville, about half-past seven o'clock on Monday evening, when a mulatto woman said to me: 'Sir, I think that General Finnigan went down that street just now.' [General F. was the commander of the rebel forces in Florida, and had charge of the battery.] She pointed down a cross road, where the forms of two persons were seen vanishing in the thickening darkness. Alone and unarmed, I could only summon the patrol, and in the delay the suspected persons escaped. But the incident shows the ready trust they place in us, and their willingness to serve us.

"We brought away some five hundred to six hundred contrabands from Jacksonville and vicinity. A very intelligent man, a resident of Jacksonville, said to me: 'The people will be ruined—they will be helpless. Here are men who have been supported by the wages their negroes have earned. Now the negroes are going away. How will they live? Next spring, when it is time to plant, who will do the work?' I saw a very intelligent negro, property of Rev. Mr. Duval, Methodist minister in Jacksonville. The man is a drayman. He used to bring in to the reverend owner from $3 to $7 a day Now he is gone, Rev. Mr. D. must henceforth ' live of the Gospel.'

" Speaking of slaveholding divines, reminds me of a reply which amused me very much.   On James Island, I employed a negro who came from a place not far from Charleston.   I asked him what was his master's name. He replied : ' His name?   Parson Prentiss, sir.'   ' Oh, he was a parson, was he? and what was his persuasion?'   I inquired.   ' His persuasion?   Oh, he lick um studdy (steady), sir,' was his reply.   A tolerably extensive branch of the Church South, is it not?

" In Jacksonville, many families were utterly desti- tute.   An officer, in charge of a picket post in the town, heard a girl, waking at midnight, cry for food, but the mother had none to give the child.   The next day he car- ried to the house a box of bread and a pail of rice.   In many houses there was literally nothing to eat.   The in- habitants said that prices were, for corn meal, from $1.50 to $2 a bushel ; salt, 50 cents a quart ; sugar $1 a pound. Fresh beef is very cheap, because there is no way of pre- serving it.

" In one of the camps at St. John's Bluff, envelopes were found cut out with scissors from the unused leaves of a ledger, with the ruled lines and the dollar-and-cent columns.

" In Jacksonville, I saw a girl making envelopes.   She

laid an old envelope, opened and spread out flat, on a piece of common *wall paper*, and cut out the envelopes, using the old one as a pattern. Surely, it is a *paper* blockade, isn't it?

" One incident, illustrating the value of the Confederate currency, was told me by an intelligent refugee, as having occurred some months ago. A shoemaker had made a pair of boots, for which he charged his customer $23. The buyer counted out the money in Confederate notes, and then put down a $10 gold piece, giving him his choice. He took the $10.

" Some time since, General Terry, who commands the Department of Fort Pulaski, St. Augustine, Fernandina, Key West, and Tortugas, when in St. Augustine was beset by a woman, who complained that her negro had been released, and who demanded his restoration and re-enslavement. She was an English woman, she said, and the Government had no right to interfere with her property. She came from the British West Indies, and brought this negro slave with her.

" ' Had not slavery been abolished in the British West Indies before you left there?' asked the general.

" ' No,' she replied, with great sharpness. ' I came in 1831, long before the emancipation.'

" ' Ah, you came in 1831?' asked the general.

" ' Yes, in 1831.'

" ' And are you aware, madam, that in 1808 Congress

passed a law making it an act of piracy, punishable with death, to bring a person into this country with a view of retaining him in slavery?'

"The female slave hunter did not press her claim further."

General Mitchel, when alluding to the contrabands not long before his death, remarked, that among the most grateful memories of the past, was the one of a *prayer-meeting* held by them, which he attended. Their unaffected worship—their faith and love, breathing the very spirit of Christianity, affected him, and his adoration rose with theirs to the God and Father of all. He knew that many of those just now "goods and chattels personal," would stand beneath the dome of unclouded light, and study with him the works of Providence and grace forever.

October 26th he was seized with the yellow fever. For a time no serious apprehensions were felt. Indeed, when the crisis of the disease was reached, the symptoms were pronounced favorable. The perspiration was free, and the physician left him with confident anticipations of his recovery. But the recent death of his devoted wife, his exile from the cherished West, and the entire field of decisive conflict, and the then threatening aspect of the national struggle for existence—all depressed him, and made recovery to his Christian heart of little consequence beyond the will of God. He was resigned to do and to suffer all that was required by loyalty to the "King im mortal and invisible."

This indifference to earthly scenes, apart from their relation to a higher love and activity, made him uncon sciously less careful to guard against exposure of his sensitive frame, than he otherwise might have been. A relapse assumed immediately an alarming type.

CHAPTER XXIV.

HE thirtieth dawned. By the bedside stood his grieving friend watching every expression of the dying face. Raising his fine eye, and extending his hand, he said, "It is a blessed thing to have a Christian's hope in a time like this." The assent was given, with "dim eyes suffused with tears." An hour passed in silent waiting on the undisputed work of death's angel, who had taken from all human interposition the illustrious captive, even then "more than conqueror" over all mortal and spiritual foes. Again the expressive orbs which had reflected unnumbered stars, opened, and his feebler hand beckoned his friend to his side. Pressing tenderly the palm, he said again: "You must not stay longer; go now, and come to me in the morning."

At this moment Major Birch, whose devotion to his

13

general had been warm and constant, entered the apartment in an agony of sorrow. He had written, at General Mitchel's dictation, his "last will and wishes." He led to the couch the Rev. Mr. Strickland, and beckoned the friend present to follow. After a few words to the clergyman, he said, "Kneel down." The prayer was offered, amid a stillness of grief too deep for any other language than the subdued utterance of the soul to the "Captain of Salvation." When the company rose from prayer, his affectionate glance once more sought his friend, and he murmured, while his hand was laid in the one so often pressed, " You can do me no good ; do not stay."

No cloud was on the splendid intellect, nor on the prospect beyond the starry darkness soon to curtain the form of the once loving gazer into its depths. At that moment two sons who were upon his staff, were sick with the same disease, and could not be permitted to know that the father was dying, and hear his last words, lest it should be fatal to them. As he reached the eternal gates, reason at times wandered. The last clear words of triumph were : "I am ready to go." The latest unshadowed glance of the princely soul rested on Rev. Mr. Strickland ; and when he came near, speech was lost ; but twice he raised his hand and pointed upward !

In four short days the manly and vigorous form which had borne all pressure of care, had sunk under the scourge of the southern latitudes, and lay in the evening quiet, cold, and still. The splendid tenant redeemed, and crowned in the skies, was stretching its tireless pinions in the glory of the Infinite !. The generous, loyal heart had ceased to throb for human wrong-doing and suffering, and was pouring the tide of its strong affections around Messiah's throne. The vision which had been so often and much among the stars, was satisfied with the shadow-less canopy of unveiled splendor above the thrones of light !

Since this record of his death and burial was written, I have seen a letter written the day of the funeral, which cannot fail to interest you :

" Port Royal, S. C., October 31.

" Last evening the announcement reached Hilton Head, ' Major-General Mitchel died at a quarter-past six this evening.' It is impossible to convey to any one out-side of the department the overwhelming sensation of grief and gloom that this news created. Every one, in every station, feels that he has lost a personal friend, in whose brilliant exploits he felt an intense pride ; that the department has lost one who was the tower of its strength and safety ; and that the country has lost a general to whom no superior is left behind. Truly, in the grand, touching words of Isaiah: ' It is as when a standard-bearer fainteth.'

" To-day I have attended his funeral at Beaufort.

The procession moved from Hospital No. 2 to the Episcopal church, the pall being borne by Admiral Dupont,
Brigadier-generals Brannan and Saxton, and other naval
and military officers of high rank.   At the church and at
the grave, the service of the Methodist Episcopal Church
was read by Rev. Dr. Strickland, chaplain of the Forty-
eighth New York, an old friend of the general.   I re-
gretted that there was not something beside the reading
of the service—some word of prayer or remark suggested
by, and growing out of, the occasion.   It seemed as if
every one present must long to hear and join in an expression of the emotions of admiration for the dead, of
grief for his departure, which burdened every heart.   It
was remembered with overwhelming emotion that two
weeks ago he had summoned together all the officers at
the post, to meet him in this church, and had, in a familiar
address, animate with patriotism, spoken to them of his
policy, and cheered them to the faithful discharge of their
duties to the country.   Alas! no more will that clear eye
flash with the instinct of genius and patriotism; no more
will that ringing voice, which seemed to emulate the
resonance and the strength of the steel by his side, call us
to duty and to glory.   In the very spot where so lately
he stood and spoke, now his body rested, enveloped in the
flag he loved so well,

"Chaplain Strickland, who, at the request of the general, came from Fort Pulaski to spend the last hours with

him, informs me that he was not only calm and resigned, but triumphant in the hopes of redemption. When his speech had failed, his eyes were turned upward, and he pointed toward heaven. It was an hour of triumph for him, but of sadness for us. God grant that his vision, illumined by the radiance of immortality, may have discerned for our country some prospects of brightness, of happiness, and of liberty, hidden as yet from us.

"He died as he had lived; for he was not alone a general, but a Christian. He was a member of the Presbyterian Church in Cincinnati, formerly under the charge of Dr. Beecher; and his life and spirit were in harmony with this profession. It was faith in God which sustained him amid the perils which he saw surrounding the nation. He said to the writer a few weeks ago, 'I am not troubled. I am standing on a rock. I have absolute confidence in the wisdom and goodness of God. He may indeed leave the country a prey to disaster. But I do not believe that He will, for then it would be of no use to contend against such a result. Rather, I believe that He will bring it out of all its perils into peace and liberty.'

"Among the many saddening attendants of the late bereavement was the fact that the general's two sons, prostrated by the same disease which had proved fatal to him, were ignorant of his death, not being in a condition to bear the shock of the announcement. It will be remembered that shortly after he offered his services to the Government, and left his home for the seat of war, his wife died suddenly, overwhelmed with solicitude in his behalf and with sorrow over his absence. Surely, no one among us has made such unparalleled sacrifices at the altar of liberty, of humanity, of the country with whose destiny he believed the interests of humanity to be inseparably linked."

Wrote another on that sad day at Port Royal : " He said to his attendant physician Wednesday morning: ' I have tried for thirty years to live the life of a Christian, and if God wills, I am prepared to go.' He was perfectly sensible until within a few hours of his death, but talked very little, and though his two sons were in the chambers above him, he did not ask for them. Doubtless he realized the impossibility of seeing them, and forbore to agitate his mind by speaking of them. They do not yet know of his death.

" As it was known to many that I had been called upon to assist in nursing their beloved general, I was accosted as I went to and fro (our houses being separated only by an alley and small yard) by officers and privates to know of his condition ; and when at last I was compelled to tell them there was no hope, it was wonderful to see the love they bore him. Not in an instance did one turn away with an indifferent or cold remark. ' He was so kind to us,' said one. ' It will be a sad blow to our troops,' said another. ' He was a good man, and good men are scarce in these days,' said a third. ' God help us, and send us another of his like,' ejaculated an old soldier who was walking with a heavy basket on his shoulder, as he passed on, the tears starting from his eyes. More than one said, ' Ah! if he could live, and some of our useless, wicked generals be taken.' But neither love nor hate could avail. He sleeps the sleep that knows no waking.

" To-day at 11 A. M. he was buried with military honors at the Episcopal church in this place. Rev. Dr. Strickland officiated, and read a part of the Episcopal service and the 90th Psalm.

" Commodore Dupont and staff were in attendance, General Saxton and General Brannan and suites, and most of the officers of the regiments stationed at this place.

" They have laid the last remains of the classic scholar, the earnest seeker after scientific truth, the eloquent orator, the humble Christian, and the successful warrior, in a sunny spot in the old South Carolina churchyard at Beaufort, around which cluster the ever-sheltering live oaks, there to repose till some state of his adoption shall call for them, to do them such honor as belongs only to the generous, true, and brave."

Farewell, thou gifted, saintly man—" lord in the domain of thought"—patriot, hero, Christian! We mourn

because so few like thee proclaim the dignity and worth
of fallen humanity when consecrated by the grace of
Christ to science, truth, and duty!

The funeral scene of the departed chief was solemn,
and deeply impressive. The coffin was laid under "the
shadow of the Episcopal church in Beaufort, S. C., near
those of his aide-de-camp, Captain Williams, who died
two days before."

I shall add to the testimony already given from many
sources, in regard to the greatness and excellence of his
character, an extract from a note received from a graduate of West Point, now occupying a high position, who
knew him well. It is not partial eulogy, but the calm
utterance of an appreciative mind and heart, though belonging to another religious denomination:

" My later acquaintance with Mr. Mitchel led me to
the conclusion that he was genial and hearty, generous to
a fault, brave as a lion, earnest and enthusiastic. A
strong, living, steamlike Christian man. As an orator,
truly extemporaneous, he had, to my knowledge, no
equal. As a soldier he combined intelligence with character, and to both he added wonderful energy. He was
exceedingly temperate in eating and drinking: indeed the
table had no charms for him but those which sprung from
association with family and friends. He was often really
hilarious from the effect of natural, not artificial spirits.
He was a man with a *very large heart.* What he loved,

he loved with a fervor which never exhibited itself in words, but always in *actions*. He loved his family better than himself, and his devotion to his wife after her illness (paralysis), was truly touching. ' He loved his friends with such simple, single-hearted affection, that they formed a brotherhood of association around him. He loved his country as few men do, even in these days of self-devotion ; and he loved his God and Church with such fervor that he could not do enough for the good cause of Christ."

His pastor in Albany, Rev. Dr. Clark, used the following language in an eloquent discourse upon the heroes that city had sent to the war :

" Of the citizens of Albany who offered up their lives for their country during the year 1862, I have the names of twenty, each of whom deserves an extended and earnest tribute. The most illustrious in this company is that of Ormsby Macknight Mitchel—a name dear to many hearts here—one who formerly worshipped within these walls, but who to-day worships in a higher, purer, more glorious temple. General Mitchel was distinguished in so many departments, that I am unable to say whether he was most eminent as an astronomer, a soldier, or a Christian. He certainly presented, in a most happy union, scientific culture, earnest patriotism, tender humanity, and devoted piety. His intellect moved among the stars, and caught their brilliancy. His thoughts partook of their harmony and grandeur. His discoveries

13*

and contributions to astronomical science are alone sufficient to render his name distinguished in the annals of
American literature. His popular lectures made him a
favorite with all, and inspired the minds of the people with
a love for the beauties and sublimities of astronomy, and
with adoration for the great Creator and his marvellous
works. He has left here an apparatus for accurate meas-
urements which bears the impress of his great mechanical
skill. But it is with the mechanism of his noble heart,
that was nicely adjusted to measure the depths of human
suffering; it is with those fine chords that vibrated to the
calls of patriotism and the claims of his country; it is
with those aspirations that nothing but the truths and
glories of Christianity could satisfy, that we are chiefly
interested. General Mitchell had a soul that could hear
the cries of humanity, and respond by toil and sacrifices
for the helpless and unfortunate. For the education and
happiness of the freedmen committed to his charge he did
what he could; and at the last great day, many of the re-
cipients of his benevolence will be ready to rise up and
pronounce him blessed. At the moment the breath left
his body, science lost a rare ornament; the army mourned
for a skilful and brave soldier; humanity wept for an
earnest defender and advocate; and the Church lost a true
Christian and humble follower of our Lord Jesus Christ."

The elegy of W. F. Williams on his death, is a
touching tribute:

" MITCHEL.

' Hung be the heavens in black.'

His mighty life was burned away
  By Carolina's fiery sun ;
The pestilence that walks by day
  Smote him before his course seemed run.

The constellations of the sky,
  The Pleiades and Southern cross,
Looked sadly down to see him die,
  To see a nation weep his loss.

' Send him to us,' the stars might cry;
  ' You do not feel his worth below ;
Your petty great men do not try
  The measure of his mind to know.

' Send him to us—this is his place,
  Not 'mong your puny jealousies ;
You sacrificed him in your race
  Of envies, strifes, and policies.

' His eye could pierce our vast expanse,
  His ear could hear our morning songs,
His mind amid our mystic dance
  Could follow all our myriad throngs.

' Send him to us ! no martyr's soul,
  No hero slain in righteous wars,
No raptured saint could e'er control
  A holier welcome from the stars.'

Take him ye stars ! take him on high,
  To your vast realms of boundless space
But once he turned from you to try,
  His name on mortal scrolls to trace.

That once was when his country's call
  Said danger to her flag was nigh,
And then that banner's stars dimmed all
  The radiant lights which gemmed the sky.

Take him, loved orbs !   His country's life,
  Freedom for all—for these he wars ;
For these he welcomed bloody strife,
  And followed in the wake of Mars !"

NOTE.

SINCE the last pages of this biography were written, I have seen a letter addressed by "J. B. S——," the widow's only son, to his mother, expressing his wish to join the army. When it was sent to her, the call was loud for volunteers.

It is given here, because it contains the soul of patriotism, guided by Christian principle. He will be surprised to see it, but it will not injure him, I think, while I hope it may do *you* good.

The words of filial obedience, along with the ardent devotion to the old flag, are the assurance of that reverent loyalty, never so much needed among American youth as now and in the future of our country. Here is the letter :

PHILLIPS' ACADEMY, July 19th, 1864.

MY DEAR MOTHER :

I have taken my pen this morning to write you on a subject which at first may seem to you unreasonable, but which if you look at in the light of duty, you will not refuse to consider.

Andover is in a whirl of excitement—Phillips' Academy on fire with patriotic fervor. Attempts are being made to raise a company from this school to defend Washington. Hon. Mr. H——, of Boston, on Monday saw the Governor, who says he will accept a company from this school for one hundred days, and he has given his son permission to go. One of our teachers, Mr. B——, a noble Christian gentleman, says he will go right into the ranks with us, if a company can be raised here. Mr. T—— is also in favor of this project, and is to speak to us this morning at prayers about it. One of the members of the school last evening drew up a paper for any who would go, provided they could receive the consent of their parents. Sixty-five names are on that paper, among which is my own.

Our country, mother, needs men to defend the Capital, that those there now may go to the front, where they are wanted. This war has continued long enough already. More men are needed. Other mothers have given their sons to their country.

This, mother, is not a rash act of mine. Is it not my duty to go? Is it not yours to let me? Can you conceive of circumstances more favorable than these? We shall all be together *there* as here; we can pray *there* as here, we can do good *there* as here; shall we not be doing our duty *more there* than here. Mr. B—— and some of the theological students being with us gives additional interest. As so many of our class are going, no doubt arrangements can be made when we return to enter college as soon as we expected to do so. All the boys are writing home to get the consent of parents, and will soon receive replies. This no doubt is a bad season of the year to be in Washington; but the rebels can work in hot as well as in cold seasons, and we must repel them. Mother, our country must be free; she must be rescued from the thraldom of civil war.

Dear mother, I now ask if I can go? Will you not give your consent? I can't go without it, therefore I must have it. Will you not, to-morrow morning early, telegraph me an affirmative answer? I know and *feel* the relation we sustain to each other, but what is that to our *country*, our bleeding, distracted country! How can I bear to think that you will refuse me this request! It seems to me we shall not be as much exposed to vice as under other circumstances, for we shall have with us earnest Christians. S——'s mother has given two sons to the war, and now he is going himself.

Your affectionate son,

J. B. S.

THE END.